THE
ANGRY MOUNTAIN

The
Angry Mountain

By
HAMMOND INNES

THE BOOK CLUB
121 CHARING CROSS ROAD
LONDON, W.C.2

I

JAN TUČEK had changed a great deal. The broad shoulders sagged, his brown hair was thinning to baldness and his eyes had retreated into shadowed sockets. It was a shock to see how he had shrunk into middle age. "Dick Farrell! So it is you." His shoulders squared as he came across to meet me. The hand he held out was soft and white with neatly manicured nails. For a fleeting moment as I shook his hand I caught a glimpse of the Jan Tuček I'd known before. He smiled. "I hope I do not keep you waiting." In the way he spoke and in the sudden eagerness of his greeting, I found my mind switched back ten years to the sight of a shattered windshield splashed with oil, a burst of flame as I went into a dive and a voice in my earphones saying: *I think I get him for you, Dick.* For a moment as I held his hand it was the reckless, fanatical Czech fighter pilot I was greeting. Then memory was swamped by the present and I was looking into the tired, withdrawn eyes of Jan Tuček, head of the Tuček Steelworks in Pilsen.

"Sit down, please." He waved me to the chair beside his desk. The secretary who had brought me in, a short, dapper little man with an uneasy smile, went out and closed the door. I became conscious then of another person in the room. He stood over against the wall, a gangling, long-limbed man with the face of a seedy intellectual. He stood there with a conscious and studied unobtrusiveness that shrieked his presence aloud. As I glanced at him uneasily, Jan Tuček said, "You see to what we are reduced here in Czechoslovakia. This is my shadow. He go with me always."

The man jerked to life. "*Mluvte česky!*" There was a sort of baffled tenseness in the way he spoke.

Jan Tuček looked across at me. "You do not speak any other language but English, you understand." It wasn't a question. It was a statement. He knew it to be false and before I could say anything he had turned to the shadow and was speaking rapidly in Czech: "Mr. Farrell does not speak any language but English. I was with him when we fought the Germans over England. He is here as representative for a British firm of machine tool manufacturers. There is nothing political in our meeting."

5

"I cannot allow you to talk without an interpreter," the man answered.

"Then you'd better find one," Tuček snapped, "for I'm not going to treat an old comrade-in-arms as though he is a stranger just because you are so badly educated you do not speak English."

The man flushed angrily. Then he turned and hurried out.

"Now we can talk." Jan Tuček smiled. The sunlight caught a flash of gold teeth. But the smile did not extend to his eyes. "But we must be quick. Soon he will return with an interpreter. Tell me, where do you stay?"

"The Hotel Continental," I answered.

"Room number?"

"Forty-four."

"Good. You see, it is only during my working hours that they have their spies with me. How long will you stay?"

"Till Friday," I answered.

"Two days. That is not long, And after that—where do you go on Friday?"

"To Milan."

"To Milan?" For the first time I saw expression come into his eyes—a quickening of interest. "If I were to come to your room very late——" He didn't finish for the door was thrown open and his shadow entered followed by a rather plain girl with a red scarf and a hammer and sickle brooch. "And you are with this machine tool company?" he said quickly as though continuing an interrupted conversation. "Why are you no longer flying?"

I thrust my leg out for him to see.

"So you lose a leg, eh?" He clicked his tongue sympathetically. "Above the knee?"

I nodded.

"But nevertheless that should not stop you flying."

"It doesn't help," I said quickly. And then, because I thought he was going to probe further, I added, "The competition's pretty keen now with so many able-bodied fliers out of a job."

He nodded sympathetically. "I understand. But when does this happen? When my squadron is posted you are all right."

"Oh, it happened much later. In Italy. I crashed up near the Futa Pass between Florence and Bologna."

"Then you are a prisoner?"

"For just over a year," I answered. "They did three operations."

"Three operations?" His eyebrows lifted. "But surely one is sufficient for an amputation."

I felt the sweat breaking out on my forehead. Even now I could feel the knife and the grating bite of the saw. "They need not have

6

operated at all," I heard myself say. "My leg could have been saved." Somehow I didn't mind talking about it to him. He was so remote, someone from another world. Here, behind the Iron Curtain, what had happened to me didn't seem to matter so much.

"Then why?" he asked.

"They wanted me to talk."

It was out before I could check myself. I saw his eyes staring at me and then they slid away to the photographs on his desk. "But you are free," he said. "Free to run your life as you wish to run it."

"Yes," I said. "Yes, I suppose so." He meant I was free of the constant supervision that surrounded him. But I wasn't free. You can never get free of the past. "Those pictures," I said to change the subject. "Are they of your family?"

"Yes. My wife and daughter." He sighed and picked up the larger photograph. "That is my wife. She is dead. The Nazis kill her. She was held up on the Swiss frontier the night I fly to England in 1939. I do not see her again." He set the photograph down gently on the big mahogany desk. "That other is my daughter. She is now in Italy with the Czech table tennis team."

He held the photograph out towards me and I found myself looking at the face of a girl with a broad forehead, high cheekbones and a friendly smile. Her auburn hair fell to her shoulders and gleamed where it caught the light. Something in her expression, in the way she held her head reminded me that Jan Tuček had not always looked tired and drawn. "Her mother was Italian," he said. "From Venice."

So the hair was real titian. "She's very beautiful," I said.

He laughed. "The photographer has been kind to her, I think. You cannot see the freckles."

It didn't matter to me whether she had freckles or not. It wasn't the face so much as the person behind the face that was beautiful. Something about the expression of the eyes, the curve of the mouth, the defiant tilt of the chin seemed to reach out to me from the plain silver frame. It was the face of a girl who possessed sympathy and understanding—and something else; self-reliance, an ability to stand on her own feet. Somehow, in my loneliness, I felt the expression on her face was something that touched me personally through my old friendship with her father.

Tuček put the photograph down again. "Fortunately she play table tennis very well." The way he said it, the words seemed to carry a message, and again, for a moment, I was conscious of the resemblance between his face and the face in the photograph.

"I'm sorry I shan't see her," I said.

"Perhaps you will—in Milan." Again his words seemed to

carry additional meaning. Then, as though he were afraid I might make some comment, he glanced at his watch and pushed back his chair. "I am sorry. I have a conference now. I will send you to the head of our retooling section. Also I will ring him so that he know who you are. I have no doubt there are things we need that you have."

I got up. "Perhaps we could meet——" I began. But something in his eyes stopped me.

"I am sorry. I am a very busy man." He came round the big, ornate desk and shook my hand. "It has been good to see you again." As I turned to go his hand was on my arm and he took me to the door. "Tell me. Do you hear anything of Maxwell these days?"

"Maxwell?" I started, wondering why the devil he had to talk to me about Maxwell. "No," I said. "No. I haven't seen him since I left Italy."

He nodded. "He is here in Pilsen. If you should see him tell him——" He seemed to hesitate for the message and then, so softly that I could hardly catch it, he whispered, "*Saturday night.*" Then aloud he said, "Tell him—I shall always remember the times we had at Biggin Hill." He opened the door for me, called to his secretary and told her to take me to *pan* Marič. "Good-bye," he said. "I will telephone him that you are coming." And he closed the heavy door.

My interview with Marič lasted nearly an hour. I was conscious of a view of one of the blast furnaces through tall, smoke-grimed windows and of alert eyes peering short-sightedly through thick-lensed, rimless glasses at my specifications. Of the details of the conversation I remember nothing. It was mostly technical. We were alone and we talked in English. I remember I answered many of his questions quite automatically, my mind going over and over again my interview with Jan Tuček. Why had he wanted to come and see me late one night? Why had he given me that message to Maxwell? I felt as though I had touched the fringe of something that could only exist on this side of the Iron Curtain.

My interview with Marič finished shortly after four. He informed me that he would examine certain of the specifications with his technical experts and telephone me to-morrow. Then he rang for his assistant and ordered him to call one of the factory cars. As I got to my feet and pushed my papers back into my brief case, he said, "Have you known *pan* Tuček long, Mr. Farrell?"

I explained.

He nodded, and then with a quick glance at the door which was shut, he said in a low voice, "It is terrible for him. He is a fine man and he did great service to this country in 1939 when he fly to

England with the blueprints of all new armament work in progress here including the Bren gun modifications. His wife is murdered. His father, old Ludvik Tuček, die in a concentration camp. Then, after the war, he come back and reorganise the Tučkovy ocelárny —that is to say the works here. He work like a man with a devil inside of himself, all day, every day, to make it what it is before the Germans come. And now——" He shrugged his shoulders.

"He looks very tired," I said.

Marič peered at me through his glasses. "We are all very tired," he said quietly. "Twice in a lifetime—it is hard to have to fight twice. You understand? It is the spirit who become tired, Mr. Farrell. Perhaps one day——" He stopped then as his assistant came in to say the car was waiting. He shook my hand. "I will telephone you to-morrow," he said.

Outside clouds had obliterated the spring sunshine and the huge steelworks belched smoke into a grey sky. I got into the waiting car and was driven out through the gates into grey, brick-lined streets.

Back in the hotel I made a few telephone calls and then had some tea brought up to my room and did some work. I'd been behind with it ever since I'd started on the trip. I had covered Scandinavia and Central Europe, constantly adjusting my mind to different atmospheres, different languages and I felt tired. It was difficult to concentrate. And though I stayed in my room till past six, I got very little work done. My mind kept running over my interview with Jan Tuček, and always it came back to that message to Maxwell. *Tell him—Saturday night.* What was Max doing in Pilsen? Why was Tuček so sure I should see him?

In the end I stuffed my papers into a suitcase and went down to the lounge. It's an odd thing, being alone in a foreign country. Impressions are heightened, everything makes a much more vivid impact. And the sense of loneliness is strong. In Prague I had had contacts. But here in Pilsen my only personal contact was Tuček and, sitting alone there in the heavy, over-ornate furniture of the hotel lounge, I had the feeling of being hemmed in—the same sort of feeling I'd had during those interminable months of captivity. The place was perfectly ordinary, the people who came in and out or sat around smoking and talking were perfectly ordinary. Yet behind the ordinariness of it all I sensed the power of something alien. I thought of Mazaryk's suicide and set it alongside Tuček's manner. And then I began to think about Maxwell.

It's a queer thing, trying to escape from the past. I'd broken with flying, with all my old contacts. I'd voluntarily taken a job that would keep me wandering round Europe like a nomad. And here, behind the Iron Curtain, I had been given a message to one of the three men who knew my story. I remembered how kind Maxwell had been when I'd reported back to him at Foggia—his damnable kindness had taught me to hate myself. And now.... My mouth felt dry and harsh. The clink of glasses at the bar drew me like a magnet. For months I'd kept clear of the stuff. But now I needed a drink. I just had to have a drink. I went through into the bar and ordered a *slivovice*, which is a plum brandy and not the sort of drink to make one want to go on.

Nevertheless, I missed out dinner that night and took a bottle of *koňak* up to my room. And there I sat with the bottle and my glass in front of me, staring out at the lights in the houses opposite, smoking cigarette after cigarette, waiting for Maxwell to come. I don't know why I thought he would come, but I did, and I was determined to be drunk when he came. I tried to analyse my state of mind. But I couldn't. It was beyond analysis, something deep down inside of me that hated myself for the weakness that had once overwhelmed me. I stuck my leg out in front of me, the one that didn't belong to me, and stared at it. I hated that leg. It would be with me till I died, always there to remind me of the heat and flies and the screams that were torn out of my own throat in that hospital overlooking Lake Como. And when I died, they'd pull it off me and give it to some other poor bastard who'd lost his flesh-and-blood leg.

It was nearly eleven and the bottle was half-empty when I heard footsteps coming down the corridor outside my room. The footsteps were heavy and solid and decisive. I knew they were Maxwell's before he opened the door. God! Hadn't I heard those footsteps night after night at the mess at Biggin Hill, night after night in our billet at Foggia? And I'd known he'd come—known it ever since Tuček had given me that message. I'd been sitting there, waiting for him, trying to get drunk enough to face him. Well, I didn't care now. Let them all come and stare at me now I was drunk. I didn't care a bloody damn for the whole lot of 'em. They hadn't fought through the Battle of Britain, flown over sixty bomber sorties in less than two years and then...God damn them! They didn't know what it was like to feel your nerves....

Maxwell shut the door and stood there looking at me. He hadn't changed much. Maybe his face was a little thinner, the eyes a little more crinkled at the corners, but there was the same quick vitality, the same thrust forward of head and chin. "Drink, Max?" I asked. He didn't say anything but came across and pulled up a chair. "Well, do you want a drink, or don't you?" My voice sounded taut and harsh.

"Of course," he answered and stretched over to the wash-basin for the tooth glass. He looked at me as he picked up the bottle and poured himself the drink. "So you've become a commercial traveller?" I didn't say anything and he added, "Why didn't you stick to aviation? A man with your experience——"

"You know very well why," I answered angrily.

He sighed and said, "You can't run away from yourself, you know, Dick."

"How do you mean?"

"You're your own worst enemy. Damn it, man, nobody but yourself——"

"Can't you leave the past alone?" I shouted at him.

He caught hold of my arm. "For God's sake keep your voice down. Nobody knows I'm here. I came up by the fire-escape."

"By the fire-escape?" I stared at him. "What are you doing in Pilsen?"

He didn't say anything for a moment. He sat there, staring at me and toying with his glass, his eyes searching my face as though looking for something inside me that he wasn't sure existed. At length he said, "You remember Alec Reece?"

I jumped to my feet, knocking over my drink. Reece! Why the hell did he have to talk about Reece? Reece was dead anyway. He'd died trying to escape. So had Shirer. They were both dead. I didn't want to think about Reece. I'd introduced him to Maxwell —got him the job. He'd been so desperately keen to succeed on that first mission to the *partigiani*. He was the part of me I wanted to forget—Reece and his sister Alice. Sentences from that last letter of hers ran in a confused jumble through my head. *I wanted to be proud of you.* . . . *I have forgiven you, but you must see that it is impossible.* . . . I fumbled on the carpet for my glass, picked it up and reached for the bottle. But Maxwell took it from my hand and placed it on the other side of the table. "Sit down, Dick," he said. "I didn't realise——"

"What didn't you realise?" I cut in. "Didn't you know I was engaged to Alice Reece, that she broke it off when she knew? Why do you think I cracked up like that? A man's mind doesn't go——" I stopped then. The room was beginning to spin and I sat down quickly. "She thought I killed him," I heard myself saying slowly. "And the hell of it is, she was right. To all intents and purposes——"

"Alec Reece is alive," he said.

I stared at him. "Alive?"

He nodded.

"I don't believe it."

"It's true."

"And—and Shirer?" I asked.

"He's alive too. Didn't you know?"

I shook my head.

"He stayed on in Italy and bought a vineyard. He's living..."

I didn't hear the rest. A great load seemed to have been lifted from me. I put my head in my hands and let that feeling of relief flood through me. When I became conscious that he was shaking me, I realised that I was crying. I felt the rim of a glass against my mouth. The drink seemed to steady me. "Sorry," I mumbled.

"I didn't know you were engaged to Alice Reece," he said.

"No," I said. "I didn't tell you because I wanted Reece to get that job on his merits. I was afraid you'd think——" I stopped and shrugged my shoulder. "It doesn't matter now. But I thought they were dead—both of them. That's what they told me at H.Q. I thought I'd killed——" He shook me then and I pulled myself together. "Why did you ask me about Reece?" I asked him.

He paused uncertainly. Then he said quietly, "He and I are both in Intelligence still. He's waiting in Milan now for me to——"

"In Milan?" I had a sudden, awful vision of our meeting face to face. I'd have to miss out Milan. Somehow I'd have to persuade my firm.... But Maxwell had caught hold of my arm. "Pull yourself together, Dick. I'm trying to tell you something. I need your help. Listen. You represent B. & H. Evans, machine tool manufacturers of Manchester. That gives you an excuse to visit any of the big industrialists in this town. Jan Tuček is here in Pilsen. Remember Jan Tuček, who commanded the Czech squadron at Biggin Hill in 1940?"

"Yes," I said. "I saw him this afternoon."

"You saw him this afternoon?" He cursed softly. "Then you'll have to see him again. I daren't go there. And I daren't go to his home either. He's too closely watched. My contacts are with Czech air force men. But I've got to get a message to him. As soon as I heard you were——"

"Funny," I said. "He gave me a message for you."

Maxwell was suddenly tense. "What was the message?" he asked quickly.

"I was to tell you—*Saturday night*," I answered.

He nodded. "The trouble is that that isn't soon enough. It's got to be to-morrow night. You've got to see him and tell him that. To-morrow night—understand? Thursday night." He was leaning forward, drumming it into me as though he thought I was too drunk to understand what he was saying. "Can you see him first thing to-morrow morning? It's urgent, Dick—very, very, urgent. Do you understand?"

I nodded.

"Can you see him to-morrow morning?"

"I don't know," I said. "Marič, the head of their tool section, is ringing me to-morrow morning. I should be able to make an appointment with him for the afternoon."

"All right then. The afternoon. But you've got to see Tuček. Tell him Saturday may be too late. It must be to-morrow night—Thursday. Understand? You know the bookshop just opposite here, on the corner?" I nodded. "I'll be there at five. Don't talk to me openly. Just tell me whether it's okay or not as you pass. Got that?"

I nodded.

"Don't fail me, Dick." He knocked back the rest of his drink and got to his feet. "Good luck!" he said, giving my shoulder a squeeze. "See you to-morrow at five."

As he turned to go, I said, "Wait a minute, Max. What is all this? Is Jan Tuček in trouble?"

"Ask no questions," he murmured.

"Are you getting him out of the country—is that it?" I demanded.

He swung round on me angrily. "Keep your voice down, for God's sake."

"Is that what's happening?" I persisted in a lower voice.

"I'm telling you nothing, Dick. It's best if——"

"You mean you don't trust me," I accused him angrily.

He looked at me. "If you like to take it that way, but——" He shrugged his shoulders and then added, "Would you mind having a look out in the corridor to see if it's all clear?"

I opened the door and peered out. The corridor was empty. I nodded to him. He went quickly down to the end and turned right. I went back to my room, closed the door and emptied the remains of the bottle into my glass.

By the time I went to bed I was very drunk—drunk and happy. Reece was alive. Shirer was alive. I hadn't killed them, after all. I managed to unstrap my leg and get most of my clothes off. Then when I'd fallen into bed, I suddenly had a feeling that I had made a mistake in the report I'd been working on earlier in the evening. I rolled out of bed, switched on the light and got the report out of my suitcase. The last thing I remember was trying to decipher the blur of writing through eyelids that kept on shutting out my vision.

I awoke to a blinding light on my eyes. I remembered that I had fallen asleep with the light on and put out my hand to switch it off. It was then that I discovered that the light was off and that it was the sun shining on my face. I sat up, trying to separate the roar of traffic outside the window from the noises in my head and wondering when during the night I had switched off the light. I looked at my watch. It was only seven-thirty and no servant would have been in the room yet. At some time during the night I must have awakened and switched it off. I lay in the bright sunlight thinking about Maxwell. His visit seemed unreal, like a dream.

I was called at eight-thirty. As soon as I was dressed I went down to breakfast. In the entrance hall I stopped to buy a paper. "Good morning, *pane*." It was the night porter. He was just putting on his outdoor things and his face had a confidential smirk. I paid for my paper and turned away. But before I was halfway across the room, the man was at my side. He was still struggling into his overcoat. "I hope you did not mind my letting a visitor up to your room so late," he said.

I stopped and glanced down at him. He was a little, rat-faced man with bulging blue eyes and a thin, greedy mouth. "Nobody came to my room last night," I said.

He shrugged the padded shoulders of his overcoat. "Just as *pana* says." He stood there and it was perfectly clear what he was waiting for. I cursed Maxwell for having been so careless. He must have mistaken my hesitation, for he added, "One o'clock is very late for an Englishman to receive visitors in a hotel in Czechoslovakia."

"One o'clock!" I stared at him. Maxwell left shortly after eleven.

He cocked his head on one side, "And *pan* Tuček is a well-known figure here in Pilsen." He shrugged his shoulders again. "But of course if *pana* says no one visit him, then I believe him and I also say no one visit him."

I remembered how the light had been off when I woke and how Jan Tuček had said he'd come to see me at the hotel. But if he had come, why the devil hadn't he wakened me? I could have given him Maxwell's message then. The porter was peering up at me uncertainly. "*Pana* must understand that I have to report everything of an unusual nature to the Party, particularly if it concerns an Englishman or an American." His lips tightened into a smile. "But life is difficult here in Czechoslovakia. I have a wife and family to think of, *pane*. Sometimes economics are more important than Party loyalties. You understand, *pane*?"

"Perfectly," I said. He was like a small sparrow searching determinedly after scraps in a cold spell. I pulled out my wallet and slipped him fifty kronen.

"*Děkuji úctivě. Děkuji.*" The notes disappeared into his trouser pocket. "I remember now. It is just as *pana* says. There was no visitor at one o'clock this morning."

14

He was turning away when I stopped him. "Did you show this visitor up yourself?"

"Oh no, *pane*. He walk straight through the entrance and up the stairs. I know he is not a resident, so I follow him. It is expected of me."

"Quite," I said. "And you recognised this person?"

"Oh, yes, *pane*." Then he smiled. "But, of course—no, *pane*. I do not recognise him any more now. I do not know to which room he go." He smirked and with a little bow, turned and walked quickly out through the hotel entrance.

I went through into the breakfast room. After several cigarettes and innumerable cups of black coffee I had got no nearer a solution of the matter. The porter wasn't lying. I was certain of that. He had been far too sure of getting a fat tip. But if Tuček had come to see me so late at night, he must have had a reason, and an important one. Then why didn't he wake me?

The problem was with me all that morning. I took a couple of aspirins to clear my head and went out into the bright spring sunshine. The buds shone fat and sticky on the smoke-black chestnut trees across the road. Birds were singing above the rattle of the trams and girls were wearing summer frocks. I paid three calls during the morning and did some business. When I got back to the hotel I was relieved to find that Marič had rung me. I was to call and see him at three-thirty. I could deliver my message to Tuček then.

At the Tuček works I was escorted by one of the factory police to the main office block. Marič had two of his technical experts with him. We discussed specifications. From a business point of view the meeting was successful. When the conference broke up, I remained seated. Marič glanced at me through his thick glasses. He got rid of the others very quickly and then, when the door was shut, he turned to me and said in English, "You wish to see me alone, Mr. Farrell?"

"Well——" I hesitated. "I didn't think I should leave without saying good-bye to Mr. Tuček. You see, he and I were together——"

"Quite, quite." Marič nodded and sat down at his desk. He took off his glasses and wiped them. Then, when he'd clipped them on to his nose again, he looked across at me.

"But I do not think you can see him." His fingers had closed on a sheet of paper and he slowly crumpled it into a ball."

"Is he in conference?" I asked. "If so I will wait."

He seemed about to say something. Then his small blue eyes retreated behind his glasses. "I do not think it will be any good waiting. But perhaps if you care to see his secretary——" His voice sounded vague and uncertain.

"Yes," I said. "I'd like to see his secretary."

He nodded and rang for his assistant. The sudden decisiveness of his movements suggested a sense of relief. His assistant came in and he instructed him to take me to Tuček's personal secretary. "Good-bye, Mr. Farrell." He dropped the crumpled ball of paper into his waste-paper basket and shook my hand. His fingers were soft and damp in my grip.

His assistant took me down two flights of concrete stairs and along a passage that was full of the noise of typewriters. Then we passed through swing doors marked *Správa závodu* and we were in the administrative block where the sound of our footsteps was lost in the deep pile of a carpeted corridor. It was the same corridor I'd walked down the previous day. We stopped at the door marked *Ludvik Novák, tajemnik ředitelství*. My guide knocked and I was shown into the office of Tuček's personal secretary. "Come in, Mr. Farrell." He was the dapper little man with the uneasy smile I'd seen the day before. There was no warmth in his greeting. "You are back again very soon. Was your meeting with *pan* Marič not satisfactory?"

"Perfectly," I said.

"Then what can I do for you?"

"I would like to see Mr. Tuček before I go."

"I am sorry. That is not possible." He gave me a rubber-stamp smile.

"Then I'll wait until he's free," I said.

"It is not possible for you to see *pan* Tuček to-day." His eyes were quite blank.

I felt as though I were up against a stone wall. "You mean he's not here?" I asked.

"I have told you, Mr. Farrell. It is impossible for you to see him." He crossed to the door and opened it. "I am sorry. We are very busy to-day."

I thought of Maxwell's strange visit the previous night. *It's urgent, Dick—very, very urgent.* "Whether you are busy or not," I said, "I wish to see Mr. Tuček. Will you please tell him."

The man's eyes stared at me without blinking. "Why are you so anxious to see *pan* Tuček?" he asked.

"I was with him in the most critical days of our fight against the Germans," I said. "I am not in the habit of leaving a town without saying good-bye to old friends." I realised that I'd got to get under the cold official to the man beneath. "You are his personal secretary," I said. "You must have fought against the

Germans. Surely you can understand that I want to see him before I leave?"

For an instant his eyes had warmth and feeling. Then they were quite blank again. "I am sorry. You cannot see *pan* Tuček to-day."

There was no more I could do. He had opened the door. I went out. It was only after the door had closed behind me that I realised he had not called anyone to escort me out of the works. I had begun to walk down the corridor before I realised this. I stopped and looked back. At the far end of the corridor was a big mahogany door. On it I saw—*Jan Tuček, předseda a vrchní ředitel*. I quietly retraced my steps and stopped outside the door. There was the sound of somebody moving inside. I turned the handle and walked in.

Then I stopped. Opposite me was a big, glass-fronted bookcase. The glass doors had been flung wide and books littered the floor. A man paused in the act of rifling through the pages of a gilt-bound tome. "What do you want?" He spoke in Czech and his voice was hard and authoritative. I glanced quickly towards the desk. Another man was seated in the chair Jan Tuček had occupied the previous day. The drawers had all been pulled out on to the floor. The carpet was littered with files. And from the midst of the pile the smiling face of Tuček's daughter looked up at me. The steel filing cabinets against the wall by the windows had also been rifled. "What do you want?" The man by the desk was also looking at me now. The sudden chill of panic crept along my spine. "I'm sorry," I said. "I was looking for *pan* Novák."

Fortunately my Czech is quite good. The two men looked at me suspiciously. Then the one at the desk said, "In the next office."

I murmured apologies and shut the door quickly. I tried not to hurry as I walked back along the corridor. But every moment I expected to hear the sound of Tuček's door opening and a voice calling me to stop. But apparently they were not suspicious. Nevertheless, it was only after I'd passed through the swing doors and heard the sound of my feet on the concrete passage beyond, that the feeling of panic left me.

At the stairs I hesitated. If I left now, without knowing what had happened, Maxwell would think me scared. I hurried up the two flights of stairs and went into Marič's department. "I think I left my gloves in *pan* Marič's office," I told his assistant. "Can I go in?" I didn't wait for him to answer, but walked straight through into Marič's office. He was sitting at his desk, staring out of the window. He turned with an obvious start as I entered.

"Oh, it is you, Mr. Farrell." The sudden panic drained out of his eyes, leaving them expressionless—as blank as Novák's eyes

17

had been when I had asked to see Tuček. "Is there—something you wish to see me about?" His voice was nervous and he fidgeted with the ruler on his desk.

"Yes," I said. I glanced towards the door and then lowered my voice. "What's happened to Jan Tuček?"

"I do not know what you mean," His voice was wooden.

"Yes, you do," I said.

He got up then. "Please go," he said. He was very agitated. "My assistant——" His mouth drooped at the corners.

"I'll go as soon as you tell me what's happened to Tuček," I said. "I've just been down to his office. There are two men there, searching it. There were files and books all over the floor."

He sat down then and for a moment he said nothing. His body, hunched in the big arm-chair, seemed suddenly shrivelled and old. "Jan Tuček has been arrested," he said slowly.

"Arrested?" I think I'd known it ever since I'd walked into his office. But to hear it put bluntly into words shook me.

"Why?" I asked.

He shrugged his shoulders. "Why is anyone arrested in Czechoslovakia to-day? He fought in England during the war. That alone is sufficient to make him suspect. Also he is an industrialist." His voice was low and somehow fatalistic. It was as though he saw in this the beginning of the end for himself.

"Is he in prison?" I asked.

He shook his head. "They do not go so far yet. That is why they search his office. They look for evidence. For the moment he is confined to his house. Perhaps he will be released to-morrow. And then—perhaps not." He gave a slight shrug of his shoulders. "This sort of thing hangs over all of us of the old Czechoslovakia. So many have disappeared already."

"But what has he done?" I asked.

"I do not know." He took off his glasses and began to polish them as though afraid of showing some emotion. There was a heavy, audible silence between us. At length he picked up a newspaper from under a pile of papers, peered at it and then held it out to me. "Column two," he said. "The Rinkstein story."

It was down-page, quite a small story headed: DIAMOND DEALER ARRESTED—RINKSTEIN ACCUSED OF IL-LEGAL CURRENCY DEALS. "Who is Rinkstein?" I asked him.

"Isaac Rinkstein is one of the biggest jewellers in Prague."

"What's his arrest got to do with Tuček?"

"Everything—nothing. I do not know." He shrugged his shoulders. "All I know is he deal in diamonds and precious stones."

18

"But he's been arrested for illegal currency operations," I pointed out.

He smiled wryly. "That is the legal excuse. It is his dealings in precious stones that will interest the authorities, I think." He bent the ruler between his two hands till I thought it must break. "I am very much afraid Rinkstein will talk." He got up suddenly and took the paper away from me. "You must go now. I have talk too much already. Please repeat nothing—nothing, you understand?" He was looking at me and I saw he was frightened. "Sixteen years I have been with the Tuček company." He shrugged his shoulders. "Good-bye, Mr. Farrell." His hand was cold and soft.

"I'll be back in Pilsen in about three months," I said as he took me to the door. "I shall look forward to seeing you again then."

His lips twisted in a thin smile. "I hope so," he said. He opened the door and called to his assistant to get me a car. It was with a feeling of relief that I was swept through the factory gates and out into the streets of Pilsen. Black clouds were coming up from the west and as I got out at my hotel the first drops of rain fell on the dry pavements.

I phoned the airport and checked that my passage to Munich and through to Milan was fixed. Then I got my raincoat and hurried across the road to the bookshop on the corner. It was not quite five. I searched through the paper backs with my eye on the door. Five o'clock struck from a nearby church. There was no sign of Maxwell. I stayed on until the shop shut at five-thirty. But he didn't come. I bought several books and after waiting for a bit in the doorway, went back to the hotel. There was no message for me at the desk. I ordered tea to be sent up to my room and tried to finish off my report. But my mind could concentrate on nothing but Tuček's arrest. Also I was worried about Maxwell.

In the end I went down to the bar. For a while I tried to persuade myself that Tuček and Maxwell were nothing to do with me. But it was no good. What had happened filled me with a sense of helplessness. It made me want to get drunk again, so I went in to dinner. And after dinner I went out to a cinema where an old English film was showing. I got back shortly before eleven. There was no message for me and nobody had called to see me. I got a drink and took it up to my room. I stayed up, waiting for Maxwell. But he didn't come and when the church clock struck midnight I went to bed. It was a long time before I could get to sleep. I kept on thinking of Jan Tuček, somewhere over on the other side of Pilsen under house arrest, and wondering what had become of Maxwell.

I was called at eight-thirty the following morning. The rain was beating in at the open window and the clouds were low and wind-blown. It looked like being a dirty trip over the Alps. But I didn't care about that. I was glad to be leaving Czechoslovakia. I knew I'd been on the fringe of a political whirlpool and it was good to know I was getting out before I was sucked down into it.

I had breakfast, paid my bill and got a *drožka*. The flight was scheduled for eleven-thirty. I paid one call on the way out to the airport and arrived well before eleven. I checked my bags and then went to the passenger clearing office. I handed my passport to the clerk. He looked at it, flicked over the pages and then nodded to a man standing near me. The man came forward. "*Pan* Farrell?"

I nodded, not trusting my voice. I knew what he was.

"You will come with me please." He spoke in Czech. "There are some questions we must ask you."

"I don't understand," I said, putting a front on it. "Who are you?"

"I am of the S.N.B." His hand was on my arm. "Come this way, please. We have a car waiting."

I looked about me quickly. I had a sudden, urgent desire to make a break for it. I'd been through all this before. I knew what it was like. I'd lost a leg and nearly lost my reason, too. But the grip tightened on my arm. There was another of them on my other side. And then suddenly I was angry. I'd done nothing, nothing at all. They couldn't arrest me without a reason. I shook my arms free and faced them. "Are you arresting me?" I demanded.

"We wish to question you, *pan* Farrell." It was the smaller of the two who replied, the one who had spoken before. He was very broad in the shoulders and his small eyes were protected by sandy lashes that blinked very rapidly.

"Then please put your questions to me here. My plane leaves at eleven-thirty."

The corners of his lips turned down slightly. "I am afraid you will miss your plane. My instructions are to take you to the *Ředitelství S.N.B.*"

"Then I am under arrest," I said. "What is the charge, please?"

"We only wish to question you." His hand was on my arm again, his face quite expressionless. I knew it was no good trying to bluff him. He had his instructions. There was only one thought in my mind, to see that somebody knew what had happened. "Very well then. But first I must telephone my Embassy in Prague."

"You can do that later."

"I'll do it now," I snapped. "You arrest me without making any charge and then try to deny me the right to inform my own

20

Embassy of what has happened." I leaned over the desk and picked up the telephone that was there. He moved to stop me, but I said, "Either I telephone or I make a scene. There are sure to be some English or Americans here at the airport. If they report what has happened you will find the repercussions at a much higher level."

He seemed to appreciate the point, for he shrugged his shoulders. Fortunately I got through right away and I was able to get the third secretary, a man named Elliot whom I'd met at a party in Prague only a few days ago. I explained what had happened and he promised to take immediate action.

I put down the telephone. "Now if you'll find my bags for me," I said, "I'll come with you. But please understand I have business appointments in Milan and I shall hold your office responsible for seeing that I have a reservation on the next plane." I took my passport away from the clerk who had been gaping at us the whole time and, after collecting my two suitcases, we went out to a waiting police car.

The moment of genuine anger which had carried me as far as the phone call to the Embassy had evaporated now, and I admit that, as we drove back through the suburbs of Pilsen, I was pretty scared. It was true that I'd done nothing. But if they checked up on me.... Suppose they'd arrested Maxwell and knew that he'd come to see me by way of the fire-escape? Had the night porter kept his mouth shut about Jan Tuček's visit? And what about the two men I'd interrupted searching Tuček's office? If they checked up on me thoroughly I'd have a job convincing them that I was completely outside the whole business. And what was the business anyway? What had happened to make them suddenly arrest me? And then I began to sweat. Suppose they'd got Maxwell? Suppose they confronted Maxwell with me? He'd think I'd given him away. My God! He'd think the mere threat of trouble had frightened me into talking. All my other fears were suddenly of no importance. They were swamped by this new and to me much more terrifying possibility.

At the *Reditelství* I was put in a dingy little waiting-room that looked out on to the ruins of a bombed building. A uniformed policeman was placed in the room with me. He stood by the door, picking his teeth and watching me without interest. There was a clock on the wall. It ticked the minutes away slowly and relentlessly. It was the old technique. I tried to relax, to ignore the slow passage of time. But as the hands of the clock slowly moved round the dial I felt the silence preying on my nerves. I tried to get into conversation with my guard. But he had his instructions. He just shook his head and said nothing.

After forty minutes a police officer entered and told me to follow him. I was taken down a stone corridor and up a flight of uncarpeted stairs, the guard following behind me. On the first floor I was shown into an office. There were shutters across the window and the place was lit by electric light. A small bearded man in plain clothes was seated at a desk. "I am sorry to have kept you waiting. Please sit down." He waved me to a seat.

I sat down. He fumbled amongst the papers on his desk. His face I remember was very pale, almost yellow, and he had bright button eyes. The back of his carefully manicured hands were covered with black hair. He found the paper he was looking for and said, "You are Richard Harvey Farrell?" He spoke in Czech.

I nodded.

"And you represent the company of B. & H. Evans of Manchester."

"Yes," I said. "I was due to catch the plane to Munich and Milan at eleven-thirty this morning. Would you be good enough to tell my why I have been arrested?"

He looked across at me with a slight lift of his tufty eyebrows. "Arrested, *pan* Farrell? Come now—all we wish is to put a few questions to you."

"If there was any way I could have helped you," I said, "surely it would have been sufficient to have sent an officer down to the hotel before I left?"

He smiled. I didn't like that smile. It was slightly sadistic. He was like a psychiatrist whose career has taken some peculiar twist. "I am sorry you have been inconvenienced." He made it clear that he enjoyed inconveniencing people. I waited and after a moment, he said, "You knew *pan* Tuček I believe?"

"That is correct," I answered.

"You are with him when he is in England in 1940."

I nodded.

"And you saw him at the Tučkovy ocelárny the day before yesterday?"

"Yes."

"What did you talk about?"

I gave him the gist of our conversation in front of the interpreter. His eyes kept glancing down to the paper on his desk and I knew that he was checking my account with the interpreter's report. When I had finished he nodded as though satisfied. "You speak our language very well, *pan* Farrell. Where did you learn?"

"In the air force," I answered. "I find languages come quite easily to me and I was stationed with Tuček's Czech squadron for several months."

He smiled. "But on Wednesday, when you see Tuček, you do not speak any language but English. Why?" The question was barked at me suddenly and his little button eyes were fixed on mine. "Why do you lie and make it necessary for an interpreter to be found?"

"I didn't lie," I answered hotly. "It was Tuček who said I spoke nothing but English."

"Why?"

I shrugged my shoulders. "How should I know? Probably he felt it was not very nice to talk to an old friend in front of a spy." I was speaking in English now and I saw him straining to translate.

"Are you sure you do not come with a message to him?" The fact that he was now speaking haltingly in English together with the negative phrasing of the question made it clear that he had nothing definite against me.

"What message could I bring him?" I asked. "I hadn't seen him for over ten years."

He nodded and then said, "Please give me an account of all that you do since you arrive in Plzeň. I wish every minute to be accounted for, *pan* Farrell."

Well, I took him through everything from the moment of my arrival at the Hotel Continental. When I had finished he sat looking down at the papers on his desk, drumming with his fingers. "Would you mind telling me why you find it necessary to question me about this meeting between Tuček and myself?" I asked him.

He looked at me. "The man is politically suspect. He has many contacts in England." He stopped short there and shouted to someone in the next office. The door opened and the man who had stopped me at the airport came in. For an awful moment I thought he was going to confront me with the night porter of the Hotel Continental. "Take *pan* Farrell back to his hotel," he ordered. Then he turned to me. "You will remain at your hotel, please. If we have no further questions to ask you, you will be allowed to leave by to-morrow's plane."

I said nothing, but followed the police officer out of the room. Outside the *Reditelství* a police car was waiting. I got in. As we drove off I found I was trembling. The reaction was setting in and I wanted a drink. The rain-wet smell of the streets was very sweet after the dead mustiness of S.N.B. headquarters. Gradually my nerves relaxed. The police car drew up at the hotel and I got out. The officer put my bags on the pavement and the car drove off. I took my things into the hotel and went through into the bar. I was ordering a drink when a voice behind me said in Czech,

"Perhaps *pana* would be kind enough to give me a light?" I turned. It was Maxwell. He made no sign of recognition and when I'd struck a match and lit his cigarette, he thanked me and went back to his seat in a corner of the bar.

II

IT was obvious that Maxwell wanted to speak to me. In the mirror backing of the shelves behind the bar I could see him seated at one of the little tables well away from the light of the windows. He was reading a newspaper and didn't once glance in my direction. I waited until the bar had filled up. Then I got myself another drink and went over to his table. "Permit me, *pane*," I said in Czech, and took the chair opposite him.

"I was beginning to get worried about you, Dick," he said without glancing up from his newspaper. "Are you being watched?"

"I don't think so," I answered.

"Good. Will they let you take the plane to-morrow?"

"I think so. They don't seem to have anything against me except the fact that I saw Jan Tuček on Wednesday. How did you know I'd been arrested?"

"I was at the airport."

"Were you catching that plane?"

"No. I was waiting to see you." I saw the whites of his eyes in the shadow of his face as he glanced quickly round the room. Then he smoothed his paper out flat on the table and leaned slightly forward. "You probably know by now why the S.N.B. police picked you up for questioning." I shook my head and he said, "We got Tuček out of the country last night. That's why I couldn't meet you as arranged. There was a lot to do."

"You got him out of the country!" I stared at him. "But—he was in protective custody. How——"

"A little diversion. The house next door caught fire. But don't worry about the details. We had an old Anson waiting at Bory airfield. There were two of them—Tuček and a senior Czech air force officer, generál letectva Lemlin. They should have been in

Milan early this morning." He was talking very fast, his lips hardly moving. "Reece wouldn't be expecting them till Sunday morning, but they knew where to contact him, and I should have had confirmation of their arrival by wire this morning." He paused and then said, "I'm very worried, Dick. I've heard nothing. When you get to Milan to-morrow, I want you to go straight to the Albergo Excelsiore, opposite the Stazione Centrale. Tell Reece to wire me immediately. Will you do that?"

"The Excelsiore! Is Reece staying there?" I asked him.

He nodded and I cursed the luck that had booked me at the same hotel. I didn't want to see Reece. I think Maxwell knew that, for he added, "It's very urgent, Dick. They may have crashed."

"All right," I said. "I'll see Reece."

"Good man. Just one other thing. A message from Tuček. He told me to tell you that he wished to see you as soon as you arrived in Milan. He was very insistent."

"All right," I said.

A waiter appeared and collected our glasses. Maxwell folded his newspaper. "Would *pana* care to have a look at the paper?" he said in Czech. I thanked him and took the paper. He collected his brief case and got to his feet. "Goodbye, Dick," he whispered. "See you again sometime," And he strolled down the length of the bar and out by the street door.

I had another drink and then went into lunch. Time passed very slowly during the rest of that day. I drank it away watching the hands of the clock over the bar move steadily through afternoon into evening. The airport had made no difficulty about transferring my booking to the following day. The only question was, would the police let me go? Everything seemed to hinge on whether the night porter kept his mouth shut about Tuček's extraordinary visit to my room. The more I thought about that, the more odd it seemed. If he had come to see me, then why hadn't he wakened me? Perhaps I'd been so drunk he couldn't wake me? But then why did he want to see me as soon as I reached Milan?

These speculations became more and more confused in my mind as I drank the evening out. And they became confused with my promise to see Reece. I didn't want to see Reece. Alive or dead, I didn't want to see him. He'd been so bitter. He'd turned his sister against me, smashed my life. Shirer I didn't mind so much. Shirer had been older. He knew what I'd been through. But Reece was young. He didn't understand. He'd never faced real pain in his life. Those letters he'd written her from the hospital —he'd told me what he was writing to her. He'd taken it out of me that way. Suddenly I didn't care about the Czech security police.

I didn't want to leave Czechoslovakia any more. Let them arrest me. I didn't care. All I knew was that I didn't want to go to Milan and see Reece. God! For all I knew Alice might be there. I began to sing *Alice Blue Gown*. That was when they got me out of the bar and I found the night porter helping me up to my room.

As we reached the landing he said, "I hear, *pane*, that you have trouble with the S.N.B. to-day?" His greedy little eyes peered up at me. I wanted to punch his face. I knew what he wanted. He wanted money. "You go to hell!" I said.

I couldn't get his face in focus, but I knew he was leering up at me. "Perhaps I go to the police."

"You can go to the devil for all I care," I mumbled.

He opened the door of my room and helped me inside. I tried to shake him off and fell on to the bed. He shut the door and came over to me. "Also I hear *pan* Tuček is escaped. Perhaps his visit to you is more important than the fifty kronen you give me, eh?" He was standing beside the bed, looking down at me.

"Get the hell out of here, you little crook," I shouted at him.

"But, *pane*, consider for a moment, please. If I tell the police what I know it will be very bad for *pane*."

I didn't care any more. As long as I didn't have to see Reece I didn't mind. "Go to the police," I said wearily. "It doesn't matter. Go and tell them what you know." I saw the baffled, frustrated look on his face and that was the last thing I remember. Whether I passed out or just fell asleep I don't know. All I know is that I woke fully clothed and very cold to find myself sprawled on my bed in the dark. It was then just after one-thirty. I undressed and got into bed.

In the morning I felt frightful. Also I was scared. Everything is much simpler when you're drunk. Perhaps it is because the urge to live is less. At any rate, in the sober grey light of day I knew that I'd rather face Reece in Milan than be held here in Pilsen by the Czech police. I'd been a fool to refuse the porter money. I dressed quickly and went down to find him. But he'd already gone. I was in a panic then lest he'd gone to the police. I tried to steady myself with cups of black coffee and cigarettes. But my hands were trembling and clammy and I knew that I was waiting all the time for my name to be called, waiting to go out and find the man with the sandy eyelashes standing by the reception desk.

But my name wasn't called and in the end I got up and went out to pay my bill. As soon as I looked in my wallet I knew why the police hadn't come for me. Most of my money was gone—all the pound notes and lire. The little swine had left me just enough kronen to pay my bill.

I got my bags down and took a *droška* out to the airport. I was sweating and my head was swimming as I went towards the passenger clearing office. I searched the faces of the men standing around the room. Several of them seemed to be watching me. I reached the desk and presented my passport. The same clerk was on duty there. He waved the passport aside with a little smile and made some crack about there being no reception committee for me this morning. I got a paper and sat waiting for my flight to be called. I tried to read, but the print hurt my eyes and I couldn't concentrate. I watched the main entrance, suspicious of every man who came in without any baggage.

The flight was called at eleven-fifteen. I walked out to the plane with four other passengers. As we queued up to enter the aircraft my heart was in my mouth. An attendant was checking the names of the passengers. Beside him stood a man in a grey trilby. I was certain he was from the S.N.B. At last my turn came. "Name, please?"

"Farrell." My mouth felt dry. The man in the grey trilby looked at me with cold, hostile eyes. The attendant made a tick against my name. I hesitated. The man in the trilby made no move. My leg seemed more awkward than usual as I negotiated the three steps of the ladder. I found a seat well up towards the front of the fuselage and slumped into it. I was sweating and I wiped my face and my hands with my handkerchief.

I got my paper out then and pretended to read. The crew came in and went through to the cockpit. The connecting door slid to. I sat there waiting. I could feel the draught from the open door of the fuselage blowing on my back. Would they never close it? The suspense was frightful. To get so far.... The devil of it was that I knew this was just the sort of cat-and-mouse game they loved. It was all part of the softening-up process.

The port engine turned over and started into life. Then the starboard engine. The door to the cockpit slid back and one of the crew looked in and ordered us to fix our safety belts. Now was the moment they'd come for me. I heard a sudden movement by the entrance door. I couldn't control myself any longer. I swung round in my seat. To my amazement the steps had been taken away. The door shut with a clang and was closed on the inside. The engines roared and we began to taxi out to the runway.

The feeling of relief that flooded through me was like the sudden plunge into unconsciousness. There was a pleasurable chill feeling along my spine and the back of my eyes were moist. I don't remember taking off. I felt too dazed. I only know that the roar of the engines changed suddenly to a steady purr and the seat was pressed hard against the base of my spine. Automatically I fumbled at the locking device of my safety belt, only to find that I'd never fastened it. Through the window at my side all Pilsen was spread out below me, tilted at an angle as we banked. I could see the onion-shaped dome of the water tower of Pilsen Brewery and the miles of sidings alongside the big factories. Through belching smoke I caught a glimpse of the Tuček steel works. Then Pilsen vanished beneath the plane as we straightened on to our course.

My sense of relief was short-lived. There was still Prague and Vienna. At each of these stops they could arrest me. But nobody disturbed me or even asked for my papers, and as we rose into the clear sunlight over Vienna with the snow-capped gleam of the Alps ahead I lay back in my seat, relaxed for the first time in two days. I was the right side of the Iron Curtain. They couldn't touch me now. I slept then and didn't wake until we were in Italy.

The plane skirted the foothills of the Dolomites and then we were on the edge of the Po Valley headed west towards Milan. I began to think of what lay ahead, of my meeting with Reece. It was odd that it should be at Milan, so close to Lake Como. It was there, at the Villa d'Este, that I had last seen him.

It had been in April, 1945, that he and Shirer had escaped. And it was that little swine of a doctor who was so like Shirer who'd fixed it for them. He'd helped them to escape and then he'd blown his brains out.

The mere thought of him brought the sweat prickling out on my forehead. Giovanni Sansevino—*Il dottore*, they'd called him. I could hear the orderly's voice saying, "Il dottore is coming to see you this morning, Signor Capitano." How often had I heard that, and always with a sly relish? The orderly—the one with the wart on his nose who was called Luigi—he'd liked pain. "Il dottore is coming to see you." He'd stay in the ward after that, watching me out of his unnaturally pale eyes, watching me as I lay sweating, wondering whether it was to be one of the doctor's little social visits as he called them or another operation.

Staring out through the window of the plane to the serrated edge of the Alps, it wasn't my reflected face that I saw in the perspex, but the doctor's face. I could remember it so clearly. It didn't seem possible that he'd been dead over five years. It wasn't an unpleasant face at all. Except for the moustache, it might have been Shirer's face, and I'd liked Shirer. It was a round, rather chubby face, very blue about the jowls with a broad forehead and an olive complexion below the black sheen of his hair. Only the eyes weren't right somehow. They were too close together, too small. He hid them behind dark glasses. But when he was operating he abandoned the glasses and I could remember staring up into those small, dark pupils and seeing the strange, sadistic excitement that stirred in them as his hands touched my skin, caressing with beastly enjoyment the flesh he was going to cut away. His breath would come then in quick, sharp pants as though he were caressing a woman and his tongue would flick over his lips.

Sitting there in the plane I felt my muscles contracting as I relived the touch of those hands. It wasn't difficult for me to recall the feel of them. My trouble had been to forget. Too often I'd wakened in the night screaming, with all my body tense, forcing myself to realise that my left leg was no longer there, that it had gone in shreds down the drains of the Villa d'Este, and that the touch of those hands, which I could still feel even on waking, was just a trick of nerve threads that had been severed long ago.

It is extraordinary how nerves can recall touch in such detail. The slow, stroking movement of the tips of his long, sensitive fingers was indelibly fixed on the nerve record of my brain. The man had been a fine surgeon and his fingers had been clever and strong. Yet somehow in their touch they had managed to convey a subtle enjoyment of pain. He must have done hundreds of operations, and all the time I felt he had been patiently waiting for the moment when I should be delivered to him and he could demonstrate his skill to the patient by operating without an anæsthetic.

And always as his fingers stroked my flesh he had said, "You think I enjoy operating on you without an anæsthetic, don't you, Signor Farrell? But I am a surgeon. I like to do a good job. This is not necessary, you know. Why not be sensible? Why not tell the Gestapo what they wish to know, eh?" It had been a formula run off like a magician's stage patter. He hadn't wanted me to talk. He'd wanted me to remain silent, so that he could operate. I could tell that by the way his breath came in his gathering excitement and by the narrowing of the black pupils of his eyes. Soon it had been only the remains of a leg that he had stroked so gently, so caressingly. Then there had come a day when he had said, "There is not much left of this leg. Soon we must begin on the other one, eh?" His gentle, sibilant voice was there in the drone of the engines and I could feel the whole of my lost leg as though it was still flesh and blood and not a tin dummy.

I put a stop to my imagination, wiping the sweat from my forehead and dragging myself back to the present by leaning forward and gazing out of the window. Padua was below and beyond the starboard wing the white teeth of the Dolomites fanged a dark cloudscape. But staring at the Alps didn't blot the thought of Reece from my mind. He was there in the past, as he'd always been. And now he was ahead of me, too. When I reached Milan I'd got to face him, give him Maxwell's message—and somehow I didn't feel I had the courage to face him. They'd brought him to the Villa d'Este with a bullet in the lung only a few hours after that last operation. They'd put him in the next bed to mine and let him find out gradually how he'd come to be picked up.

Shirer they had picked up about the same time. But he went to a P.O.W. camp. He was brought to the Villa d'Este early in 1945 after a course of poison gas treatment. It was a burning gas and they'd used him as a guinea pig, partly to make him talk, partly as an experiment. They put him in the bed on the other side of me and Il dottore was put to work on him. There in the plane I could still hear his screams. I think they were worse than my own remembered screams. And all the time, through the barred window, we looked out on to the blue of Lago do Como, with the white villas opposite and the Swiss frontier only a few kilometres away.

Sansevino did a good job on Shirer. Within two months he was almost well again. Once the little doctor said to him, "I take trouble with you, signore, because you are so like me. I do not like to see a man who is so like myself disfigured." The likeness was certainly extraordinary.

In April the three of us were moved to a separate ward. It was then that Sansevino first intimated that he would help them to escape. His condition was that we all three signed a statement that he had been kind and considerate to all Allied patients and that he had taken no part in German guinea-pig experiments. "The Allies will win the war now," he had said. "And I do not wish to die because of what they force me to do here." We had refused at first. I remembered that I had enjoyed the momentary flicker of fear I had seen in his eyes as we refused. But we'd signed the document in the end, and after that we had got better food. It was almost as though he were fattening us up. He was particularly interested in Shirer's condition, having him weighed repeatedly, examining him again and again as though he were a prize exhibit in some forthcoming show. This special treatment worried Shirer. He was worried, too, about his resemblance to the Italian doctor. He became obsessed with the idea that it was because of this he had been brought to the Villa d'Este and he was filled with a premonition that he would never see America again.

For my part I thought it was all a part of the twisted mentality

30

of the little doctor that he should bring these two, Reece and Shirer, to the hospital and then move us to a separate ward. It was hell for me being cooped up in that tiny room, forced in to the company of the two men I had destroyed. They should have been out in the hills above Bologna organising the *partigiani*. Only the fact that my plane had been hit by ack-ack and crashed after dropping them had led to their being captured. It was hell having them for company—a worse hell than the frightful pain of those operations. Shirer had understood, I think. He wasn't a young man and he had seen a good deal of suffering in the coal mines of Pittsburgh, which was his home. The fact that he was an American Italian also probably had something to do with it—it made him more sensitive and perhaps his code wasn't so rigid.

Reece, on the other hand, was solid and unimaginative. He came from Norfolk of a long line of Puritan ancestors and for him right and wrong were as clear as white and black. Two years in Milan as an engineering student had hardened, rather than softened his outlook on life. From the day he arrived at the Villa d'Este and Sansevino explained to him how it was that he had been captured, he never spoke to me. The fact that I had been engaged to his sister made his reaction all the more violent. He didn't take Sansevino's word for it. He cross-examined me. And when he realised that it was the truth, that the third operation had finished me, then he withdrew into himself, hating me for being the cause of his not finishing the job he'd been sent out to do.

It wasn't so bad in the big ward. But when we were moved into the little room overlooking the lake, it had been torture to me. I could feel the silence still. It would grow and grow until suddenly Shirer would break it, going out of his way to talk to me. He had made a little chess set and we played by the hour. But all this time I was conscious of Alec Reece's presence. knowing that sooner or later he would inform his sister of what had happened.

The memory of those days was so vivid that even the sounds of the plane and the sight of the Alps standing white along the horizon couldn't blot out their memory. Then, thank God, the two of them had gone. Sansevino had arranged it. I was up and about then, getting my stump accustomed to the pain of bearing my weight on the cup of the wooden leg they'd given me. But I couldn't go. And I was glad I couldn't go.

They left on the 21st April. Sansevino had given them civilian clothes and all the necessary documents. They left just after midnight—first Shirer, then Reece. They were to rendezvous at the vehicle park, take an ambulance and drive to Milan where they would be looked after by Sansevino's friends.

I thought at the time that Sansevino had been relying on the document we had all signed to save him from being arrested for war crimes when the war was over. It never occurred to me that in arranging their escape he was trying to come to terms with his conscience. Yet that must have been the reason for his sudden act of generosity, for next morning he was dead at his desk. His orderly had been instructed to bring me to him first thing in the morning, at 7 o'clock. It was we who found him. He was in full uniform with all his Fascist decorations, slumped in his chair, his head lolling back and a black bloodstain on his shoulder. The little Beretta with which he'd shot himself was still clenched in his hand. Oddly enough his dark glasses still covered his eyes, though the force of the explosion had driven them almost to the end of his nose. Some queer sense of justice must have induced him to arrange it so that I should actually be one of those to see him after he'd taken his life.

As for Reece and Shirer, something had gone wrong. I heard afterwards that they'd been stopped at an unexpected road block and had been killed whilst attempting to climb to the Swiss frontier. That's what I had been told and I had never doubted the truth of it. Certainly I had made no attempt to check up on it. Why should I? The very last thing Reece had said to me was, "I have written to Alice telling her everything. That letter may not reach her and I may not come through. But God's curse rest on you, Farrell, if you ever try to see her again. You understand?" And I had nodded, too emotionally destroyed to say anything. His letter, however, had got through. Her reply was waiting for me when I rejoined my unit at Foggia. Maxwell himself had handed it to me.

God! I could remember it all so clearly. And here I was, flying through the Po valley to see Reece again. Ahead of us I could see Lake Maggiore, like a piece of lead laid flat in the brown fold of the hills. And beyond, in a golden shimmer of sunshine, the Plain of Lombardy was rolled out like a map. I wiped the sweat off my brow and picked up the paper. My eyes drifted aimlessly over the headlines until they were caught and held by a story headed: ISAAC RINKSTEIN CONFESSES. One paragraph stood out from the rest: *Rinkstein has admitted to making heavy sales of diamonds and other precious stones to certain industrialists, the chief among them being Jan Tuček, chairman and managing director of the Tučkovy ocelárny. This is regarded as indicating that he has been active against the State. Men who convert their fortunes into such easily portable goods as precious stones usually have a guilty conscience. Tuček is believed to have been selling vital industrial and military information to the Western Powers.*

I put the paper down and stared out of the window. We were over Verona now and the road from Venice to Milan cut like a grey ribbon through the green sheet of Lombardy. I was hoping that if Tuček had crashed, as Max feared, he had crashed beyond the Czech frontier. At least he'd have a chance then. But through the farther window I could see the jagged molars of the Alps grinding against the black vault of a storm. I knew what it was like to crash—the tearing, shattering impact and then the sudden stillness of intense pain and the smell of petrol and the fear of fire. That's how it had been when I'd crashed in the Futa Pass. But there I'd managed to find an open stretch of moorland. Up here in the Alps it would be into a snow-covered peak or against some pine-clad slope they'd crash. There was all the difference in the world.

Thinking about Tuček, I forgot myself, and it was not until the sound of the engines slackened and the port wing dipped that I looked out of my window again. Milan lay along the horizon, sunlight glittering on long streamers of smoke blown by the wind from the tall factory chimneys on the outskirts. The solid bulk of a gasometer came up to meet us. Then we were skimming the spire of a church and running in towards a line of pylons. The lights came on in the indicator ordering safety belts to be fixed. The door to the cockpit slid back and one of the crew repeated the order. The sun-baked flat of the airfield came up to meet us and in a moment the concrete of the runways was streaming by and we had landed in Milan.

The main hall of Milan Airport looked very much as it had done when I passed through it on my way down to Foggia in May, 1945, after the German capitulation. The same air maps sprawled across the walls publicising Mussolini's empire. But now the sun shone through the tall frosted windows on to the motley of civilian dress and the public address system announced the flights in Italian and French as well as English.

I checked baggage and passports and was just going out towards the waiting bus when I saw Reece. He was over near the airfield entrance talking to a small, bearded Italian. Our eyes met across the heads of the crowd. I saw sudden recognition and the shock of surprise in his eyes. Then he deliberately turned away and continued his conversation with the Italian.

I hesitated. I had a message to give him and the sooner he got it the better. But somehow I couldn't face it. The blankness that followed that sudden glance of recognition seemed to block me out. I found I was trembling and I knew then I must have a drink before I faced him. I went quickly out to the bus and climbed in. "*Dove, signore!*" The attendant stared at me suspiciously.

"*Excelsiore*," I answered.

"*Excelsiore? Bene.*"

A few minutes later the bus moved off. I knew then that I ought to have gone over to Reece and given him Maxwell's message. I cursed myself for letting my nerves get the better of me. After all it was a long time ago and ... But all I remembered was the blank look that had followed recognition. It had taken me straight back to that little room in the Villa d'Este. He didn't seem to have changed at all. A bit fuller in the face perhaps, but the same broad, stocky figure and determined set of mouth and chin. Well, I'd got to face it sooner or later. I'd have a drink or two and wait for him at the hotel.

The Excelsiore is in the Piazzale Duca d'Aosta facing the Stazione Centrale, that exuberant monument to Fascist ideals that looks more like a colossal war memorial than a railway station. A porter took my two suitcases and I climbed the steps and entered the marble-pillared entrance hall of the hotel. At the reception desk the clerk said, "Your name, please, signore?"

"Farrell," I answered. "I have accommodation booked."

"*Si si, signore.* Will you sign please. *Numero cento venti.*" He called a page. "*Accompagnate il signore al cento venti.*"

The room was small, but comfortable. It looked out across the Piazzale to the railway station. I had a bath and changed and then went down to the lounge to wait for Reece. I ordered tea and sent a page for my mail. There wasn't much; a letter from my mother, a bill for a suit I'd bought before leaving England and the usual packet from my firm. The last included a letter from the managing director. *We expect big things of you in Italy.... When you have been in Milan a week send me a report on the advisability of establishing a permanent agency.... You have my permission to take a holiday there as and when you please and trust you will be able to combine business with pleasure by making social contact with potential customers for our machine tools.* It was signed Harry Evans. I folded the letter and put it away in my brief-case. Then I sat back, thinking of the possibilities of a holiday in Italy, and as I did so my eyes strayed over the room and riveted themselves on the far corner.

Seated alone at a small table by the window was Alice Reece. The sight of her hit me like a blow below the belt. As though drawn by my gaze, she turned her head and saw me. Her eyes brightened momentarily as they met mine across that dimly-lit lounge. Then they seemed to go cold and dead, the way her brother's had done, and she turned away her head.

I think if I'd hesitated I'd have fled to my room. But I was

34

gripped by some strange urge to justify myself. I got to my feet and walked across the room towards her table. She saw me coming. The green of her eyes was caught in the sunlight from the window. She looked into my face and then her gaze fell to my leg. I saw her frown and she turned away towards the window again. I was at her table now, standing over her, seeing the sunlight colouring the soft gold of her hair and the way her hands were clenched on her bag.

"Do you mind if I sit down for a minute?" I asked, and my voice was trembling.

She didn't stop me, but as I pulled out the chair opposite her she said, "It's no good, Dick." She had spoken in a tone of pity.

I sat down. Her face was in profile now and I saw she was older, more mature. There were lines in her forehead and at the corners of her mouth that hadn't been there before. "Eight years is a long time," I said.

She nodded, but said nothing.

Now that I was here, sitting opposite her, I didn't know what to say. No words could bridge the gulf between us. I knew that. And yet there were things I wanted to say, things that couldn't have been written. "I hope you're well," I said inanely.

"Yes," she answered quietly.

"And happy?"

She didn't answer and I thought she hadn't heard. But then she said, "You had all there was of happiness in me, Dick." She turned and looked at me suddenly. "I didn't know about the leg. When did that happen?"

I told her.

She looked away again, out of the window. "Alec never told me about that. It would have made it easier—to understand."

"Perhaps he didn't want to make it easier for you to understand."

"Perhaps."

An awkward silence fell between us. It grew so that I felt at any moment our nerves would snap and we'd cry or laugh out loud or something equally stupid.

"What are you doing in Milan?" I asked.

"A holiday," she replied. "And you?"

"Business," I answered.

Silence again. I think both of us knew that small talk was no good between us. "Will you be here long?" I asked. "I mean— couldn't we meet some——"

She stopped me with an angry movement of her hand. "Don't make it more difficult, Dick," she said and I noticed a trembling in her voice.

35

Her words took us over the edge of small talk, back into the past that we'd shared; a holiday in Wales, the Braemar Games where we'd first met, her fair hair blown by the wind on a yacht on the Broads. I could see her slim body cutting the water as she dived, see her face laughing up at me as we lay under the shade of an old oak in the woods above Solva. Memories flooded through me bringing with them the bitter thought of what might have been between us—a home, children, life. Then her hands were on the table, moving blindly among the tea things, and I knew she had not married.

"Can't we go back——" I began. But the look in her eyes stopped me. She hadn't married, but there was no going back. The eyes that met mine were full of sadness. "Please go now, Dick," she said. "Alec will be back soon and——"

But suddenly I didn't care about Alec. "I'll wait," I said. "I've a message for him—from Maxwell in Czechoslovakia."

Her eyes tensed and I knew then that she had some idea what her brother was doing. "Are you in this, too?" she asked. "I thought——" Her voice stopped there.

"I got drawn into this by chance," I said quickly.

Her eyes were searching my face now as though she expected to see some change there. Suddenly she said, "Tell me about your leg. Was it very bad? Did you have a good surgeon?"

I laughed. Then I told her what had happened. I kept nothing back. I wallowed in self-destruction, explaining how it felt to have the bone sawn through without any anæsthetic, knowing that it would happen again and again. I saw that I was hurting her. But she didn't stop me and I went on. "You see, I don't remember anything. All I know is I went under again, screaming and half delirious and when I came round I was told there would be no more operations, that they had got all——"

I stopped suddenly for I was conscious of a figure standing over us. I looked up. It was Alec Reece. I saw the muscles in his throat tighten and the blood come up into his face as anger gripped him. "I told you once, Farrell, that I'd break your neck if you ever tried to speak to my sister again." I had risen to my feet. "I suppose you thought I was safely out at the airfield." His inference was obvious and I felt my anger rising to match his.

"Sit down, both of you." Alice's voice was calm. I saw her hand catch her brother by the arm. "Dick has a message for you from Max."

There was a baffled look in his eyes as he said, "Where did you see Maxwell?"

"In Pilsen yesterday," I said. I turned to Alice. "Excuse us a minute." He followed me over to the window. "Has Tuček arrived?" I asked.

He stared at me. "What about Tuček?" he asked. He didn't trust me. I could see that.

"Jan Tuček was arrested on Thursday," I told him. "Maxwell got him away to Bory airfield that night. Tuček and a senior Czech air force officer flew out in an Anson trainer. They should have arrived at Milan early yesterday morning."

"I don't believe a word of it," he said.

"I'm not interested whether you believe me or not," I exclaimed angrily. "Maxwell asked me to see you when I got to Milan and tell you to notify him whether or not they'd arrived. He's afraid they may have crashed since they were told to contact you immediately on arrival and he's not heard from you."

He fired a lot of questions at me then. At length he said. "Why the devil didn't you give me that message at the airfield?"

"Your own attitude made it impossible," I answered.

"What were you doing in Pilsen?"

I told him.

"Have you any proof that you represent this machine tool company?"

He was still suspicious.

"Yes," I said. "But you'll bloody well have to take my word for it."

"All right," he said. "I'll start checking up. But I warn you, if I find you're playing some game of your own——" He turned on his heel, and then stopped. "And keep clear of Alice whilst you're here." He went back to his sister then. He bent over her for a moment, talking to her, then with a quick glance at me, he hurried out of the lounge.

I went over to the table. Again I was conscious of her gaze on my leg. She began to put the tea things together as though she were going to carry them out herself. As she didn't speak I said, "How long will you be in Milan?"

"Not long," she said. "I am going to Rapallo and then to stay with some friends of Alec's at Cannes."

"I hope you have a nice time," I murmured.

"The sun will be nice, and I think we shall enjoy ourselves." Her voice was barely audible. Then she suddenly said: "Please go now, Dick."

I nodded. "Yes. I'll go now. Good-bye then."

"Good-bye."

She didn't look up. I went back to my table and collected my things. As I passed her on the way out she didn't look at me. She was staring out of the window. I hesitated in the doorway. But she made no sign and I went up to my room.

They were gone next morning. I don't know what hotel they went to. All I know is that I didn't see them at breakfast and when I inquired at the reception desk I was told they had left.

It was useless trying to do any business that day. It was Sunday. So I went for a walk. Spring had come to Milan. The sun shone out of a cloudless sky and the wide tram-lined streets blazed with warmth. There were tables out on the pavements and some cafés even had their awnings down. I walked up the Via Vittor Pisani and into the Giardini Pubblici. I was thinking of nothing but the fact that the girls were in summer frocks and that the olive-skinned, laughing crowds looked gay and happy. The mystery of Tuček's disappearance and my encounter with the Czech security police seemed very far away, part of another world. In the gardens the trees were showing young green. Everything was bursting with life. I sat down on one of the seats and let the warmth of the sun seap through me. It was wonderful just to sit there and relax. To-morrow there would be work to do. But to-day, all I had to do was sit in the sunshine.

I always remember that hour I spent sitting in the Giardini Pubblici. It stands out in my mind like an oasis in a desert. It was my one breathing space—a moment that seems almost beautiful because it had no part in what had gone before or what came after. I remember there was a little girl and a big yellow rubber ball. She followed it relentlessly, teeth flashing, black hair gleaming and her dark eyes bubbling with laughter. And her mother sat suckling a baby discreetly under a shawl and telling me how she hoped to go to Genoa for a holiday this year. And all the time Milan streamed by, their gay clothes and constant, liquid chatter seeming so light-hearted after the sombre atmosphere of Czechoslovakia. It was like listening to Rossini after a course of Wagner.

Feeling warm and happy I went out into the Viale Vittorio Veneto and sat for a while at one of the café tables drinking cognac. I sat there till twelve-thirty, reviving my Italian by listening to scraps of the conversation that flowed around me. Then I went back to the hotel. As I crossed the entrance hall towards the lift the clerk at the reception desk called me over, " Signor Farrell."

"Yes?" I said.

"I have a message for you." He pulled a slip of paper out of the pigeonhole marked F. "Signor Sismondi telephone half an hour ago to say will you ring him please." He handed me the slip of paper on which was scribbled a telephone number and the name Sismondi.

"Who is he—do you know?" I asked.

"Signor Sismondi? I think perhaps it is Signor Riccardo Sismondi. He have a big *fabbrica* out on the Via Padova, signore."

"What's the name of his company?" I asked.

"I do not know if it is the same man, signore. But the one I speak of is *direttore* of the Ferrometali di Milano."

I went up to my room and got my notebook with the list of Italian firms with which B. & H. Evans had done business before the war. Among them I found the Ferrometalli di Milano. I picked up the telephone and asked for Sismondi's number. A woman's voice answered. "*Casa Sismondi. Chi Parla?*"

"This is Mr. Farrell," I answered. "Can I speak to Signor Sismondi?"

"*Un momento.*" Very faintly I heard the woman's voice call "Riccardo." Then a man's voice came on the wire, rather harsh and grating. "Signor Farrell? *Bene.* You know who I am per'aps?"

"Ferrometalli di Milano?" I asked.

"*Sì, sì, signore.* I do business with your company before the war. I hear you arrive in Milano yesterday—from Pilsen?"

"That's correct," I murmured.

"Do you see Signor Tuček of the Tičkovy ocelárny while you are in Pilsen?"

It was the suddenness of the question that rattled me. I hadn't expected it. I naturally thought he'd rung me on business. Instead he was asking me about Tuček. The happy, laughing Milan I'd walked through that morning faded in my mind. I felt as though a long arm had been stretched out across the borders of Czechoslovakia, to fetch me back into the clutches of the Czech security police.

"'Ullo, 'ullo, signore. Are you there plees?" The voice sounded impatient—harsher and more grating.

"Yes?" I said.

"I ask you do you see Signor Tuček when you are in Pilsen?"

"Yes."

"You are a friend of his per'aps—from the war?"

"Yes," I said. "Why?"

"And he know you are coming to Milano?"

"Yes."

"Good. Then per'aps all is not lost."

"Look," I said. "Do you mind telling me what this is all about?"

"Very well. I tell you. I am a business friend of Signor Tuček. Things are very bad for him in Czechoslovakia. He intend to leave the country and we are going into business together with a new factory 'ere in Milano. I am expecting him 'ere for three days now. But he do not arrive. I am very worried, Signor Farrell."

"What's this got to do with me?" I asked him.

"I tell you. We are to start a new business together. He is bringing with him specifications of some new types of machines we are to produce. On Friday I receive a letter from him to say that he will not bring them himself. It is too dangerous. He give them to an Englishman who fly to Milano the next day. I have checked with the airport, Signor Farrell. You are the only Englishman who arrives from Czechoslovakia since I receive his letter."

"And you think I've a package for you from Tuček?" I asked.

"No, no. I think per'aps you have a package as you say to deliver to Tuček here. But Tuček is not 'ere. He do not arrive. It is terrible. I do not know what is happened. But business is business, Signor Farrell, and I have special workers ready waiting to begin the building of the tools to make these new machines. If I could plees have the specifications——"

"But I haven't got any package for you," I told him.

"No?" The voice had risen a shade. It was hard and metallic. "But Signor Farrell, in his letter he say——"

"I don't care what he said to you in his letter," I interrupted him. "I can only repeat, I have not got a package for you. I saw him once in Pilsen, that's all. It was in his office and an official interpreter was with us all the time."

He started to say something and then his voice vanished suddenly as though he had cupped his hand over the mouth-piece of the telephone. There was a pause and then he said, "Are you sure you only see him once, signore?"

"Quite certain," I answered.

"He does not come to see you at your hotel?"

Was it my imagination or was there a sudden emphasis on his words. "No," I answered.

"But he tell me——"

"Once and for all," I said angrily, "will you please understand that I have no package either for you or Tuček."

There was another pause and I thought perhaps he'd rung off. I was sweating and I wiped my face with my handkerchief. "Per'aps, Signor Farrell, we do not understand each other, no?" The voice was softer, almost silky. "You see, if I have the specifications and can proceed with the organisation of the new factory, then I need several of the sort of machine tools fabricated by your company. Per'aps I require them in a hurry and pay a bonus to you for arranging the quick delivery, eh? Now you have another

40

look through your baggage, signore. It is possible you cannot remember what is in it until I remind you, eh?"

It was a straight bribe and I wanted to tell him what I thought of him. But after all he was a potential customer, so all I said was, "I'm sorry, Mr. Sismondi. I just haven't got what you want. I will call on you later at your office if I may and talk about equipment for the Ferrometalli di Milano."

"But, Signor Farrell——"

"I'm sorry," I said quickly. "I cannot help you. Good-bye." And I put the receiver back on its rest.

For a while I stood there, staring out of the window at the colossal bulk of the Stazione Centrale. The grey stone stood out almost white against the dark under-belly of the cumulus that was piling up across the sky. Sismondi knew that Tuček had visited me at the Hotel Continental. That was the thing that stood in the forefront of my mind. I told myself I was imagining it. Sismondi couldn't possibly know. But the thought stayed there and I felt as though the fingers of that imaginary arm stretched out across the Czech frontier were closing round me. The sunshine streaming in through the open window faded. The Piazzale Duca d'Aosta looked suddenly grey and deserted. I shivered and closed the window.

I started towards the door and then stopped. Suppose Tuček had put a package amongst my things that night. I hadn't searched through my suitcases. It could have lain there without my noticing it. My hands were trembling as I got out my keys and unlocked the two cases. But though I searched even the pockets of my suits and felt the linings there was nothing there. I searched the clothes I was wearing and my overcoat and went through the papers in my brief-case. I found nothing and with a feeling of relief went down to the bar.

It was lunch-time and the place was half empty. I sat down at the bar and got a drink. I felt less alone with a glass in my hand and the cognac was comforting. There was a paper on the bar counter and I concentrated on that, trying to forget Sismondi and that damned telephone conversation. But even the paper contained something to remind me of Tuček. On the inside page I found a paragraph headed: CZECH TABLE TENNIS STAR TO STAY IN ITALY. The story began—*When the Czech table tennis team, which has been touring Italy, left Milano yesterday, Sgna Hilda Tuček was still in her hotel. She refuses to return to Czechoslovakia. She intends to remain in Italy for the present. Hilda Tuček is the daughter of . . .*

I stared at the paragraph, remembering how Jan Tuček had

said—*Fortunately my daughter play table tennis well.* So that was what he had meant. Father and daughter had planned to be together and now.... I pushed the paper away. Poor kid! She must be wondering what had happened.

A hand touched my arm and I spun round with a start.

It was Alec Reece. "Can I have a word with you?" he said.

"What about?" I asked.

I didn't want to talk to him. I'd had enough for one day. I suddenly felt very tired.

"Come over here," He took me to a secluded corner of the bar. We sat down. "What are you having?"

"Cognac," I answered.

"*Du cognaci,*" he told the waiter. Then he leaned forward. "I've been checking up on Tuček," he said. His face looked pale and there were lines of strain round his mouth. "The Anson arrived at the airport here shortly after four on Friday morning."

"Then he's in Milan?" I felt relieved. It was nothing to do with me. But I was glad he was safe.

"No," Reece said. "He's not in Milan. And the devil of it is I don't know where he is—or what's happened to him. The plane was met by two Italians. I gather that neither Tuček nor Lemlin ever got out of it. The aircraft was refuelled and took off again immediately. I've checked up on every airport in Italy, also in Switzerland, France and Austria. I've tried Greece and Jugoslavia as well. The plane and its occupants have completely disappeared."

He was looking at me hard as though I were responsible.

"Why come to me?" I asked.

"I thought you might know something," he said.

"Look," I answered wearily. "I know nothing about this business."

"You saw Maxwell in Pilsen."

"Yes. And he gave me a message to deliver to you."

"Was that before or after your interview with the police?"

"After." Then I saw what he was driving at and I could have hit him. He thought I might have got out of the clutches of the Czech security police by giving information to them. I got to my feet. "I see no point in continuing this discussion," I said. "I'm glad to know Jan Tuček didn't crash. As to where he is now, I can't help you."

"For God's sake sit down," he said. "I'm not suggesting you had anything to do with it. But I must find him. It's vitally important. Sit down—please." I hesitated. He pushed his fingers through his fair hair. He looked damnably tired.

"All right," I said, resuming my seat. "Now, what do you want to know?"

"Just tell me everything that happened to you in Pilsen—everything, however unimportant. It may help."

So I told him the whole story. When I had finished he said, "Why was Tuček so anxious for you to see him when you got to Milan?"

"I've no idea."

He frowned. "And he came to your hotel that night?" He looked across at me. "Has anybody tried to contact you since you've been in Milan?"

"Yes," I said. I told him then about the telephone conversation I'd just had. Somehow the sense of menace I'd attached to it seemed to recede as I told it to Reece.

When I'd finished he didn't say anything for a moment, but sat lost in thought, toying with the drink the waiter had brought him. At length he murmured the name Sismondi, rolling it over his tongue as though by repeating it aloud he could make contact with something hidden away in his memory. But then he shook his head. "The name means nothing to me." He swilled the pale liquor of his cognac round and round in the glass as though he couldn't make up his mind what line to take. "I wish to God Maxwell was here," he said. Then he suddenly knocked back the drink. "I want you to do something," he said quietly, leaning across the table towards me. "You probably won't like it, but—" He shrugged his shoulders.

"What is it?" I asked.

"I want you to go and see Sismondi."

"No," I said quickly. "I don't want anything to do with it. It's none of my business and——"

"I know it's none of your business. But Tuček was a friend of yours, wasn't he? You were in the Battle of Britain together."

I thought again of that shattered windshield with the black oil smoke pouring through it, the flames fanning out from the engine cowling and a voice in the headphones saying: *Okay, I get him for you, Dick.* Jan had probably saved my life that day. "Yes," I said.

"Very well then. You can't just abandon the poor devil because you're afraid of getting involved in something unpleasant. All I want you to do is go and see Sismondi. Find out what he knows. Evidently he thinks you've got something he wants. Play on that."

I remembered the silky tone in which Sismondi had offered me that bribe. Hell! It wasn't my pigeon. "I'm sorry," I said. "I don't want to get mixed up——"

"Damn it, Farrell, don't you realise Tuček's life may be in

43

danger. Listen! This is the second time in two months that somebody important has come through from the other side and then disappeared here in Italy. There have been others, too. Our people have been offered information that could only have been brought through by people who have completely disappeared. They've had to pay through the nose for it. Now do you understand? The man's life is at stake."

"That's your affair," I answered. "You and Maxwell were organising the thing. It's up to you to see that he's safe."

"All right," he answered in a tone of sudden anger. "I've slipped up. I admit it. Now I've come to you. I'm asking you to help me." He was forcing his voice under control, suppressing his anger, trying desperately to assume humility.

"I've given you all the help I can," I answered, "I've told you everything that's happened. I've given you a complete account of my telephone conversation with Sismondi. It's up to you now. Go and see him. Batter the truth out of him."

But he shook his head. " I've thought of that. It wouldn't work. Sismondi won't be the man we're looking for. He probably knows very little. But if you were to suggest that you had the papers they're after——"

"No," I said. "I'm through with that sort of game. You should know that better than anyone," I added in a tone of sudden bitterness.

"Then you won't help?"

"No." I felt obstinate. Maxwell could probably have persuaded me. But not Reece. There was a personal barrier. I finished my drink and got to my feet.

Reece got up also and came round the table. He didn't make any further attempt to play on my friendship with Tuček. He didn't even try to tell me it was my duty as an Englishman to help him. He just said, "All right. I was afraid you might feel like that so I brought someone with me. I think you'll find it more difficult to say No to her."

For an awful moment I thought he'd got Alice with him. But he must have realised what was in my mind, for he said quickly, " It's someone you've never met before. Let's go through into the lounge." He had hold of my arm then and I had no option but to go with him.

She was sitting in the far corner—a small, red-haired girl with her head bent over a newspaper. As we approached she looked up, and I knew her at once. She was Jan Tuček's daughter. Reece introduced us. "I have heard of you from my father," she said. The grip of her hand was firm. The set of the chin was as deter-

mined as her father's, and her eyes, set rather wide on either side
of the small upturned nose, looked straight at me. "He often used
to speak of his friends in the R.A.F." She glanced down at my leg
and then pulled up a chair for me. "Mr. Reece said you might be
able to help us." Her voice was rather husky and she spoke English with a queer mixture of accents.

I sat down, comparing the girl in front of me with the memory
of the photograph in Tuček's office. Some trick of the light caused
her hair to gleam just the way it had gleamed in the photograph.
It was beautiful hair—a reddish gold, the real Venetian Titian.
And she had freckles just as Tuček had said. They mottled the
pale golden skin of her face in a way that gave it a gamin quality.
But the face wasn't quite the same as the face in the photograph—
it was older, more set, as though she had had to come to grips with
life since the photograph had been taken. I remembered how I'd
last seen that photograph, smiling up at me from the floor of
Tuček's ransacked office. She wasn't smiling now and there was
no laughter in her eyes. Her face looked small and pinched and
there were dark rings under her eyes. And yet, as I met the level
gaze of her eyes, I was conscious again of that sense of something
personal in her face. It suddenly became important to me that she
should smile again as she'd been smiling in the photograph. "I'll
do anything I can," I murmured.

"Thank you." She turned to Reece. "Is there any news please?"

He shook his heed. "Not much I'm afraid. Farrell saw your
father only once." He hesitated, and then said, "Does the name
Sismondi mean anything to you, Hilda?"

She shook her head.

"Your father never hinted that he might be forming a business
partnership with Sismondi?"

"No."

"He wasn't planning to form a company here in Milan?"

Again she shook her head. "No. We were to have a holiday
here, and then we were going to England." Her voice sounded
puzzled. "Why all these questions?"

Reece gave her the gist of what I'd told him. When he had
finished she turned to me. "You will go and see this Sismondi?"
I think she knew at once that I didn't want to. "Please," she
added. "He may know where my father is." She reached out and
caught hold of my hand. Her fingers were cold and their grip was
hard and urgent. "This is our last hope, I think." Her eyes were
fixed on my face. "Can you imagine what it has been like for him
in Czechoslovakia all these months since they take over? It has
been terrible—always living on the edge of catastrophe. And it

45

had happened before, you see—with the Germans. My mother was murdered. And his father. To have to leave Czechoslovakia twice—that is very hard, I think. We plan to build a new life in England. And now——" She shrugged her shoulders. I thought, *if she breaks down now it will be horrible.* But she didn't. Somehow she kept control of herself and in a small, tight voice, she said, "So you must help me, please."

"I'll do anything I can," I said. I was completely under the spell of her urgency.

"And you will go to speak with this Sismondi?"

"Yes."

"Thank you. As soon as I hear you are the Dick Farrell who is a friend of my father's I know you will help." She leaned suddenly closer. "Where do you think he is? What do you think has happened?"

I didn't say anything and when she saw I had nothing to tell her she bit her lip. Then she got quickly to her feet. "I would like a drink please, Alec."

They went through into the bar. She didn't say anything to me as she left. She kept her face turned away. I think she didn't want me to see how near she was to breaking point.

III

I HAD all afternoon to think it over. And the more I thought about it, the less I liked it. What they'd asked me to do was to let Sismondi think I'd got whatever it was he wanted and by that means to find out what he knew about Tuček's disappearance. It doesn't sound much. But then remember, this was Italy, a country where real life crosses the footlights to emerge with melodrama. Last time I'd been in Milan I'd seen the mutilated bodies of Mussolini and his mistress strung up by the heels for the public to jeer at. A bloodthirsty mob had cut the woman's heart out. And the farther south you get the cheaper life becomes. Moreover, it was very different from the war-time Italy. I'd been very conscious of that since I arrived. There was none of that sense of security induced by the constant sight of British and American uniforms.

I had dinner early and went to the bar. I thought if I had a few drinks I shouldn't feel so unhappy about the whole business. But somehow they seemed to have the reverse effect. By nine o'clock I knew I couldn't put it off any longer. I called a taxi and gave the driver Sismondi's address, which was Corso Venezia 22.

It was raining and a cold, damp smell hung over the streets. A tram was the only thing that moved in the whole of the Vittor Pisani. The atmosphere of the city was very different from the morning when I'd sat in the sun in the public gardens. I shivered. I could feel one of my fits of depression settling on me. The stump of my leg ached and I wished I could go back to the hotel, have a hot bath and tumble into bed. But there was no turning back now.

In a few minutes the taxi had deposited me at Corso Venezia 22. It was a big, grey house, one of several that ran in a continuous line facing the Giardini Pubblici. There was a heavy, green-painted wooden door with a light showing through a fanlight. I watched the red tail light of the taxi disappear into the murk. The wind was from the north. It came straight off the frozen summits of the Alps and was bitterly cold. I climbed the half-dozen steps to the door. There were three bells and against the second was a small metal plate engraved with the name Sg. Riccardo Sismondi. Evidently the house was converted into flats. I rang the bell and almost immediately a man's voice said, *"Chi è, per favore?"*

The door had not opened. The voice seemed to come from somewhere up by the fanlight. I realised then that I was faced with one of those electrical contrivances so beloved by Italians. "Mr. Farrell," I said. "I've come to see Signor Sismondi."

There was a pause and then the same voice said, "Come in, please, Signor Farrell. The second floor." There was a click and a crack of light showed down one side of the door. I pushed it open and went in to find myself in a big entrance hall with a hothouse temperature. The heavy door swung-to behind me and locked itself automatically. There was something final and irrevocable about the determined, well-oiled click of that lock. Additional lights came on in the narrow Venetian chandelier that hung from the ceiling. Thick pile carpets covered the tiled floor. There was a big grandfather clock in one corner and on a heavily carved table stood a beautiful model of an Italian field-piece in silver.

I climbed the stairs to the second floor. The air of the place was suffocatingly hot and faintly perfumed. The door of the flat was open and I was greeted by a leathery-faced little man with dark, rather protruding eyes and a glassy smile. He gave me a thick, podgy hand. "Sismondi. I am so glad you can come." The smile was automatic, entirely artificial. His almost bald head gleamed

47

like polished bone in the light from the priceless glass chandelier behind him. "Come in, please, signore." There was no warmth in his tone. I got the impression that he was upset at my unexpected arrival.

He shut the door and hovered round me as I removed my coat. "You like a drink, yes?" He stroked his hands as though smoothing down the coarse black hair that covered the backs of them.

"Thank you," I said.

The lobby led into a heavily furnished lounge where my feet seemed to sink to the ankles in the thick pile of the carpets. Dark tapestries draped the walls and the furniture was ornate and carved. Then he pushed open a door and we went through into a softly-lit room full of very modern furnishings. The contrast was staggering. A fat pekinese got up from a silk-covered pouff and waddled towards me. It sniffed disdainfully at my trousers and returned to its couch. "My wife like those dogs very much," Sismondi said. "You like dogs, signore?"

I was thinking how very like the dog he was himself. "Er—yes," I said. "I'm very fond——" And then I stopped. Reclining on the piled-up cushions of a big couch was a girl. Her figure merged into the green of the silk cushionings. Only her face showed in that soft lighting—a pale, madonna oval below the sweep of her jet black hair. The eyes caught the light and shone green like a cat's eyes. The lips were a vivid gash in the pallor of her skin. I thought I knew then why Sismondi had given me such a glassy smile of welcome.

He bustled forward. "Signor Farrell. The Contessa Valle."

I bowed. The girl didn't move, but I could see her eyes examining me. I felt the way a horse must feel when it is being appraised by an expert. Sismondi gave an uncertain little cough. "What can I give you to drink, Signor Farrell? A whisky, yes?"

"Thank you," I said.

He went over to an elaborate modern cocktail cabinet that stood open in the corner. The girl's silence and immobility was disturbing. I followed him, very conscious of the drag of my leg.

"I am sorry my wife is not 'ere to welcome you, signore," he said as he poured the drink.

"She have—how do you call it?—the influenza, eh?" He shrugged his shoulders. "It is the weather, you know. It has been very cold here in Milano. You like seltz?"

"No. I'll have it neat, thank you," I said.

He handed me a heavy, cut-glass goblet half-full of whisky. "Zina? You like another benedictine?"

"Please." Her voice was low and slumbrous and the way she

48

said it the word became a purr. I went over and got her glass. The tips of her fingers touched mine as she handed it to me. The green eyes stared at me unblinking. She didn't say anything, but I felt my pulse beat quicken. She was dressed in an evening gown of green silk, cut very low and drawn in at the waist by a silver girdle. She wore no jewellery at all. She was like something by one of the early Italian painters—a woman straight out of the medieval past of Italy.

When I took the drink back to her she slipped her legs off the couch. It was one single movement, without effort. Her body seemed to flow from one position to the next. "Sit down here," she said, patting the cushions beside her. "Now tell me how you lose your leg?"

"I crashed," I said.

"You are a flier then?"

I nodded.

She smiled and there was a glint of amusement in her eyes. "You do not like to talk about it, eh?" When I didn't answer, she said, "Perhaps you do not realise what an advantage it gives you?"

"How do you mean?" I asked.

She gave a slight, impatient shrug of the shoulders. "I think you are perhaps quite an ordinary man. But because of that leg you become intriguing." She raised her glass. "*Alla sua salute!*"

"*Alla sua, signora!*" I replied.

Her eyes were watching me as her lips opened to the rim of her glass. "Where are you staying in Milano?"

"At the Excelsiore," I answered.

She made a small face. "You must find some friends," she said. "It is not good at a hotel. You will drink too much and sleep with the chambermaid and that will not be good for your work. You drink a lot. Am I right?" She smiled. "Is it to forget the leg?"

"Do I look as dissipated as all that?" I asked.

She put her head slightly on one side. "Not yet," she said slowly. "At the moment it only makes you look intriguing. Later——" She shrugged her shoulders.

Sismondi gave a little cough. I'd forgotten all about him. He came across the room, pushed the pouff with the peke on it out of the way and drew up a chair. "You come to tell me something, I think, Signor Farrell," he suggested.

"A little matter of business," I said vaguely.

"Because of my telephone conversation this morning?"

I nodded.

"Good!" He cupped his hands round the big brandy glass and drank. "You like a cigar?"

49

"Thank you," I said. He seemed in no hurry. He went over to the cocktail cabinet and returned with a box of cigars. I looked across at the girl. "Do you mind?" I asked.

She shook her head. "I like it. I may even take a puff of yours." Her voice was silky, an invitation to be stroked.

Sismondi and I lit our cigars. After that the conversation became general. I think we talked of Russia and Communism and the future of the Italian colonies. But I'm not really certain. My impression is one of soft lights, the night scent of perfume penetrating through the aroma of cigars and the oval of the girl's face against the green silk of the cushions. I had a feeling that we were waiting for something. Sismondi did not again refer to the matter that had brought me to his flat.

I was half-way through my cigar when a buzzer sounded outside the room. Sismondi gave a grunt of satisfaction and scrambled to his feet, spilling cigar ash on to the carpet. As he left the room the girl said, "You look tired, signore."

"It's been a very busy trip," I told her.

She nodded. "You must take a holiday during your stay in Italy. Go down to the south where it is warm and you can lie in the sun. Do you know Amalfi?"

"I was there during the war."

"It is very beautiful, yes? So much more beautiful than the Riviera. To see the moon lie like a streak of silver across the warmth of the sea." Her voice was like the murmur of the sea coming in over sand.

"I'm due for a holiday," I said. "As soon as I can——"

But she wasn't listening. She was looking past me towards the door. I half turned in my seat. There was the murmur of voices and then Sismondi came in rubbing his hands. He went over to the cocktail cabinet and poured a drink. A silence hung over the room. Then the door opened again and a man came in. I got to my feet and as I did so he stopped. I couldn't see his face. It was in shadow and he was just a dark silhouette against the light of the open doorway. But I could feel his eyes fixed on me.

Sismondi came hurrying forward. "Mistair Farrell. I wish to introduce you to a friend of mine who is very interested in the matter which brings you here. Signor Shirer."

I had moved forward to greet him, but I stopped then. Walter Shirer! It couldn't be. It was too much of a coincidence just after I'd met Reece again. But the man had the same short, rather round figure. "Are you—Walter Shirer?" My voice trembled slightly as I put the question.

"Ah! So you know each other already?"

50

The figure in the doorway made no move. He didn't say anything. I felt the sudden tension in the room. I began to sweat. "For God's sake say something," I said.

"I have nothing to say to you." He had turned on his heel.

"Damn it, man!" I cried. "You don't hold it against me now, surely? At the Villa d'Este you were so decent about——"

But he had left the room, closing the door behind him.

I stood there for a second feeling helpless and angry. Then I brushed Sismondi aside and wrenched the door open. The lounge beyond was empty. Somewhere in the flat a door closed. Sismondi had hold of my arm now. "Please, signore. Please." He was almost whimpering with fright. I realised then that my drink was no longer in my hand. Vaguely I remembered flinging it on to the carpet. A sudden sense of hopelessness took hold of me. "I'm sorry," I mumbled. "I must go."

I got my hat and coat. Sismondi fussed round me. All he seemed able to say was, "Please, signore."

I flung out of the flat and banged the door behind me. The lights brightened in the chandelier in the hall. The front door clicked softly open. I stopped outside, staring at the glistening tram lines of the Corso. The door closed with a final click, and I went down the steps, turned right and hurried towards my hotel.

I had got almost as far as the Piazza Oberdan before the bitterness inside me subsided. My mood changed then to one of self-reproach. Why the devil hadn't I stayed there and brazened it out? Shirer had probably been as surprised as I had at the suddenness of the meeting. He'd had no time to adjust himself to it. He'd hesitated and I'd flown into a rage. I had slowed my pace up and now I stopped. I'd made a fool of myself and what was worse I'd failed completely to do anything about Tuček. Well, there was nothing I could do about that now. I couldn't very well go back to the flat. It would have to wait till to-morrow. But I could go back and wait for Shirer to come out. I was certain he wasn't staying there and I suddenly had an overwhelming urge to set things right between us.

I turned and walked very slowly back along the Corso. I reached the steps leading to the massive door of Number Twenty-two. I hesitated. I had only to walk up to the door and ring the bell. I could speak to Sismondi from the street. But I knew he'd want me to come up—he'd be slimy and ingratiating and then I'd be back in that softly lit room.... I was honest with myself then. I couldn't face the mocking eyes of that girl. She'd guess the truth and somehow I couldn't take it. I went on up the street and after walking perhaps fifty yards I turned and walked back.

51

I suppose I paced up and down outside Number Twenty-two for nearly half an hour. I know a church clock struck eleven, and then shortly afterwards a taxi drew up. The driver got out and rang a bell. I could see him talking to the voice above the door and then he got back into his taxi and sat there, waiting. I strolled forward. I'd have to catch Shirer before he drove off. But suppose he took the girl home? I knew if he came out with the Contessa Valle I wouldn't be able to talk to him. But perhaps it would be better that way. Then I could go up and see Sismondi and settle the Tuček business.

I had reached the steps now. There was no crack of light down one side of the door. It was still firmly closed. I went on past the house and stepped out into the street behind the taxi. I waited there, screened by the rear of the car. The brilliant light of a street lamp shone on the green paint of the door I was watching.

At last it opened. It was Shirer and he was alone. For a moment he was a black silhouette against the lights of the chandelier in the hall. Then he was out in the full glare of the street light and the door closed behind him. He had on a grey overcoat and a wide-brimmed American hat. He paused on the top step, pulling on his gloves. Then he glanced up at the night and I saw his face. It was still round and chubby with high cheekbones, but the chin looked bluer, as though he had forgotten to shave, and there was a hint of grey at the temples. His eyes caught the light and seemed contracted as though the pupils had narrowed against the glare. He caressed his upper lip with the tip of a gloved finger as though he still. . .

I was suddenly in a cold sweat of panic. It was as though he were fingering a moustache and making a diagnosis, as though he were saying, *"I think we must operate to-day."* A hand seemed to touch my leg, caressing it—the leg that wasn't there. Shirer was dissolving into Sansevino before my eyes. I tried to fight back my sudden panic. *This is Shirer*, I kept telling myself—*Walter Shirer, the man who escaped with Reece. You saw Sansevino dead at his desk with a bullet through his head.* I could feel my finger-nails digging into the flesh of my palms and then it was Walter Shirer again and he was coming down the steps. He hadn't seen me. I tried to go forward to meet him, but somehow I was held rooted to the spot. He vanished behind the bulk of the taxi. *"Albergo Nazionale."* The voice was crisp and sibilant and I felt fear catching hold of me again. Shirer hadn't talked like that surely?

The door of the taxi closed. There was the sound of a gear engaging and then the glossy cellulose-finished metal of it slid away from me and I was staring at a fast-diminishing speck of red.

I passed my hand over my face. It was cold and clammy with sweat. Was I going mad or was I just drunk? Had that only been Shirer or... I shook myself, trying to get a grip on my thoughts. I'd been standing over the exhaust, that was all that had happened. I was tired and I'd breathed in some of the exhaust fumes. My sound leg felt weak at the knee. I was feeling sick and dizzy, too.

I turned and walked slowly down the Corso towards the Piazza Oberdan. The night air gradually cleared my brain. But I couldn't get rid of the mental picture of Shirer standing at the top of those steps looking down at me, looking down at me and stroking his upper lip with the tips of his fingers. It had been the same gesture. I'd only to think of it to see the blasted little swine leaning over my bed fingering that dirty smudge of a moustache. Of course without that moustache the two would have looked very similar. It was Shirer I'd been introduced to and Shirer who'd come out of Number Twenty-two. It was my damned imagination, that was all.

Reece was waiting for me in the entrance hall when I reached the hotel. I didn't even notice him until he caught me by the arm at the foot of the stairs. "What happened?" he asked, peering at me.

"Nothing," I snapped and shook his hand off my arm.

He gave me an odd look. I suppose he thought I'd drunk too much. "What did Sismondi say?" he asked. "What did you find out?"

"I didn't find out anything," I answered. "I didn't get a chance to talk to him alone."

"Well, what was your impression? Do you think he knows where Tuček is?"

"I tell you, I didn't get a chance to talk to him. Now leave me alone. I'm going to bed."

He caught me by the shoulder then and spun me round. "I don't believe you ever went to Sismondi's place."

"You can believe what you damn' well like," I answered.

I tried to shake myself free, but he had hold of my shoulder in a grip of iron. His eyes were narrowed and angry. "Do you realise what that poor kid's going through?" he hissed. "By God if this wasn't a hotel I'd thrash the life out of you." He let me go then and I stumbled up the stairs to my room.

I didn't get much sleep that night. Whenever I dozed off the figures of Shirer and Sansevino kept appearing and then merging and changing shape as though in a trick mirror. I'd be running through Milan in a sweat of fear with first one and then the other materialising from the crowd, appearing in the lighted doorways of buildings or seizing hold of my arm in the street. Then I'd be awake in a clammy sweat with my heart racing and I'd begin thinking over the events of the evening until I fell asleep and started dreaming again.

I have a horror of going mad—really mad, not just sent to hospital for treatment. And that night I thought I really was going round the bend. My mind had become a distorting mirror to the retina of my memory and the strange coincidence of that meeting with Shirer became magnified into something so frightening that my hair literally crawled on my scalp when I thought about it.

I got up with the first light of day and had a bath. I felt better then, more relaxed and I propped myself up in bed and read a book. I must have dozed off after a time for the next thing I knew I was being called. My mind felt clear and reasonable. I went down and ate a hearty breakfast. Shafts of warm sunshine streamed through the tall windows. I steered my mind clear of the previous night. I'd obviously been drunk. I concentrated all my energies on the work that had to be done. I could see Sismondi again that evening.

When I had finished my breakfast I went straight up to my room and began a long session of telephoning. I had the window on to the balcony open and the sun lay quite warm across the table at which I was seated. A maid came in and made the bed, managing, like most Italian servants, to make me conscious of her sex as she moved about the room.

I was about half-way through my list of contacts and had just replaced the receiver after completing a call when the clerk at the reception desk came through. "A lady to see you, Signor Farrell."

I thought of the scene with Reece the previous night and my heart sank.

"Did she give you her name?" I asked.

"No, signore. She will not give me her name."

I suppose she'd been afraid I wouldn't see her if she said who she was. "All right. I'll come down." I replaced the receiver and got to my feet. Her arrival had broken the spell of my concentration on work and I found myself thinking again of the events of the night before. The sunlight seemed suddenly cold. There was a slight breeze blowing on to the table and ruffling the papers that spilled across it from the open mouth of my brief-case. I shut the windows and then went out down the corridor to the main stairs, mentally bracing myself to face Tuček's daughter.

She wasn't in the entrance hall and I went over to the reception desk. The clerk gave me an oily smile, "She is gone to the bar, Signor Farrell," I turned and went up the stairs again.

But it wasn't Hilda Tuček who was waiting for me in the bar. It was the girl I'd met at Sismondi's flat—the Contessa Valle. She was dressed in a black coat and skirt with a fur cape draped round her shoulders. Her black hair was drawn tight back from a central parting and it gleamed in the sunlight. Her oval face was pale by comparison and the only spot of colour was a blood-red carnation pinned above her left breast, the colour exactly matching the shade of her lips. She still looked like a painting by one of the early masters, but in the morning sunlight her madonna features seemed to have a touch of the devil in them.

"Good morning, signore." Her voice was soft like a caress. The lazy smile she gave me made me think of a cat that has found a bowl of cream. She gave me her hand. I bent and touched the warm flesh with my lips, and all the time I knew her green eyes were watching me. "I hope you do not mind my coming to see you, like this?"

"I'm delighted," I murmured.

"I wait for you in the bar because I think perhaps you need a drink—after what happen last night."

"Yes," I said. "Yes, I could do with a drink. What will you have?"

"It is a little early for me. But to keep you company I will have a crème de menthe."

I sat down and called a waiter. All the time I was trying to control the sudden sense of excitement that her presence had induced and at the same time to figure out just why she had come to see me. The waiter came over and I ordered a crème de menthe and a cognac and seltz. Then I said awkwardly, "Why have you come to see me, Contessa?"

A glint of amusement showed in her eyes. "Because you interest me, Signor Farrell."

I gave a little bow. "You flatter me."

She smiled. "It is a pretty scene you make last night, throwing your glass on the floor and walking out on poor little Riccardo. Also Walter was very upset. He is sensitive and——" She must have seen the tenseness in my face for she stopped then. "Why do you behave like that, signore?"

The unexpected directness of the question took me by surprise. "I was drunk," I answered tersely. "Suppose we leave it at that."

She smiled and shrugged her shoulders. The waiter arrived with the drinks. "Salute!" She raised the glass to her lips. The green of the crème de menthe was a shocking contrast to the red gash of her lips, but it matched her eyes. I emptied the bottle of seltz into my glass and drank.

There was an uncomfortable silence which was broken by her saying, "I do not think you were drunk last night. You were very strung up and you had been drinking. But you were not drunk."

I didn't answer. I was thinking of Shirer, seeing him again in the glare of the street light stroking the side of his upper lip with the tips of his fingers. "Have you known Walter Shirer long?" I asked.

"Two or three years perhaps. I am from Napoli and he has a vineyard there. He is producing a very good Lachrima Christi. You know him before you meet him last night, eh? That is why you are so upset."

"Yes," I said. "I knew him during the war. We were in the Villa d'Este together."

"Ah, now I understand. That is the place he escape from. But you are not the Englishman who accompany him."

"No."

"Are you angry with him because he go and you cannot?"

Damn the woman! Why couldn't she pick on some other subject. "Why should I be?" My voice sounded harsh.

"You do not like to talk about it, eh? I hear from Walter that there is a doctor in the Villa d'Este who is not very kind."

"Yes. There was a doctor." I stared at my drink, thinking of the tone in which Shirer had said *Albergo Nazionale* as he'd directed the taxi driver. "He was very like Shirer," I murmured. And then suddenly I remembered. God! Why hadn't I thought of it before? Upstairs amongst the files in my baggage I had a photograph of Il dottore Sansevino. I'd liberated it from the files of the Instituto Nazionale Luce. Some perverse sense of the morbid had made me keep it. I got to my feet. "I have a photograph I would like you to see, Contessa," I said. "If you'll excuse me, I'll go and get it. I won't be a minute."

"No, please," Her hand was on my arm. "I have to go in a moment and I did not come here to look at photographs."

"I'd like you to see it," I insisted. "It won't take a second for me to get it."

She started to argue, but I was already walking away from the table. I took the lift up to my floor and went down the corridor to my room. The next door to mine was open and I could see the maid making the bed. As I put the key in the lock of my door something banged inside. I entered to find that the windows to the balcony had blown open. The sudden through draught slid my papers across the table and on to the floor. I shut the door quickly, retrieved the papers and closed the windows again.

Then I stood stock still, remembering suddenly that I had closed them and locked them before going down to meet the Contessa. I turned quickly to my bags and checked through them. Nothing seemed to be missing and I cursed myself for being so jumpy. I found the photograph and shut my case again.

As I left my room the maid came out of the next door. She stopped and stared at me, mouth agape in astonishment. "Whatever's the matter?" I asked her in Italian.

She stared at me stupidly and I was just going to go on down the corridor when she said, "But Il dottore said you were ill, signore."

The words *il dottore* brought me spinning round on her. "How do you mean?" I asked. "What doctor?"

"The one who come through this room when I am making the bed, signore." She looked pale and rather frightened. "He say that the signore is not to be disturbed. But the signore is not ill. Please—I do not understand."

I took hold of her by the shoulders and shook her in my sudden, intuitive panic. "What did he look like—the doctor? Quickly, girl. What was he like?"

"I do not remember," she murmured. "He came in from the balcony, you see, and he was against the light so that——"

"From the balcony?" So that was why the french windows had been open. Somebody had been in my room. "Tell me exactly what happened?"

She stared at me, her eyes very large. She was frightened. But I don't think she knew quite why she was frightened.

"What happened?" I repeated in a more controlled voice, trying to calm her.

She hesitated. Then she took a breath and said, "It was whilst I was making the bed, signore. I had opened the windows to the balcony to air the room and then this man came in. He frightened me, appearing suddenly like that. But he put his fingers to his lips and told me I was not to disturb you. He said he was a doctor. He had been called because you were taken ill, signore, and he had given you some medicine. He added that you had gone to sleep now and he had come out by way of the balcony because he was afraid the door might make a noise when he closed it and wake you."

"And he said he was a doctor?"

"*Si, si, signore.* He was not the hotel doctor. But sometimes guests call in other doctors. Are you better now, signore?"

"I haven't been ill and I didn't call a doctor," I told her.

She stared at me, her eyes like saucers. I could see she didn't believe a word of it. Probably I looked pretty wild. I was in the grip of a horror that seemed to come up from right deep down inside of me. I had to fight all the time to keep myself under control. "Can you describe this man to me?" I asked her.

She shook her head. She was beginning to edge away from me. At any moment I felt she'd run away down the corridor. "Was he short or tall?" I persisted.

"Short."

I suddenly remembered the photograph I was still holding in my hand. I covered the uniform with my hand and showed her just the head. "Was that the man?"

Her gaze slid reluctantly from my face to the photograph. "*Si, si, signore.* That is the man." She nodded her head emphatically and then frowned. "But he do not have a moustache." Her voice had become uncertain. "I cannot tell, signore. But it is very like him. Now, please. I must go. I have many, many rooms——" She edged away from me and then hurried off down the corridor.

I stood there, staring at the photograph. Sansevino's dark, rather small eyes stared back at me from the piece of pasteboard. It wasn't possible. Damn it, Sansevino was dead. I'd seen him myself with his brains spattered from his head and the little Beretta gripped in his hand. But why should Shirer want to search my room? And then there was that story about being a doctor. In an emergency a man thinks up something that appears reasonable to him. Shirer wouldn't have thought of calling himself a doctor. But Sansevino would. It would leap automatically to his mind as a perfectly natural excuse for his behaviour.

I felt a shiver run up my spine: a tingle of horror, of anticipation—an unholy mixture of glee and instinctive fear. Suppose it was Sansevino I'd met last night? Suppose.... But I discarded the idea. It was too fantastic, too horrible.

I turned and walked slowly along the corridor and down the stairs. But all the way back to the bar I couldn't get the idea out of my mind. It would account for the man's odd behaviour the night before. It would account, too, for my involuntary sense of fear. But I wasn't afraid now. I had a feeling of exultance. Suppose it were Sansevino. Just suppose that it was Sansevino who had escaped from the Villa d'Este. Then I had him. Then I could repay all he'd done to me, repay the pain, the hours of mental torture waiting for the...

"What is the matter, Signor Farrell? Has anything happened?"

I had reached the table where I had left the Contessa. "No," I answered quickly. "Nothing has happened." My glass was still half-full and I drained it at a gulp.

58

"You look as though you have seen a ghost," she said.

"A ghost?" I stared at her. Then I sat down. "What made you say that?"

Her brows arched slightly at the abruptness of my tone. "Have I said something wrong? I am sorry. I am not good at idiomatic English. What I mean to say is that you look upset."

"It's nothing," I said, wiping my face and hands with my handkerchief. "I get these attacks sometimes," I was thinking of that time in Naples when I'd been waiting at the Patria for a boat to take me home. I'd had the same feeling of tightness inside my head. It had been like an iron band being slowly screwed down across the brain cells. I'd been two months in hospital then. Was I going the same way again? "Hell! I can't be imagining it all."

"What is that you say?" She was staring at me curiously and I realised I must have spoken aloud.

I called the waiter. "Will you have another drink?" I asked her. She shook her head and I ordered a double cognac.

"You should not drink so much," she murmured.

I laughed. "If I didn't drink——" I stopped then, realising that I was in danger of saying too much.

She reached out and her fingers touched my hand. "I am sorry," she said softly. "I think something terrible has happen in your life."

The waiter brought my drink and I gulped at it thirstily. "Do you recognise that man?" I asked and thrust the photograph across the table towards her.

She stared at it, her forehead wrinkling in a frown. "Well?" I said impatiently. "Who is it?"

"I do not understand," she said. "He is in Fascist uniform."

"And he has a moustache, eh?"

She looked across at me. "Why do you show me this?"

"Who is it?" I asked.

"You know who it is. It is the man you meet last night."

I knocked back the rest of my drink. "The name of the man in that photograph is Dottore Giovanni Sansevino." I picked up the pasteboard and slipped it into my wallet.

"Sansevino?" She stared at me uncomprehendingly. "Who is Sansevino?"

I thrust my leg out. "He was responsible for that." My voice sounded harsh and blurred in my ears. "My leg was smashed up in an air crash. He could have saved it. God knows, he was a good enough surgeon. Instead he did three amputations on it, two below the knee and one above—all without anæsthetics." Anger was welling up inside me like a tide. "He deliberately sawed my leg to pieces." I could see my fingers whitening as they tightened on each other. I had them interlaced and I was squeezing them as though they were closed around Sansevino's throat. Then suddenly I had control of myself. "Where will I find Walter Shirer?" I asked her.

"Walter Shirer?" She hesitated. Then she said, "I do not know. I think he is not in Milano to-day."

"He's staying at the Albergo Nazionale, isn't he?"

"Yes, but——" Her fingers were on my hand again. "You should learn to forget the past, signore. People who think too much of the past——" She shrugged her shoulders. "Everyone has things inside them that are better forgotten." Her eyes were looking beyond me, not seeing the details of the room.

"Why do you say that?" I asked her.

"Because you are all tense inside. Walter reminds you of the man in that photograph and you are bitter." She sighed. "I also have the past that I must forget," she said softly. "I have not always been dressed like this, you see. Life has not been easy for me. I was born in a slum off the Via Roma in Napoli. You know Napoli?" She smiled as I nodded. It was a wry, hard smile. "Then you know what that means, signore. Fortunately I can dance. I get to know a man at the San Carlo and he gets me into the Corpo di Ballo. After that it is much better. Now I am a Contessa, and I do not think too much of the past. I think I should go crazy if I think too much of what my girlhood is like." She leaned towards me and her eyes were fixed on mine. They were large eyes—pale brown with flecks of green and the whites were not quite white, more the colour of old parchment. "Think of the future, signore. Do not live in the past." Her fingers squeezed my hand. "Now I must go." Her voice was suddenly practical as she reached for her handbag. "This afternoon I go to Firenze."

"How long will you be in Florence?" I was thinking it was a pity she was going. She was exciting, unusual.

"Not long. I stay two nights with some friends and then I motor to Napoli. I have a villa there. You know the Palazzo Don Anna on the Posillipo?"

I nodded. It was a huge medieval building, the base of its stone arches planted in the sea just north of Naples.

"My villa is just near the Palazzo. You will come and see me I hope when you are in Napoli. It is called the Villa Carlotta."

"Yes, I should like to," I said.

She had risen to her feet and as I escorted her to the entrance hall, she said, "Why do you not take a holiday? It would do you good to lie in the sun and relax yourself." She glanced at me with

60

a swift lift of her brows. "Milano is not good for you, I think. Also I should like to see you again. We have something in common, you and I—our pasts." She smiled and gave me her hand.

I watched her as she went out and got into the car that was waiting for her. Then I turned and went back into the bar. *Milano is not good for you, I think.* What had she meant by that? And why had she come to see me? I realised then that she had not given me any really satisfactory reason for her visit. Had she come by arrangement with the man who had searched my room?

What did it matter anyway? The bug eating into my mind was Shirer. The idea that he was really Sansevino clung with a persistence that was frightening. I had to know the truth. I had to see him again and make certain. The thing was ridiculous, and yet... it was the sort of thing that could happen. And if it were Sansevino.... I felt anger boiling up in me again. I had another drink and phoned the Albergo Nazionale. Signor Shirer wasn't there. He wasn't expected back till the evening. I rang Sismondi at his office. He told me Shirer had said something about going out of town.

I had lunch then and after lunch I called on various firms. I didn't get back to the hotel till nearly eight and by then the whole idea seemed so fantastic that I discarded it completely. I had a quick dinner and then went into the bar. But after a few drinks, I began to feel I must see him and make certain.

I got a taxi and went straight over to the Nazionale. It was a small and rather luxurious hotel almost opposite La Scala. There was an air of past grandeur about it with its tapestried walls and heavy, ornate furnishings. In this setting the lift, which was caged in with a white-lacquered tracery of wrought-iron, seemed out of place whilst at the same time adding to the expensive impression already given by the furnishings, the deep-piled carpet and knee-breeches uniform of the servants. I went over to the hall porter's desk and asked for Shirer.

"Your name, please, signore?"

"Is Mr. Shirer in?" I repeated.

The man looked up at the sharpness of my tone. "I do not know, signore. If you will please give me your name I will telephone his suite."

I hesitated. Then some devil in me prompted me to say, "Just tell him a friend of Dr. Sansevino wishes to see him."

The porter picked up the telephone. He gave my message. There was a pause and then he was talking fast, looking at me all the time, and I knew he was describing me to the person at the end of the line. At length he put down the receiver and called one of the pages. The boy took me up in the lift to the top floor, along a heavily carpeted corridor and rang the buzzer of a door marked B. It was opened by a manservant, or it might have been a secretary. It was difficult to tell. He was neatly dressed in a lounge suit and his small button eyes were quick and alert. "Please to come in, signore." He spoke English in a manner that suggested he hated the language.

He took my hat and coat and then showed me into a large, surprisingly modern room. It was decorated in white and gold, even the baby grand was white and gold, and it was lit by concealed lighting. The floor was carpeted in black. The effect was startling in contrast with the rest of the hotel. "So it's you, Farrell." Shirer came forward from the fire, his hand held out in greeting. "Why in the world didn't you say who you were?" His voice was irritable, his face pale and his eyes searching my face.

I looked past him and saw Zina Valle in a big armchair by the electric fire, her legs curled up under her and a sleepy, rather satisfied smile on her face. She looked somehow content and relaxed, like a cat that has been at a bowl of cream. "A friend of Dr. Sansevino." Shirer patted my arm. "That's rich coming from you." He caught the direction of my gaze and said, "You know the Contessa Valle, I think."

"Yes," I said. And then as Shirer took me towards the fire I said to her. "I thought you were in Florence."

She smiled. "I could not go to-day. I shall go to-morrow instead." Her voice was slurred and languorous.

"Queer running across you again like this," Shirer said. "It takes me back to things I'd rather forget. I guess you'd rather forget them, too—eh? Sorry about last night. Afraid you caught me off balance. It was just that I wasn't expecting to find you there. Care for a drink?"

"Thank you," I murmured.

"What will it be? Whisky and soda?"

"That'll do fine."

He had turned to an elaborate cocktail cabinet. "I had no idea you were in Milan. I suppose you're here on business. Sismondi never entertains anyone unless there is some business behind it."

He was talking too fast—too fast and with a sibilance that did not belong to Shirer. The room, too. Walter Shirer had been an ordinary, simple sort of person. Maybe he'd reacted against his environment. He'd been a coal miner. But even then the room didn't seem to fit and I was filled with uneasiness.

He handed me my drink Then he raised his glass. "Up she goes!" I remembered Shirer in agony over those gas blisters raising a glass of filthy medicine to his lips and saying "Up she goes!" He'd always said that as he drank.

An awkward silence developed. Zina Valle had closed her eyes. She looked relaxed and almost plump. A clock on the mantelpiece ticked under a glass case. "How did you know I was at the Nazionale?" Shirer asked.

"Oh—somebody told me," I replied.

"Who?"

"I'm not sure." I couldn't tell him I'd overheard him give the address to the taxi-driver last night. "I think perhaps it was the Contessa, this morning when she came to see me."

He turned quickly towards her. "Zina. Did you give Farrell my address this morning? Zina!" She opened her eyes. "Did you tell Farrell I was at the Nazionale?"

"I heard you the first time, Walter," she replied sleepily. "I don't remember."

He gave an impatient shrug of his shoulders and then turned back to me. "Well now, suppose you tell me why you're here?"

I hesitated. I wasn't really sure. I wasn't sure about anything; the room, the man himself—it was all so strange. "I'm sorry," I murmured. "Perhaps I shouldn't have come. It was just that I didn't want to leave it as it stood between us last night. I quite realise how you must feel. I mean—well, at the time I thought you'd understood. I stood two of their damned operations, but the third——" My voice trailed away.

"Forget it," he said.

"But last night.... I felt——"

He didn't let me finish. "I was surprised, that's all. Damn it, Farrell, I don't bear you any grudge for what happened. It wasn't your fault. A guy can stand so much and no more. I wouldn't have stood up to even two of that little swine's operations." He said *that little swine's operations* so easily that I found myself relaxing.

He turned to Zina Valle. "Can you imagine what it's like to have your foot amputated without any anæsthetic? The foot was damaged when he crashed. But it wasn't badly damaged. It could have been saved. Instead they let it become infected with gangrene. Then they had an excuse for operating. Once it was gangrenous they had to operate in order to save his life. And then when they got him on the operating table they found they'd run out of anæsthetic. But it was made perfectly clear to him that if he cared to talk, to tell them who he'd dropped behind the lines and where, the anæsthetic might be found. But he kept his mouth shut and they strapped him down and gagged his mouth and sawed his foot

63

off. And he had to lie there, fully conscious, watching them do it, feeling the bite of the saw teeth on his own bones...."

I wanted to tell him to shut up, to talk of something else. But somehow I couldn't say anything. I just stood there, listening to him describing it with every nerve in my body shrieking out at the memory of it. And then I saw his dark eyes looking at me, watching me as he described how they'd done everything possible to hasten the healing of the wound. "And then, when it was nearly healed, they artificially infected the stump with gangrene again. Within a few days——"

But I wasn't listening now. I was staring at him with a sense of real shock. I'd never told anyone that they'd infected the leg with gangrene each time to give them an excuse to operate. I'd told Reece and Shirer about the operations, of course. But I'd never told them about the gangrene. It was bad enough knowing that they were there in that ward through my weakness without giving them any reason to think that the operations had been necessary. Of course, it was possible one of the orderlies, or even Sansevino himself, had told Shirer, but somehow I was sure they hadn't. If they had, Reece at any rate would have made some comment.

I stared across the room with a sense of growing horror. The man was watching me, telling the story of my operations for the sheer pleasure of seeing my reaction. I felt suddenly sick. I finished off my drink. "I think I must go now," I said.

He stopped then. "You can't go yet. Let me give you another drink." He came across the room and took my glass. As he bent to pick it up from the table where I had placed it, his neck was within reach of my hands. I had only to stretch forward.... But in the moment of thinking about it he had straightened up. Our eyes met. Was it my imagination or was there a glint of mockery there? "I'm sorry, I didn't realise how the memory of pain would affect you." He turned to the cocktail cabinet and I wiped the sweat from my face. I saw Zina Valle glance from me to the man she thought was Walter Shirer. Her eyes were suddenly sharp and interested. Had she guessed the truth?

"Zina. Another drink?"

"Please. I will have a whisky this time, Walter."

"Do you think that wise?"

"Perhaps not. We are not always wise."

"I really think I should be going," I muttered. I was feeling dazed, uncertain of being able to control myself. It was Walter Shirer I'd seen dressed up in Fascist uniform sitting dead at that desk. Anger rose up and choked me. The words *Il dottore* were on the tip of my tongue. I wanted to say them, to see him swing round

64

under the shock of discovery and then to close with him and choke the life out of him. But I stopped myself in time. I'd never get away with it. I'd never convince the authorities. And anyway he'd be armed. And then suddenly I knew that if he realised that I was aware of his true identity I'd never get out of the room alive. The ghastly game had got to be played out to the end now. That, and that alone, was clear in my mind. He was coming over to me now with the drink in his hand. "Here you are, Farrell. Now just you sit down and relax."

I took the drink and sank into the nearest armchair. If I was to get out of the room alive I'd got to convince him that I still thought he was Shirer. "Funny thing," I said. "I only discovered a few days ago that you and Reece were alive. The hospital authorities gave out that you'd both been shot while trying to escape."

He laughed. "We damn nearly did get shot. The ambulance we got away in broke down and we had to take to the hills. Didn't you ever come across Reece? I thought you and his sister——"

"She broke it off."

His eyebrows lifted. Shirer had never looked like that. This man was considering the mental impact of a thing like that, considering it as a doctor.

"That was not very kind of her," Zina Valle said.

I shrugged my shoulders.

"I would like my drink, please, Walter."

He took it across to her and went back to the cabinet for his own. Zina Valle slid her feet to the floor and came across to me. "You do not seem to be very lucky in love, signore," she said.

I didn't say anything. She placed her drink on the table where I had placed my own. "Perhaps you make a lot of money with the cards?"

"I don't play cards," I replied.

She laughed. "Always I am trying to prove that proverb. I do not think it is a true one." She yawned. "I am getting sleepy, Walter."

He looked at his watch. "It's only half-eleven."

"Yes, but I must be up early to-morrow." She glanced down at me. "Perhaps you would see me home, Mr. Farrell?"

It was almost as though she were offering me a means of escape from that room. "Of course," I said.

Shirer rang the bell and as the door opened behind me, he said, "Pietro. Order a taxi."

Zina Valle had moved back to her chair. I reached out for my drink. And then I glanced across at her, for my glass wasn't where I'd placed it. She had taken mine and left me hers on the far side of the table. I was about to mention it, but something in her expression made me keep silent. Anyway, she had already finished the drink.

The man, Pietro, came in to say that the taxi was waiting. I got up and helped her on with her wrap. "How long will you be in Milan, Walter?" she asked.

"I can't say. But don't worry. I'll see you get what you want. Farrell. You've left your drink." He held the glass out to me. "Scotch is too valuable these days to be wasted." He watched me while I knocked it back. *Like a doctor seeing that his patient takes his medicine,* I thought. And then I saw that Zina Valle was looking at him with an odd expression in her eyes.

He took the glass and put it down for me on a side table. Then he accompanied us to the lift. "It was nice of you to come and see me, Farrell," he said. His hand held mine and I felt a tingle run up my spine. The touch of his smooth fingers made me want to jerk him towards me and break him, smash him into little pieces. The hand I held, I knew, had never mined coal. I dropped it as though it was something that was dangerous to touch. "I hope this won't be the last time we meet." He smiled. The lift gates closed and we went down. My last sight of him was peering down at us as we descended, the light catching his eyes and making them appear black like sloes.

In the taxi, Zina Valle took my arm and leaned close. "You do not like Walter, eh?"

I didn't answer and she added: "You hate him. Why?"

I didn't know what to say. To change the subject I said jokingly, "You took my drink, you know."

"But of course. Why do you think I take the trouble to get up when I am very happy sitting in my chair?"

I stared at her. "Do you mean you did it purposely? Why?"

She laughed. "Because I do not think it is good for you. Tell me, why was Walter so strange to-night? And that name—Sansevino. It frightened him. When he hears that a friend of Dr. Sansevino is wanting to see him, he turns very white. And when you come in—for a moment I think he is afraid of you. Is he afraid of you?"

"Afraid of me?" The phrase echoed in my mind like a peal of bells. Afraid of me! Sansevino afraid of me? I felt a sudden surge of power, of exultance. I had him now. I knew his secret. I could play the same game with him that he'd played with me. There was a saltness in my mouth; the taste of revenge.

"Well? Is he?"

"Perhaps."

"Why?"

"One day, if I get to know you better, I may tell you."

"Is it because of something he has done—something he has done to you?" Her voice was eager, questing, as though she wanted the power that I possessed.

"Why do you ask?" I said. "Don't you like him?"

The taxi stopped with a jerk. She was looking straight into my face, her eyes very wide and luminous. "I hate him," she breathed. Then the door was opened and she got out. "Don't forget—if you come to Napoli I am at the Villa Carlotta."

"No," I said. "I won't forget. Good night."

"*Buona notte.*" She blew me a kiss and was gone, swallowed by a big modern block of flats.

"Where to, signore?"

"Albergo Excelsiore."

"*Bene.*"

The taxi turned into the Corso Buenos Aires, and I sat, watching the street lamps flash by, hugging to myself the thought that I had Sansevino alive and in my power. It was a mood of elation that took me back to my hotel and stayed with me when I reached my room. I was too tensed up to think of sleep. I paced up and down, my imagination running ahead of time, picturing just how I would handle the situation.

Looking back on it now I think my mood must have been a very queer one. I was excited, fascinated and afraid, all at the same time. For over a year I had lived in daily fear and dread of what this man could do to me. I had thought him dead. And now I knew that he was alive. Unless I were stark, raving mad, the man I had met was Sansevino. It was a frightening thought.

But even whilst my nerves cringed the mood of elation in which I had returned to the hotel still remained with me and I kept on repeating to myself: *Sansevino is alive. I've got him now. This time he is in my power.*

What should I do? Go to the police? No, no. That would be too straightforward. Let him learn what it was like to be afraid. Yes. That was what Zina Valle had said—*I think he is afraid of you.* Afraid! That was the thought that filled my mind. Sansevino was afraid of me. And he'd go on being afraid. All the rest of his life he'd be afraid.

I laughed out loud at the thought. No, I wouldn't go to the police. They might not believe me, anyway. I wouldn't say anything. But I'd keep in touch with him. And from time to time I'd let him know that I was still alive, that I knew who he was. Let him sweat it out through the long nights as I had sweated it out in the heat of summer on Como. Let him know what it was not to sleep for fear—fear of the rope that I could put round his neck.

And then I thought of Tuček. *God! Has he anything to do with Jan Tuček's disappearance!* I remember how Sismondi had been waiting for him that night. Was there some connection there? A man who could do what Sansevino had done—who had cold-bloodedly organised....

There was a sudden knock at the door.

I swung round, my breath caught, gazing at the plain painted panels. Was it a knock, or had I imagined it?

Then it came again. It was real enough. Suppose it were Sansevino? The palms of my hands pricked with sweat and I was trembling.

"Who is it?" I called.

"My name's Hacket. I'm in the next room to you. I'm trying to get some sleep." It was an American voice, but much deeper than Shirer's. I crossed the room and opened the door. A big, broad-shouldered man emerged from the shadows of the corridor blinking his eyes sleepily behind rimless glasses. His grey hair was ruffled and he had the appearance of a surprised and rather angry owl. He peered past me into the room. "Are you alone?"

"Yes. Why?"

He looked at me rather oddly. "I thought you must be having an all-night conference. Suppose you go to bed and let other folk get some sleep."

"Have I been disturbing you in some way?" I asked.

"Disturbing me?" His voice was almost a snarl. "Just take a look at this." He tapped the wall that separated my room from the next. "Paper thin. Do you realise I've been listening to your voice for nearly two hours now? I guess maybe I'm a little peculiar—I like it quiet when I sleep. Good night to you."

His purple dressing-gown merged again into the shadows of the corridor and I heard his door close. It was only then that I realised that I must have been talking aloud to myself. I glanced at my watch. It was past two. With a rather guilty feeling I closed my door and began to undress. Now that I was going to bed I realised that I was terribly tired. I didn't even bother to unstrap my leg. I just fell into bed and switched off the light.

My mind was still hammering away at the same problem. At what point I went to sleep, I don't know. Probably almost at once, for I barely seemed to have turned the light out before my thoughts had merged into fantasy and I was off on a crazy chase after Sansevino through a ward planted with cacti that all looked like Shirer. I cornered him in an operating theatre where lights started as far-off pinpoints and came rushing towards me till they burst in blinding flashes inside my brain. I had Sansevino in a corner. He was the size of a mouse and I was wrestling with the spring of a trap baited with my own foot. And then he began to swell. In a moment he had filled the cockpit of my plane and was looking down at me as I descended slowly into the ground. His hands reached out towards me. They were huge hands, long-fingered and smooth. They touched my clothes, undoing the buttons, and then I felt them against my skin.

I woke then, my body rigid, all the muscles tense as though I'd been subjected to an electric shock. A slight draught touched my face and I knew the windows to the balcony were open. The bedclothes had been flung back and I was cold, particularly round the stomach where my pyjama trousers had been pulled away. There was a slight movement to my left and the sound of breathing.

Somebody was in the room with me.

I lay quite still. My muscles seemed frozen. I wanted to run, but it was like it is in a nightmare when you try to run but can't. I was rigid with terror. The breathing came nearer, bending over me. Hands touched my bare stomach, sliding across the cringing flesh till they touched the stump of my left leg. They felt where it fitted into the cup of my artificial leg. Then they began to move up my body, feeling their way in the darkness as though they knew the shape of every muscle, every bone.

I stiffened in sudden, mortal terror. *I knew those fingers.* Lying there I knew who it was bending over me in the dark. I knew the touch of his hand and the way he breathed as certainly as if I could see him, and I screamed. It was a scream torn from the memory of the pain those hands had caused me. And as my scream went shrieking round the room, I lashed out with the frenzied violence of a man fighting for his life. But all I hit was air.

I thought I heard the sound of soft shoes on tiles and then a click of the windows closing. The air in the room no longer stirred. I sat up, gulping for breath in great sobs. My chest was heaving so that I thought my lungs would burst. I couldn't still my panic.

Then with a shock the windows flew open. Somebody floundered against the table. I screamed at him to go away. I could hear him moving blindly across the room. Panic gripped me so that I could scarcely breathe. And all the time I was screaming at him the only sound that came out of my mouth was an inarticulate retching for breath.

The central light clicked on and I was blinking at a figure in scarlet pyjamas. It was the man from the next room. "What's the trouble?" he asked. "What's going on?"

69

I tried to explain, but I couldn't get any words out. My heart was pounding and I seemed to have no control over my tongue. My breath just came in great sobs. Then I was sick, a dry retching. "Are you ill? Would you like a doctor?"

"No," I gasped. I could feel my eyes dilating in horror at the suggestion. "No. I'm all right."

"Well, you don't look it." He came over and stood staring down at me. "You must have had one hell of a nightmare."

I realised I was half-naked and fumbled with the buttons of my pyjama jacket. "It wasn't a nightmare," I managed to get out. "There was someone here, in the room. His hands were——" It sounded so absurd when I tried to put it into words. "He was going to do something to me. I think he was going to kill me."

"Here, let me pull the bedclothes round you. Now then, you just lie still and relax."

"But I tell you——"

"Take it easy now."

"You don't believe me," I said. "You think I'm making it up." I thrust my artificial leg out from beneath the bedclothes. "Do you see that? A Dr. Sansevino did that. It was during the war. They wanted to make me talk. To-night I met him again, here in Milan. Don't you see—he was here in this room. He was going to kill me." I remembered how Zina had changed the drinks over. Of course. It all fitted in. "He thought he'd drugged me. I tell you, he came here to kill me. If I hadn't woken up——"

I stopped then. He had picked up a packet of cigarettes and was holding one out. I took it automatically and he lit it for me. "You don't believe me, do you?"

"Just draw on that and relax," he said.

I knew he didn't believe me. He was so solid and practical. But somehow I'd got to make him believe me. It was suddenly very important. "Have you any idea what it's like to have three operations on your leg and be conscious all the time?" I stared at him, trying to will him to believe what I was telling him. "The man was a sadist. He enjoyed doing it. He'd caress my leg with his fingers before he operated. He liked the feel of the flesh he was going to cut away." I could feel the sweat breaking out on my forehead. I was working myself up into a lather again in my effort to convince him. "I know the touch of those fingers as I know the feel of my own. They touched me to-night. I was dreaming about him, and then I woke and his fingers were moving over my body. It was dark, but I knew they were his hands. That's when I screamed. You've got to believe me. It was Sansevino. He was here in this room."

70

He pulled up a chair and sat down, lighting one of my cigarettes. "Now, listen to me, young fellow. There was no one in this room. I came in here as soon as you started screaming. The door was locked. The room was quite empty. You've had——"

"But I tell you Sansevino was here," I shouted at him. "He was here, in this room. He was bending over me. I could hear his breathing. He went out by the windows. I know it was him. I know it, I tell you. I know it." I suddenly stopped with my hand in mid-air. I had been beating at the bedclothes in my agitation.

"All right. He was here. But in your imagination. Not in reality. Listen. I was skipper of a LST at Iwo Jima. I know what war neurosis is like. And afterwards—you get relapses. You had a tough time. You lost a leg. All right, but don't let it prey on your mind. What's your name?"

"Farrell." I lay back against the pillows, feeling utterly drained of energy. It was no good trying to explain to him. He just wouldn't believe me. Probably no one would believe me. I wasn't sure I believed myself. It all seemed so vague now as though it were part of that nightmare. There had been a mouse and an operating table and that lift descending slowly as Sansevino peered down at me. Perhaps I'd dreamed it all.

The American was talking again. He was asking me something. "I'm sorry," I murmured. "What did you say?"

"I asked what you were during the war."

"I was a flier."

"Are you still flying?"

"No. This leg——"

"What are you doing in Milan then?"

"I represent a firm of machine tool manufacturers."

"When did you last have a holiday?"

"A holiday? I don't know. I was looking around for a job for a long time and then I joined this firm. That was about fourteen months ago."

"And you haven't had a holiday?"

"Not since I've been with them. I can take one when I like now. The managing director said so in his last letter. But I don't need a holiday. What happened just now has got nothing to do——"

"Just a minute. Answer me one question first. Have you ever had a nervous breakdown?"

"No. I—don't think so."

"Never been in hospital because you were upset mentally?"

"I had a couple of months in hospital before I left Italy. That was after the war ended and I was released from the Villa d'Este, the German hospital where they amputated my leg."

He nodded. "I thought so. And now you're all wound up like a clock that's ready to burst its mainspring. If you don't take a holiday you're going to have a nervous breakdown."

I stared at him angrily. "You're suggesting there's something wrong with my mind. That's what you're suggesting, isn't it? My mind's all right, I tell you. There's nothing wrong with it. You think I imagined all this to-night. But it happened just as I told you. He was here in this room. It wasn't a nightmare. It was real."

"Reality and nightmares sometimes get confused, you know. Your mind——"

"There's nothing wrong with my mind," I snapped.

He pushed his hand through the tousled mop of his white hair and sighed. "Do you remember me knocking on your door earlier to-night?"

I nodded.

"Would it surprise you to know that you had been talking to yourself for two solid hours?"

"But I was——" I lay back then, a wave of exhaustion sweeping over me. What was the good? How could I possibly explain to this stolid, practical American the mood of elation I'd been in? It would be as difficult to convince him of that as it was to convince him that Shirer was Sansevino. Perhaps he was right anyway. Perhaps my mind was getting out of control. They say it's possible to believe anything, if you want to. Perhaps I'd wanted to believe that Shirer was Sansevino. No, that didn't make sense. Perhaps the shock of meeting Shirer suddenly like that had been too much for me.

"See here, Farrell." The American was talking again. "I'm over here on a vacation. To-morrow I'm flying down to Naples. Why don't you come, too? Just wire your outfit that you're under doctor's orders to take a rest. No need to actually go and see a doctor. They'll never check up. You come down to Naples with me and take a week or so lying out in the sun. What do you say?"

Naples! The blue peace of the Bay came to my mind like a sunny picture postcard. We'd sailed out between Sorrento and the Isle of Capri. We'd been homeward bound then. Perhaps he was right. At least I'd be right away from it all then—from Shirer and Reece and that business of Jan Tuček's disappearance. Lying in the sun I could forget it all. And then I began to think of Hilda Tuček. Her freckled, determined little face was suddenly there in my mind, desperate and unhappy, accusing me of running away. But I couldn't help her. There was nothing I could really do to help her. "I'll think it over," I said.

But he shook his head. "No. You make the decision now.

Thinking it over is the worst possible thing. You decide now. Then you'll sleep."

"All right," I said. "I'll come."

He nodded and got to his feet. "That's fine. I'll fix your passage for the same flight first thing in the morning. Now you just relax and go to sleep. I'll leave the balcony window open, and mine, too. If you want me, just call out."

"It's very kind of you," I muttered.

He glanced at his watch. "It's nearly four. It'll be light in an hour. Shall I leave the light on?"

I nodded. I'd be happier with the light on. I watched him go out through the windows. For an instant his pyjamas were a scarlet patch against the velvet darkness of the night outside. Then he was gone and I was alone. I felt exhausted and strangely relaxed. I think I was asleep almost before he'd reached his room.

I must have slept like a log because I don't remember anything until Hacket woke me. "How are you feeling?"

"Fine," I murmured.

"Good. I booked your passage on the plane. It leaves at eleven-thirty. It's now just after nine, so you'd better hustle. Shall I tell them to send some breakfast up?"

"Thank you." It was slowly coming back to me, all that had happened during the night. It seemed vague and unreal with the sun streaming in through the windows. "I'm afraid I gave you a rather disturbed night," I murmured.

"Forget it," he said. "It was lucky I was in the next room. I know a bit about this sort of thing. You'll be all right when you've nothing to do but lie in the sun and watch the girls."

When he had gone I lay back, trying to sort the whole thing out. Had Sansevino really been in this room or had I dreamed it? But whether it was a nightmare or not didn't seem to matter. It was real enough to me and I was glad I was going to Naples, glad the decision had been taken out of my hands. Hacket was so solid, so reasonable. I felt like a kid running away from something seen in the dark, but I didn't care. Lying there, waiting for my breakfast, I knew that I was scared. There had been a moment early on in the night when I'd been exultant with the thought of revenge. But that was gone now. The touch of those hands had swept all sense of mastery away as though I had been plunged back five years in time to the hospital bed in the Villa d'Este.

I was still going over in my mind the events of the night when my breakfast arrived. I had some toast and coffee and then dressed and packed my things. Then I went down to the entrance-hall and cancelled my room. As I drew out the lire to pay my bill the

73

photograph of Sansevino fell to the floor. I bent down to pick it up and a voice said, "Mr. Farrell." It was Hilda Tuček. "I must speak to you, please."

I straightened up. Facing her in the act of settling my bill I felt as though I had been caught doing something I shouldn't. "What is it?" I asked. She had someone with her; an Italian in a wide-brimmed American hat.

"This is Captain Caselli. He is investigating the disappearance of my father. Alec Reece thought you might be able to help him."

"Why?" My tone was automatically defensive. I didn't want to get involved in this—not now.

"I do not understand you." She was staring at me with a puzzled, frustrated look. "The other day you are willing to help and then——" She hesitated and I could see she didn't know what line to take. "What happened when you go to see this man, Sismondi?"

I couldn't face the look of helplessness in her eyes and my gaze fell. I saw then that I was holding the picture of Sansevino in my hand.

Caselli was talking now. He said, "We have spoken with Signor Sismondi. He said you behaved very strangely. The only persons present were the Contessa Valle and Signor Shirer, an American. Perhaps you can tell us why you behave so strangely, yes?"

An idea took hold of me. Caselli was a police officer. I knew that. If I could implicate Shirer, if I could start them making inquiries.... I thrust the photograph towards him, my thumb over the uniform. "Do you recognise that man?" I asked him. He peered forward. His breath smelt faintly of garlic. "He has no moustache now."

"Yes. That is the American the signorina speak of. It is Shirer."

"You think it's Shirer," I said. "But it isn't. His name's Sansevino. You go and see this fellow you think is Walter Shirer at the Nazionale. Go and talk to him. I think maybe——"

"Ah, here you are." It was Hacket who had interrupted me. "I've just ordered a car so maybe we can go out to the airport together, eh?" He had halted, looking from me to Hilda Tuček and the police officer. "Is anything wrong?"

"Nothing," I said quickly. And then to Caselli, "You can keep the photograph. It may help Shirer to remember what he did at the Villa d'Este."

Caselli stared at the photograph and then at me.

"Wasn't Shirer the man who escape with Alec?" Hilda Tuček asked.

"Yes," I said.

"And you are suggesting this Walter Shirer has something to do with my father's disappearance?"

"No. I mean——" I shrugged my shoulders. Probably he had nothing to do with it. But I wanted Caselli to investigate. That was all I wanted. "Reece thinks he escaped with his friend, Shirer," I said. "But he didn't. He escaped with that man." I pointed to the photograph. "He was an Italian doctor. He wanted to escape from being tried as a war criminal. Now he pretends he's Walter Shirer. But he isn't. He's Doctor Sansevino. Go and see him," I told Caselli. "Check the details of his escape. You'll find——"

"I do not have to," Caselli interrupted. His small eyes were looking at me hard. "I know Signor Shirer."

I turned to Hilda Tuček. She was staring at me blankly. I felt suddenly as though they were all against me. It was no good telling them the truth. They didn't believe it. No one would believe it.

"Steady." Hacket's hand gripped my arm. Then he turned to Caselli. "A word with you," he said. He shepherded them across to the other side of the entrance hall. I could see him talking to them and they were staring at me. Then he was coming back to me and they were leaving the hotel. Hilda Tuček paused momentarily in the doorway, looking at me with a strange uncertainty as though she were reluctant to leave. Then she was gone and Hacket was at my elbow.

"What did you tell them?" I asked angrily.

He shrugged his shoulders. "I just explained that you were a little upset this morning—that you weren't yourself. It's all right. They won't worry you now." He grinned. "I said I was your doctor and had advised a holiday. Have you settled your hotel bill?"

I felt helpless as though I had no will of my own and was drifting on the tide of Hacket's good nature. I turned and looked at the bill the clerk was pushing towards me.

"I hope you are not in trouble, signore?" The clerk beamed at me as though he had said something funny.

"How do you mean?" I asked.

He shrugged his shoulders. "Do you not know who that is? It is Il capitano Caselli of the Carabiniere. A very clever man, Capitano Caselli—very clever indeed."

I handed him four thousand lire notes. "You can keep the change," I said and picked up my bag. "I'm ready now, Mr. Hacket," I told the American. "Can we stop at a post office? I must send off a cable." All I wanted now was to get out of Milan.

"Sure we can. We've plenty of time."

We arrived at the airport at ten to eleven and the first person I

75

saw as I went into the passenger hall was Reece. He was talking to a stout little man with a bald head and long sideboards. He didn't see me as we went through. We checked our bags and passports and then sat waiting for our flight. Shortly after eleven the flight from Prague was announced and I saw Reece go out to meet it. I wondered whether Maxwell was arriving. I didn't see why else Reece should be meeting the Prague plane. A few minutes later our own flight was called and we went down the ramp to the aircraft.

For the second time in the space of a few days I felt a sense of great relief as I found a seat and sank back into it, safe inside the fuselage of an aircraft. The door was fastened and we began to taxi out to the runway. We had a smooth take-off and as the plane rose and Milan vanished below us in a haze of smoke, a great weight seemed to be lifted from my mind. Milan was behind me now. Ahead was Naples, and all I had to do was lie in the sun and relax, just as Hacket had said. Almost for the first time since I'd met Jan Tuček in his office at the Tuček steelworks I felt safe and free.

IV

TO land at Pomigliano Airport we made a wide sweep that carried us right over Naples. The Bay was a deep blue and Capri an emerald isle. White blocks of flats clawed their way up to the Vomero where the brown bulk of the Castel San Elmo looked out over the city. In the distance the grey ash heap of Vesuvius shone white in the sunlight, a little plume of smoke hanging like a trick cloud over the crater.

"Looks kind of peaceful, doesn't she?" Hacket said. He hadn't stopped talking since we left Milan. I knew all about his wife and family and the colliery screening business he owned back in Pittsburgh, and I welcomed the change of subject. "You wouldn't think to look at her that she'd produced some sixty major eruptions in the last four hundred years." His pale grey eyes gleamed behind the thick, rimless glasses. He gave a chuckle and dug me in the ribs. "See Naples and die—eh? Guess the fellow who dreamed that one up must have been here when she was in eruption." He sighed. "But she doesn't look very active now. And I come all the way from Pittsburgh to see that mountain. Geology is my hobby."

I noticed another puff of gas above the great circle of the crater. "Well, she's more active than when I last saw her in 1945 if that's any encouragement to you," I said.

He had his camera out of its case and was taking a shot of the mountain through the window. When he'd taken it he turned to me again. "You were here during the war?"

I nodded.

"Did you see the eruption in 1944?"

"No, I just missed it."

He clicked his tongue sympathetically. "You missed something big there, sir. My boy—the one that's running a road haulage business back home now—he was out here. He was driving one of the AMG trucks when they evacuated San Sebastiano. He saw Somma Vesuviana wiped out by the lava flow and watched San Sebastiano gradually engulfed by it. Well, I just had to come and see for myself. He says the dome of the church is still showing just above the solidified surface of the lava rock. And you missed it all?" He shook his head pityingly as though I'd missed a good film.

"You can't choose where you'll be when there's a war on," I said rather tersely.

"I guess that's so."

"Anyway, I climbed Vesuvius only a week or two before the eruption."

"You did?" He had swung round in his seat to face me and his eyes gleamed behind the thick lenses. "That's something my boy never done. I kept on asking him, what was it like before the eruption. But he didn't seem to have taken much notice of Vesuvius until it happened—sort of took it for granted. Now tell me, what was it like? I suppose it was much the same as it is now. Did you go right to the top?"

"Yes." I was thinking how we'd gone up by the tourist road from Torre Annunziata to where it was blocked by an old lava flow and how we'd climbed the rest of the way on foot. I'd had both my legs then. "It was very different," I murmured.

"It was? Gee! This is a bit of luck for me meeting someone who saw it before the eruption. What was it like?"

His excitement was infectious. "The lower slopes were quite gentle," I said. "But the last bit was steep, like a battlement of lava. And the top was a plateau about a mile across which steamed with the heat pouring out of the fissures. The whole plateau was

77

composed of solidified lava which rang hollow like metal casing as we walked across it. Right in the centre of the plateau was a huge heap of cinders about 300 feet high. From Naples it looked like a small pimple right at the very top, but close to it was more like a slag heap."

"And that was where the crater was?"

I nodded. "We climbed the slag heap and from the top we were able to look down into the crater mouth."

"Could you see anything?"

"Oh, yes. She was blowing off about every thirty seconds then, sending stones whistling up to a height of about 2000 ft."

"You don't say. Wasn't it dangerous?"

I laughed. "Well, I'll admit I wished I'd got a tin hat with me. But fortunately the funnel of the crater was sloped slightly away from us. We could hear the stones falling on the other side of the plateau. And inside the mouth of the crater great slabs of red hot, plastic rock were rising and falling like phlegm in the throat of a dragon."

He nodded, eyes gleaming. "A remarkable experience. I must tell my boy about this. A very remarkable experience. And you say the mountain is greatly changed?"

"It was the ash," I pointed out.

"Ah yes, the ash." He nodded. "My boy told me that it blew right across to the Adriatic coast—six inches of ash in the streets of Bari, two hundred kilometres away, he told me."

One of the crew came aft at that moment and ordered us to fix our safety belts. A few minutes later we touched down at Pomigliano. The airport was hot and dusty. The sun blazed out of a cloudless sky. The air was almost tropical after Milan and I wished I'd changed into lighter clothing.

The airport bus took us into Naples through narrow, squalid, tram-lined streets where the houses opened straight on to the road and bare-footed children played half-naked in the gaping doorways. Naples hadn't changed much—the same poverty and dirt. The white-painted hearses of the children would still be winding up the Via di Capodimonte to the cemetery and for all I knew the homeless would still be dying of mal-nutrition in the quarry vaults under the Via Roma. We came in by way of the Piazza Garibaldi and the Corso Umberto and as the bus ground its way through the chattering, laughing crowds time seemed suddenly to have stood still and I was back in 1944, a flight-lieutenant with nineteen German planes and more than sixty bomber sorties to my credit and nothing worse than a bullet scar across my ribs. That was before Maxwell had got me posted to Foggia, before I'd started those damned flights up to the north, dropping officers and supplies to the *partigiani* in the Etruscan hills.

At the air booking office I said good-bye to Hacket. He had been kind and helpful, but I wanted to be on my own. To be honest, I found him a tiring companion. "Where are you staying?" he asked me as we stood on the hot pavement.

"I don't know," I said. "I'll find some little hotel along the waterfront, I expect."

"Well, you'll find me at the Hotel Grand. Any time you feel like a drink, just give me a call."

"Thank you," I said. "Perhaps you'll come and have dinner with me sometime." A taxi drew up and I got in with my suitcase. "And thank you again for being so kind to me last night." Then I ordered the driver to go to the Porto Santa Lucia. "I'll telephone you," I said as the taxi drove off. I looked back and he waved his grey homburg to me, his rimless glasses catching the sunlight so that he looked like an owl surprised by the noontide glare. He looked very American, standing there in the sun with his sleek grey suit and the camera slung across his shoulders as though it belonged there permanently, like a piece of equipment issued to him before he left the States.

The taxi crossed the Piazza del Plebescito, past the Palazzo Reale where the big Naafi Club had been during the war, and slid down to the waterfront. The sea was flat like a mirror, a misty blue burnished by the sun. The sails of yachts gleamed like gliding pyramids of white, and humped against the skyline was the dim outline of Capri, half lost in the haze. I stopped at the little port of Santa Lucia that nestles against the dark, rocky mass of the Castello dell'Ovo. Sitting there in the warmth of the sun, watching a fishing boat preparing to sail, with the sweep of Naples Bay spread before me and Vesuvius standing in the background like a huge, battered pyramid, Milan faded away, a nightmare only vaguely remembered. I felt relaxed and at peace with the world, like a ghost that has come back and found his youth again—sight, sound, smell, it was the same Naples, a wonderful heady concoction of riches and squalor, sun and dust and ragged, thieving urchins. Probably they still sold their sisters in the Galleria Umberto and stole from every unguarded vehicle that ran down the Via Roma. But I didn't care. I didn't care about the mixture of wealth and poverty and the thousands who died every day of starvation and horrible, incurable diseases and filled the hearses that the gaunt horses dragged up to Capodimonte. It was all romance to me and I just sat there, drinking it in and letting the lotus of Naples take hold of me.

79

I hadn't booked accommodation. But I knew it would be all right. I just felt that nothing could go wrong now.

For that day, at any rate, I was right. There was a bright, newly-painted hotel that looked out across the port of Santa Lucia and when I ordered the taxi to drop me there they welcomed me as though they had been expecting me. They gave me a room on the second floor looking out over the Bay. There was a little balcony and I sat there in the sun and went to sleep with the blue of the Mediterranean glittering below me.

Later I got a taxi and went to a little restaurant I'd known out beyond Posillipo. The night was warm and there was a moon. I had frutti di mare and spaghetti, and Lachrima Christi, eating at a table in the open with the inevitable Italian fiddler playing *O Sole Mio* and *Sorrento*. The stillness and beauty of the night brought a sense of loneliness. And then I remembered that Zina Valle was arriving in Naples the next day and something primitive stirred in my blood. At least I ought to thank her for changing over those drinks. She'd probably saved my life. It was an excuse to call on her at any rate.

That night, when I got back to the hotel, I asked for the telephone directory. *Valle, Cssa. Zina, Villa Carlotta.* She was there all right and I made a note of her telephone number.

I woke next morning to sunshine and a lovely warm, scented air coming in through the open balcony windows. Sitting up in bed I looked out on to the blue of Naples Bay with the fishing boats and the yachts putting out from Porto Sanazarro Barbaia. I had breakfast on the balcony in my dressing-gown and then sat with a cigarette and a long cognac and seltz, dreaming of what I would do with myself all day in that golden, sunlit world. It seemed so wonderful that I couldn't believe that the spell could ever be broken. I would go out to the restaurant for lunch and then I'd lie in the sun on the rocks by the water's edge. And later I would telephone the Villa Carlotta.

I reached the restaurant just after twelve and as I was paying off my taxi a big cream-coloured Fiat swung into the parking place. There was nobody in it but the chauffeur. He got out, tossed his cap into the back and unbuttoned the jacket of his olive-green uniform. He wore nothing under the jacket. He undid the belt of his trousers and slipped them off, revealing a pair of maroon bathing trunks. I stood there, staring in fascination at this transformation from chauffeur to bather. He must have been conscious of this, for when he'd tossed jacket and trousers into the car he turned and scowled at me. He was a well-built, broad-shouldered youth of about twenty with a strong face and a mass of long, black hair which he had a habit of tossing back from his wide forehead. His eyes looked very black under the scowl. And then the scowl was replaced by a wide, urchin grin.

I knew him at once then. Instead of the chaffeur I saw a ragged little urchin with a broad grin and a white American sailor's hat. He'd been in this car park to greet us every time we'd come out here in that spring of 1944. "I know you," I said in English.

He came towards me. "Me watchee," he said, grinning all over his face.

That had been his business slogan. He would jump on the running board or run beside the trucks shouting, "Me watchee. Me watchee." I had never heard him say anything else in English. He and his gang had kept the parking place clear of thieves and as long as you paid for your protection you could leave anything in the truck and know it would be safe. When I had come back to the restaurant in 1945 there had been the same cry of "Me watchee" but the boy who ran beside the truck had been smaller. It had been his younger brother. Roberto, the original "Me Watchee," had made enough to buy a boat and we had found him jostling the fishermen at the foot of the steps.

"What happened to the boat?" I asked him in Italian.

He shrugged his shoulders. "The American and English soldiers go, signore. There is no trade, so I sell and buy a truck. Then that fall to pieces and I become a chauffeur."

"Come and have a drink," I suggested.

"*Gracia, signore. Gracia.*"

We went down to the restaurant and I had a bottle of vino brought out to a table on the balcony. The reflection of the sun on the sea was blinding. We talked of fishing and the tourist trade. Then we got on to politics and I asked him about the Communists. The corners of his lips dragged down. "Only the Church saves Napoli from the Communists, signore," he said. "But the Church cannot fight arms."

"How do you mean?"

He shrugged his shoulders. "I know nothing. It is all talk. But the arms come in and disappear to the south. They say there is a Communist army in Calabria."

"There's always an army in Calabria," I said. When I'd left Naples there had been rumours of a brigand force of 20,000 fully armed with field pieces, even tanks.

He nodded. "That is so, signore. But it is different now. It is all organised. I have heard the Conte Valle speak of it with *Comandante delle Armate del Sud.* He is in the *Governo* and he say arms are arriving all the time and everything go underground."

"Did you say the Conte Valle?" I asked.

"*Si, si, signore.* Il conte is in the *Ministero della Guerra.*"

His mention of the Conte Valle took me by surprise. Somehow I'd got the impression she was a widow. "Is that the husband of the Contessa Zina Valle?" I asked him.

His eyes narrowed. "You know the Contessa, signore?"

"I met her in Milano," I said. "Conte Valle is her husband?"

"*Si, signore.*" He was frowning and his brown fingers had tightened round his tumbler. "Where do you meet the Contessa?" he asked.

"At the house of a business man named Sismondi," I answered.

The scowl was still on his face. "Was anyone else there with her?" His voice sounded thick and angry. It seemed strange for a chauffeur to show such interest in a member of the aristocracy and I said so. He gave me a quick shrug and then grinned. "It is all very simple, signore. I am chauffeur to the Contessa. I like to swim. When the Contessa is away I can come out here and enjoy the sea. But I am always afraid she will come back too soon and be angry because I am not there at the Villa Carlotta. She is very bad when she is angry. She telephone that she arrive this afternoon. Did she tell you anything about her plans?"

"She was staying the night in Florence." I answered his question almost automatically. I was thinking what a strange coincidence it was that I should meet her chauffeur like this and find I knew him from the war days. It was almost as though I had conjured him here. He had finished his wine and was getting to his feet. "*Scusi, signore.* Now I must have my swim."

I nodded. "Will you give the Contessa a message? My name is Farrell. Tell her I propose to call on her at the Villa Carlotta this evening at six-thirty and that I would like her to have dinner with me."

Again I was conscious of that slight narrowing of the eyes and the beginnings of a scowl. "I will tell her, signore," he said. "*Molte gracie.*" He gave me a little bow which seemed strange, dressed as he was in nothing but his bathing trunks. "*Arrivederla, signore.*"

"*Arrivederci.*" I watched him as he disappeared down the steps. I felt as though somewhere a string had been pulled, tightening my contact with Zina Valle. A moment later I saw his brown body cleave the brazen surface of the water below me with hardly a splash. He swam with strong, powerful strokes straight out to sea. The soles of his two feet beat the surface like a propeller. I got up quickly and went into the restaurant.

That evening, just after six-thirty, a taxi deposited me at the entrance of the Villa Carlotta. It was a big, white house approached from the Via Posillipo by a long curving drive overhung with the trailing fronds of palm trees. Through a little group of firs I caught a glimpse of the frowning rock arches of the Palazzo Don Anna, golden brown against the blue backcloth of the sea. A man-servant showed me into a room on the first floor. My only impression of it is one of soft, powder blue with glass doors open to a balcony that had for background the picture postcard blue of Naples Bay with Vesuvius in one corner and Capri, looking remote and mysterious, in the other. Zina Valle came in from the balcony. "It is very kind of you to visit me so soon," she said in that soft, husky voice. She was dressed in a black evening gown. Her bare shoulders were covered by a white ermine wrap, which hung loose so that I could see that the top of the gown barely covered her breasts. A shiver ran down my spine as I took her hand and kissed it.

A servant brought in drinks and she handed me one. "Is it business or pleasure that bring you to Napoli?" she asked, raising her glass to her lips.

"A holiday," I replied.

"So you take my advice, eh?"

"How do you mean?"

"That day I come to see you at the Excelsoire—I advise you to take a holiday. Remember?"

"Yes, I remember," I answered. She'd said something else, too. "You told me Milan was bad for me. Why?"

She shrugged her shoulders. "In Milano it is business, always business," she answered evasively. "You work too hard."

But I knew she hadn't meant it like that. *Milan is not good for you.* She had meant it as a warning. "You were right, you know."

Her brows lifted. "How so?"

"That night at the Albergo Nazionale when you took my glass —you didn't drink it, did you?"

She shook her head.

"Why?"

She shrugged her shoulders again. "I think perhaps the flowers want a drink, too."

"It was drugged, wasn't it?"

"Drugged?" She laughed. "Now you are being melodramatic. And they say the English——"

"I'm not being melodramatic," I cut in. "About three-thirty in the morning someone came to my room. If I'd had that drink— I don't think I should be standing here now. You saved my life."

"Oh, come now, you are being ridiculous. It was all a joke."

She lowered her eyes. "I will be honest. I thought you very attractive. I wanted to make you think me mysterious. That is all."

"Someone tried to murder me." My voice sounded obstinate.

"Why should anyone wish to do that?" She turned and put her glass down on the tray. "I think I was right when I say you must have a holiday. Either you pull my leg, or if you really think such nonsense, then the fact that you have been overworking has made you imagine things." She pulled the wrap closer round her shoulders. "Come now. You invited me to dinner. But please, no more silly jokes about people trying to murder you."

We went out to the car and then drove to a restaurant high up on the Vomero where we had dinner looking through tall glass windows out across the Bay. I don't remember what we talked about. I only know that I didn't refer again to what had happened in Milan and soon I had forgotten all about it in the pleasure of her company. The moonlight and the warmth seemed to fill all the dark corners of my mind, so that Milan and Pilsen were forgotten and I was free of the past, alone with her on a cloud where yesterday and to-morrow were nothing and only to-day mattered. We danced a little, talked a lot, and in a moment, it seemed, the evening was over. "I must go now," she said. "At midnight my husband will telephone me from Rome."

That mention of her husband broke the spell. "He always telephones me at midnight." She smiled as she said this as though it was amusing that her husband didn't trust her. I helped her on with her wrap and then she said, "Will you have them call Roberto please."

When Roberto had driven us up to the Vomero his face had been wooden and impassive. But now, as he held the door open for us to get in, it was dark and alive with something that made him look more of the peasant and less of the grown-up urchin I had known. His eyes didn't once glance at me and as he closed the door I saw he was watching Zina.

The car moved off and she slipped her hand under my arm. "It has been a lovely evening," she murmured. Her eyes were deep like velvet, her lips slightly parted. Her skin looked very white against the black of her dress. I wanted to touch it, feel her lips against mine. And then something made me look up and I saw Roberto's eyes watching us through the driving mirror. I stiffened and she said something violent in Italian. Then she removed her hand from my arm.

As I was getting out at my hotel, she said, "Would you like to have a bath with me to-morrow?" She was smiling as though she had purposely phrased it to sound naughty. When I hesitated, at

84

a loss quite what to reply, she added, "I always go to the baths at the Isola d'Ischia when I come back. It is very good for the skin after the chemical atmosphere of Milan. If you would like to come I shall be leaving in the launch at eleven. We could have lunch there." She smiled. "You do not have to have the bath, you know."

"It's very kind of you," I said awkwardly. "I'd love to."

"*Benone*. At the Villa Carlotta at eleven then. *Buona notte*, Dick."

Roberto was watching me from the driving seat. "Good night," I said.

Next day was as warm and blue as the previous one. I breakfasted on the balcony, dressed leisurely and then drove out to the Villa Carlotta. Zina was waiting for me in the garden. She wore white slacks, white sandals and a white silk shirt. The white emphasised the warm olive tan of her skin and the raven-gleam of her hair. A blue wave of wisteria cascaded over the summer-house in which she was sitting. She took me down a rock path, heavy with blossom, to a wooden jetty where Roberto waited for us with a smart little motor launch, white-painted with chromium fittings sparkling against the glossy brown of the teak hull.

"*Buon giorno, Roberto*." It was said softly, silkily and like that it seemed to have significance. Roberto looked at her as though he hated her. Then he turned quickly and started the engine.

Lounging on the cushions as the powerful engine thrust us out into the glare of the Bay I felt lazy and content as though I were a child again and had never known what it was like to be scared. The sound of the water creaming back from the bows and the touch of Zina's hand on mine merged to form something beautiful that I wanted to grasp and keep. It was the lull before the storm and if I'd had my wits about me I'd have known it, for it was all there could I but have seen it—in the baffled hatred of Roberto's glance, in the puff of vapour at the top of Vesuvius and in what happened at Casamicciola.

The sea was smooth as glass and as we roared westward at nearly twenty knots a liner was steaming into the Bay between Capri and the Sorrento peninsula, looking very big by comparison with the yachts whose white sails scudded round it. We passed Procida with its castle prison and the crater harbour of Porto d'Ischia. At Casamicciola, where we landed, the villas and hotels shone in the sunlight and the air was laden with the scent of blossom.

Zina took me to a small hotel where she was apparently known. We had a drink whilst our baths were prepared and I asked her what they were like. She shrugged her shoulders. "They are natural hot springs. They say that they are radio-active. I do not

85

know anything about that. All I know is that you feel good afterwards." She glanced down at my leg. "Is that made of metal?" she asked.

"Yes," I said. "Some aluminium alloy."

She nodded. "Then I should not take it inside the cubicle. The steam will not be good for it."

"The steam won't hurt it," I answered. My voice sounded angry and I could feel the blood coming up into my face. I hate being reminded that the damned thing isn't a part of me.

"Do you never take advice?" she asked, smiling.

"Sometimes," I answered.

"Very well then. Do not be stupid about your leg. The steam will do it no good. When you are inside, pass it out to the attendant."

I laughed. "I'll do no such thing. As for the steam being bad for it, there's one advanatge about an artificial limb, you can always go to a shop and get another if it gets rusty."

Her eyes were suddenly violently angry. "You have not had one of these radio baths before, no?"

"No."

"Then you do not know what damage it does to metal. Anything metal—watch, cuff-links, anything—should be given to the attendant. You cannot buy a new leg here in Napoli."

"I'll give it an extra polish to-night," I said in an endeavour to allay her fears. "You've no idea the amount of care and attention I lavish on this leg of mine."

She didn't smile. She sat and stared at me as though I were a child and she would like to whip me. Then she relaxed and gave a little pout to her lips. "You are a stubborn man." She smiled. "I should not have tried to reason, eh? A woman should know nothing about radio-activity, she should be all emotion and no brain. Very well then." Her voice softened. "Will you let me look after your leg for you while you are in your bath?"

The idea of her even seeing it seemed quite horrible. It made me into a piece of machinery that unscrewed and took to pieces so that it could be passed part by part through bathroom doors. "No," I said sharply.

She gave an angry sigh. "You are an obstinate fool," she said and got to her feet. "I ask you to do something and all you say is No. I shall not speak to you again unless you do as I ask." She left me then, cold as ice, quite remote. I couldn't see what all the fuss was about. The obvious thing was to do as she said, but somehow I couldn't. The queer contraption that was my leg was my own affair, whether it got rusty or not.

86

A few minutes later the attendant came in to say that my bath was ready. "Is the Contessa having her bath?" I asked him.

"*Si, si, signore.*" He leered up at me as we crossed the lounge. "She is in the next cubicle to yourself, *signore,* so that you will be able to talk. I arrange it myself." Apparently his clients enjoyed bathing with only a partition between them. I gave him some lire.

He took me through to the back of the hotel and down some stone steps. The atmosphere became hot and humid as we descended. By the time we had reached the electrically-lit cellars of the hotel I could see the steam and feel the moisture settling on the inside of my lungs and throat. He took me through to a room lined with doors. He opened one and as I entered the steam-filled interior he said, "Please pass your clothes out very quickly, otherwise they will become damp. Also anything of metal, even rings, signore. The steam is very bad for metal, you understand."

I passed out everything, but I was damned if I was going to hand him my tin leg. I unstrapped it and wrapped it up in my towel. Then I got into the bath. It seemed to me much the same as any other bath. I could hear Zina splashing in the next cubicle. Then the splashing ceased, there was the sound of a door opening and a whispered conversation. I heard the bath attendant say, "*Non, non, Contessa.*" Then the door was closed and the splashing began again. I called out to her, but she didn't answer.

I lay and wallowed, wondering why she had been so insistent about my leg. I even began to think I'd been a fool not to do as she suggested. After all, she knew what effect the steam would have on it. And then I tried to remember whether radio-activity could be transmitted through steam. Surely the steam would be just plain water? Anyway it didn't seem to matter.

After half an hour I got out, dressed and left the bath-house. My body seemed overcome with lassitude so that it was a great effort to climb the steps to the hotel. I went through to the balcony and then stopped. Seated at a table with a tall glass in front of him was Hacket. He had seen me before I had time to turn back into the lounge. "Well, well—Mr. Farrell. This is a surprise. I see you've been having one of their damned energy-sapping baths. Guess you could so with a drink, eh? What will it be?"

"Cognac and seltz," I said as I sat down.

He gave the order. "Just had a bath myself. It left me weak as a kitten. Feeling better for your holiday?"

"Much better, thanks."

"That's fine. You look better already."

"What brings you to Casamicciola?" I asked him.

"Oh, I just came out to have a look at the crater harbour of

Ischia and this afternoon they're taking me up to the top of Epomeo on a donkey." He gave a fat, jovial laugh. "Imagine me on a donkey. I'll have to get a picture of that to show the folks at home. They tell me there's a hermit lives on the top of this mountain. I wonder what the beggar pays the local authorities for a pitch like that, eh?" Again the fat chuckle. My drink arrived and I sat back enjoying the warmth of the sun and the clink of ice in the glass. "Ever been to Pozzuoli, Mr. Farrell?" he asked.

"Yes."

"Now there's an interesting place. I went there yesterday—a lake crusted with plaster of Paris in the hollow of a crater. I don't reckon there's another place like that anywhere in the world. Just a twelve-inch thick crust over liquid lava. Couldn't understand at first why the guide said we weren't to walk too close to each other. Then over in one corner he showed us a place where the crust was broken away and there was stuff that looked like black mud bubbling up. Guess I understood then, all right." He chuckled. "And when you light a torch of paper and hold it to a crack, the whole rim of the crater, five hundred feet above you, begins to smoke as the sulphur gases are ignited. A very remarkable sight, Mr. Farrell. And they say it's linked underground with Vesuvius."

"I see you're not going to miss anything," I murmured.

"No sir. That's why I've come out to Casamicciola to-day. Did you know that Epomeo is a volcano?" He showed me a little red-bound book he had with him. "This is an old Baedeker I found amongst my father's things. It's dated 1887." He flipped the pages. "This is what it says about Casamicciola. *The terrible earthquake of 28th July, 1883, laid it almost entirely in ruins and cost thousands of lives and most of the few houses that are still standing have suffered severely.*" He waved his arm towards the town. "Do you realise what that means, Mr. Farrell? It means that when this little book was printed there was almost nothing here but the ruins of that earthquake."

I believe he would have gone on reading passages to me out of that old Baedeker if Zina hadn't appeared. I introduced them and she slumped exhausted, into a chair. "Phew! It is very relaxing, no?" She smiled. "But a little later you will feel like a million dollars."

"What will it be, Countess?" Hacket asked her.

"I do not think I will drink yet." She looked across at the American. "Are you here on business or pleasure, signore?"

"Mr. Hacket has come here to look at volcanoes," I said quickly.

"Volcanoes?" Her brows lifted. "You have your wife with you perhaps?"

"No." He looked puzzled. "The wife is a bad sailor. She doesn't like travel."

"You are here alone and you are only interested in our volcanoes?" Zina smiled.

"I am interested in everything geological—in rock formation, everything," Hacket said. "But down here, of course, my interest is in volcanic eruptions. Yesterday I was at Pozzuoli. This afternoon I'm going up to take a look at Epomeo. And——"

"You have not been out to Vesuvius yet?"

"No. I guess I'll leave that to the last."

"Well, don't forget to have a look at Pompei." Zina gave me a quick glance. She was paying me back for my earlier obstinacy. "That will show you better than anything else what Vesuvio can do."

"I thought of taking a quick look at Pompei on my way out to Vesuvius."

"Pompei is not a place you can take a quick look at, signore." Zina was smiling at him. "The *Ruggiero*—that is the director—is a friend of mine."

It was an obvious bait and the fish rose. "You don't say. Maybe you could—I mean if you were to give me an introduction——"

"I will do better than that." Zina turned to me. "Are you doing anything to-morrow afternoon?"

I shook my head.

"Then we will all three go out to Pompei. You have a car, Mr. Hacket? Then, shall we say three o'clock at the entrance to Pompei?"

"That's very kind of you, Countess. I'll look forward to that with great interest. In the meantime perhaps you will do me the honour of being my guest at lunch to-day?"

Zina accepted at once and there was nothing I could do about it. For a solid hour I had the two of them talking volcanic eruptions across me. Zina seemed remarkably well informed on the history of Pompei so that I began to wonder if this *Ruggiero* fellow had been her lover at some period.

At last we were back at the boat. As we left Casamicciola Zina looked at me and said, "You do not like our American friend, no?"

"It isn't that," I said quickly, remembering how kind he had been to me in Milan. "It's just that he will go on talking."

She laughed. "Perhaps he does not get any opportunities to talk when he is at home." She sprawled back on the cushions with a little sigh. After a while she said, "Do you wish to hear Rossini's *Barbiere* to-night? It is at the San Carlo. I have a box."

So I went with her to the opera that night and that was the end of my idyll in Naples. Sitting in the box with the crystals of the chandeliers ablaze with lights and the orchestra tuning up, I looked down on a sea of faces, a constantly shifting mass of colour stretching from below the crimson red of the curtain right back to the dim recesses of the theatre. And in all that eddying mass, my gaze was caught and held by one pair of eyes staring up at me. It was Hilda Tuček. I saw her nudge her companion and then he, too, looked up and I saw she was with John Maxwell.

"What is the matter?" Zina's hand touched my arm. "You are trembling Dick. What has happened?"

"Nothing," I said. "Nothing at all. Just someone I know."

"Where?" I didn't answer and she said playfully, "A girl?" I still didn't say anything, but she must have seen the direction of my gaze, for she focused her opera glasses on the centre of the stalls. "An English girl—in a white frock?"

"No—Czech," I corrected. "Why did you think she was English?"

"She look so damn' superior," she answered venomously. Then I heard her suck in her breath quickly. "What is the name of the man who is with her? I think I have met him before."

"John Maxwell," I answered.

She shook her head. "No. I do not meet him."

The lights began to fade as the conductor took his place on the platform. Then they were out and the overture had begun. I was glad to sit back in the darkness and absorb the gaiety of Rossini's music. But somehow it failed to lift me out of the fit of depression that had enveloped me. Maxwell's arrival in Naples had shaken me. I had a queer feeling of being trapped and in imagination I felt unseen eyes watching me across the dark pit of the theatre. The knowledge that Maxwell was down there in the body of the theatre stood between me and the music and I got no enjoyment out of it.

"You are cold?" Zina's lips almost touched my ear. Her hand closed over mine.

"No—I'm quite warm, thank you."

"But you are trembling, and your hand is like ice." Then her fingers closed violently on mine. "What is it you are afraid of?" she hissed.

"Nothing," I answered.

"Is the girl an old love affair?"

"No," I answered frigidly.

"Then why do you shiver? Or is it the man who frighten you?"

"Don't be ridiculous," I said irritably and got my hand out of the clutch of her fingers.

"So. I am being ridiculous, am I? But it is you who tremble."
She leaned suddenly close to me again. "What does he want, this
Maxwell?"

"Do you mind dropping the subject, Zina?" I turned away
towards the stage where the curtain was just rising.

"You are obstinate again." Her voice sounded petulant. I found
myself thinking of the ridiculous scene at Casamicciola when she
had tried to get me to give my leg to the attendant. I was still
thinking of this and listening to the music at the same time when
a hand came out of the darkness of the box behind me and gripped
my shoulder. I spun round to see the gleam of a white shirtfront
and Maxwell leaning down towards me.

"A word with you, Dick."

I hesitated, glancing at Zina. She'd noticed the interruption and
was looking up at Maxwell. He bowed, a slight inclination of the
head. "Signorina Zina Bestanto, isn't it?"

She gave a slight nod of assent. "That was my name before my
marriage. But I do not think I have met you before, signore?"

"No," Maxwell answered. "I know your name because I happened to see a photograph of you—at the Questura."

Zina's eyes narrowed. Then the lids dropped and she smiled.
"One day, signore, I hope you are very poor, then perhaps you
understand many things that seem strange to you now." She
turned back towards the stage. Her face looked very white in the
glare of the footlights and for an instant I thought I caught a
gleam of intense anger in her eyes. Then Maxwell touched me on
the shoulder and nodded towards the door of the box.

I followed him out. He shut the door and produced a packet of
cigarettes. "You certainly do have a way of picking trouble, Dick,"
he said.

"How do you mean?" I asked him.

"That girl." He nodded towards the closed door of the box.

"Well? What about her?"

"She's dynamite. The photograph I saw of her was in a dossier
about an inch thick. It was shown to me by one of the AMG police
at the Questura in Rome during the war."

"You mean she was a German agent?" I asked.

"There was no definite proof, but——" He shrugged his
shoulders. "The Field Security Police kept a close eye on
her."

"If there was no proof, then——"

He stopped me with a quick movement of his hand. "I didn't
come to see you about your girl friend," he said. "Why did you
skip out of Milan like that?"

"Reece was getting on my nerves," I answered quickly.

He drew on his cigarette until the point of it glowed. "I don't think that was the reason," he said softly.

"Then what was the reason, since you know?" I found it difficult to keep the tremor out of my voice.

In the same quiet tone, he said, "I think you were scared."

"Scared?" I tried to laugh it off, but it didn't sound right and I let it trail away uncertainly.

"Suppose you tell me what scared you so badly that you sent a cable to your firm saying you were under doctor's orders to take a rest?"

I didn't say anything and after a moment he said, "Where does that girl come into it?"

"How do you mean?" I asked.

"She comes into it somewhere. What's her name now?"

"Zina Valle. She's a contessa."

"Valle's wife? I wonder." He stroked his chin. "Where did you meet her?"

"At Sismondi's flat."

"And then?"

"She came and saw me at the Excelsiore. Later I met her again."

"Where?"

"At Shirer's suite in the Albergo Nazionale."

"Was that the night before you left for Naples?"

I nodded.

He frowned. "You're holding something back. Suppose you give me the whole story?"

I hesitated. But I knew it was no use. He and Reece were in the thing together. Reece would never believe it and therefore Maxwell wouldn't. "I've nothing to tell you," I said.

"I think you have." His voice suddenly had a bite to it. "For a start you could tell me what made you leave Milan like that."

"Look," I said. "If I could help you over Tuček's disappearance I would. Damn it!" I added angrily. "You surely believe that? The man was a friend of mine. He saved my life once during the Battle of Britain. Just leave me out of it, will you."

"I wish I could," he said. "But somehow you're a part of it whether you like it or not. Somehow it's all connected with you."

"What do you mean by——"

"Don't ask me why. I don't know. But——" He stopped and looked at me. "The morning you left Milan you were hinting to Hilda that Shirer had something to do with her father's disappearance."

"That's not correct," I answered. "There was a carabiniere captain with her. He was investigating her father's disappearance. I showed him a photograph I had of Sansevino, the doctor at the Villa d'Este."

"You told him to go and interview Shirer."

"Yes. Did he go?"

"I don't think so. There was an American doctor with you who told them you were balmy. However, Reece went along, but Shirer had left Milan." He gripped my arm. "What do you know about Shirer? Why did you tell Caselli to interview him?"

I hesitated. "I don't know," I said. I had been on the point of telling him that Walter Shirer didn't exist, that the man he thought was Shirer. . . . But in the moment of putting it into words I was assailed by doubts. He'd only think I was crazy. And here in Naples the reason for my suspicions seemed vague and unreal.

"You were going to say——?"

"Nothing," I answered quickly.

"You were going to tell me something. What was it?" And then as I remained silent, he said, "For God's sake, Dick, tell me where you come into it. You come into it somewhere. That I'm certain."

"I can't help you," I said.

He looked at me for a moment as though testing my mood. "All right," he said at length. "If you won't talk, I can't make you— not yet. But watch your step. I think you're out of your depth. Perhaps you don't know it. I hope for your sake——" He ground his cigarette out on the carpet. "If you change your mind I'm staying at the Garibaldi." He turned quickly and went down the corridor. I went slowly back into the box and sat down again in the seat beside Zina. She didn't move, but I knew she had seen me. "What did he want?" she whispered.

"Nothing," I said.

Her lips were compressed into a thin line and for a moment she looked almost haggard.

When the curtain came down on the first act and the lights went up I saw there were two empty seats in the centre of the stalls. "Your friends have left?" Zina's eyes were narrowed and watchful. I didn't reply and she said, "Let us go and get a drink." When we were seated in the bar she said, "Are you shocked to learn that I work for the Germans?"

"No," I said.

She looked down at her drink. "I was in cabaret then. My father had been injured in the bombing of Napoli. My mother was dying of tuberculosis. I had a brother prisoner of war in Kenya

93

and two sisters, one ten, the other twelve. They gave me the choice of working for them or going to the campo di concentramento. If I had refused then my sisters would have become prostitutes in the bordellos off the Via Roma. I do not think I have much choice, Dick." She looked up at me and smiled. "But now everything is all right. The war is over and I am married to a conte. Only, you see, I do not like to be reminded of the past, by people who do not understand. This Maxwell, he was a British police officer?"

"No. R.A.F. Intelligence."

"And what does he do now?"

"I don't know," I said.

She shrugged her shoulders, "What does it matter anyway. Who cares what he does? He has ruined the evening, that is all I know." She finished her drink and got to her feet. "I wish to go home now, Dick. You are not good company any more and I am upset."

I followed her out of the bar and down the wide staircase to the crowded foyer. The car was parked in the Piazza Trieste, but there was no sign of Roberto. I found him in a café in the Galleria Umberto. As we drove down to the waterfront Zina slipped her hand over mine. "Dick. I do not think this Maxwell is very good for you. Why not come away with me for a little? I have a friend who has a villa on the other side of Vesuvio. It is very quiet there among the vineyards. You can rest and relax, and nobody will know you are there. That is what you want, isn't it?" I could feel the warmth of her body very close to mine. I felt my nerves begin to relax as though they were being gently, subtly caressed. It was exactly what I wanted. If I could get right away, so that Maxwell, nobody knew where I was. "Yes," I said. "That's exactly what I want. But there is your husband."

"It does not matter about my husband," she murmured. "He is in Rome. He will be there for several weeks yet. I often go out to this villa. He can ring me there as easily as at Possillipo. What do you think?"

"Can I ring you in the morning?"

"No. Come and see me between eleven and twelve. I will be ready to leave if you want to go. Roberto can drive us."

The car had stopped at my hotel. "Good night," I said. "And thank you. I'll see you to-morrow."

"*Buona notte.*"

I watched the red tail-light of the Fiat disappear round the bend by the entrance to the Castello dell'Ovo and then I went into the hotel and straight up to my room. But when I'd gone to bed I couldn't sleep. Something Maxwell had said kept running through my mind—*Somehow you're a part of it whether you like it or not*. At length I got up, put my dressing-gown on and went out on to the balcony. The night air was cool after the warmth of the room. A rippled path of silver ran to meet the moon and I could hear the water lapping at the stone breakwater of Santa Lucia. Away to the left a red glow showed for an instant in the night sky and was gone. I watched and it came again, high up, a reflected glow against the under-belly of a cloud. But the stars shone brightly and there wasn't a sign of any cloud.

Footsteps sounded on the pavement below and I heard an American voice say, "It's just the same as it was in 1944." Just the same as in 1944! I knew then what that glow was. It was Vesuvius. The molten lava tumbling about inside the crater was being reflected on the cloud of gases each time she blew off. I lit a cigarette and stood watching it, wondering how it would look from a villa on the slopes of the mountain itself. At the moment it was only a faint flash of red in the sky, no brighter than the glowing tip of my cigarette, far less bright than the moon's path.

I shivered and went back into my room. To-morrow I would leave Naples. To-morrow I would go with Zina to this villa. Maxwell wouldn't find me there. And in a week's time I'd go back to Milan and start work again.

V

IN the morning I told myself I was a fool to be driven out of Naples by Maxwell. Why should I go up to a hot, dusty villa on the slopes of Vesuvius when I could stay down in Naples and lounge by the sea? Better to go over to Capri or Ischia or down the coast to Amalfi and Positano. The fact that Maxwell seemed to think I was in some way connected with Tuček's disappearance didn't seem so important as I sat on the balcony having breakfast in the sunshine.

It was a very close day. The sky overhead was blue, but cotton-wool banks of cumulus were piled up over Sorrento. Vesuvius looked remote and misty as though the air round it were curtained with dust. The red flashes of fire I'd seen the night before were no longer visible. The mountain looked serene and entirely dormant.

A thing that puzzled me was why Zina should want to go up to a villa on the slopes of Vesuvius. She seemed so much a creature of the popular bathing beaches. Not that it mattered. She would be exciting wherever we went. Lying back in my chair with a cigarette between my lips and the warmth of the sun seeping through the silk of my dressing-gown my mind conjured a picture of her body that was so clear I felt I could stretch out my hand and caress it.

The sound of a taxi stopping in the street below broke the spell and I leaned curiously over the balcony. It had stopped at the entrance to the hotel and a girl got out. Her titian hair glinted in the sunlight as she paid off the driver. It was Hilda Tuček. I turned quickly back into my room and grabbed the telephone. But by the time I got through to the hall porter it was too late—she was on her way up to my room.

As I put down the receiver there was a knock at the door. "Signor Farrell."

"Yes?"

"*C'è una signorina che la cerca, signore.*"

I tightened the belt of my dressing-gown and went to the door. When I opened it I was shocked to find how tired she looked. She seemed to have got no benefit from the sunshine of the past few days. Her skin was pale, almost transparent, and the freckles were more noticeable. "May I come in, please?" Her voice was low and hesitant.

"Of course." I held the door open. "Come through on to the balcony. Would you like something to drink?"

"Please. A lemonade. It's so hot."

I sent the boy for it and took her through to the balcony. She stood quite still with her hands on the railing looking out across the bay.

"Won't you sit down?" I suggested.

She nodded and sank into my chair. I brought out another. An awkward silence developed. I was waiting for her to tell me why she had come and she seemed to find it difficult. At length she said, "It is so beautiful." Her voice sounded wistful.

The boy brought her the drink and she sipped at it. I offered her a cigarette. When I had lit it for her, she said, "I am afraid I was rather rude to you that morning at the Excelsiore."

I waited for her to go on, but she was gazing out towards Capri again. "Did Maxwell tell you to come and see me?" I asked.

She glanced at me quickly and then dropped her eyes to the

handkerchief she was slowly twisting round her fingers. "Yes." She looked up suddenly and I realised how tensed-up she was inside. "He thinks you know something. He thinks you're connected with it in some way. Please, Mr. Farrell, you must help me." There was desperation in her voice and somehow it hurt me.

"I wish to God I could help you," I said. "But I can't. Maxwell's wrong. I know nothing about your father's disappearance. If I did I'd tell you."

"Then why did you leave Milan so hurriedly?"

"I told Maxwell last night—because I needed a holiday."

"He doesn't believe you." Her eyes were watching me closely and I realised that, however pathetic she might seem, she was a girl of iron determination. She was going to sit there and batter away at me until she got the truth out of me. I felt suddenly ill-at-ease, as though I was faced with something that I couldn't beat down. "Why *did* you leave Milan?"

"Look," I said. "The reason I left Milan has nothing whatever to do with your father's disappearance. You've got to believe that."

She looked at me hard, and then said, "Yes—I think I believe that. But Maxwell is convinced there's some connection between——"

"Maxwell knows nothing about it," I snapped.

She turned her head and looked out to sea. "Would you be willing to tell me about it?" she asked.

I hesitated. "No," I said. "You've got enough troubles without listening to mine."

"I'm sorry," she said softly. "I would have liked you to feel you could trust me." She paused for a moment and then said, "When John Maxwell arrived in Milan he brought a message for me from my father. It was given to him at the airfield before they left—on that flight. My father said, if anything went wrong I was to contact you."

"Contact me?" I stared at her in surprise. "Why contact me?"

"I don't know, Mr. Farrell. I thought you might know. You were his friend years ago. I think he must have communicated something to you."

I remembered then the extraordinary telephone conversation I had had with Sismondi.

"Won't you tell me what it was, please?"

"I can't," I said. "There's nothing to tell you."

"But surely——"

"I tell you there's nothing. I saw him once, that's all. It was in his office and there was an interpreter with us the whole time. All he did was to give me a message for Maxwell which I delivered."

"And you didn't see him again?"

"No." I hesitated and then added, "The night porter at the hotel where I was staying told me your father visited me late one night. If he did, he didn't wake me. He left no message, nothing. I've searched my baggage, even my clothes. I can only imagine the porter made it up in order to blackmail me into giving him some kronen to keep his mouth shut."

"I don't understand," she said, looking at me hard. "Maxwell is convinced you're mixed up in this——"

"Damn Maxwell!" I said, rising suddenly to my feet. "He knows nothing about it. He wasn't there."

"But this business of Sismondi telephoning you about some blueprints you were to deliver to him?"

"I think it was a try-on."

"You went to his house. What happened, please?"

"Nothing happened." I was getting agitated. She was forcing my mind back to Milan, to things I wanted to forget.

"Alec told me you were very upset when you got back."

"I was drunk," I said. Damn it, why did she have to cross-examine me like a public prosecutor?

"Mr. Farrell, please. I have a great deal at stake in this. I love my father very much. I have run his home ever since we have been able to return to Czechoslovakia. He means a great deal to me." There were tears in her eyes now. "What happened at the flat of this man Sismondi?"

I didn't know what to say. I wanted to help her. But it wouldn't help if I started telling her again about Shirer and Sansevino. "Nothing happened," I said. "I met someone I hadn't seen for a long time, that's all. It upset me."

"Walter Shirer?"

I nodded.

"Captain Caselli is satisfied he has got nothing to do with it. Also Alec Reece swears that Shirer would never have become involved in a thing like this."

"The man he knew wouldn't," I answered.

"What do you mean by that?"

"Nothing." I was thinking back now to the scene in Sismondi's flat. I'd thrust it out of my mind. But now I remembered how Sismondi had been waiting...

"Walter Shirer is very like the man whose picture you had."

"Yes. He was very like Sansevino. Have you—met Shirer?"

"Yes. John Maxwell took me to see him."

"In Milan?"

"No. Here in Naples. We saw him last——" She caught hold of my arm. "What is the matter?"

"It's all right," I muttered. I felt for the back of my chair and sank into it.

"You went quite white."

"I'm not at all well. That's why I had to have a holiday."

"It was when I said Walter Shirer was here in Naples." She was leaning forward, staring at me. "Why did the name Shirer upset you?"

"I told you, that day in Milan when I was leaving—only you wouldn't believe me. His name's not Shirer. It's Sansevino. Tell Maxwell that. Tell him that the man Reece escaped with was Sansevino."

I saw her eyes widen. "But this Dr. Sansevino is dead—he died in 1945. Besides, Alec has seen Shirer in Milan. He would have known if it wasn't Shirer." She was looking at me oddly. "I think that doctor was right. You are ill."

I felt frustration and anger mounting inside me. "Do you think I don't know who the man is? That last night in Milan—I lay in bed in the dark and felt his hands on my leg. I knew those hands. I'd know them if a thousand hands were touching my leg."

Her eyes had dropped to my artificial limb. The metal of it was showing beneath my pyjama trousers. "I'm sorry." she said. "Last night Maxwell told me what happened to you when you are a prisoner. I did not mean to——" She didn't finish and got to her feet.

"You don't believe me, do you?" I, too, had risen.

"I think perhaps you were right. You do need a holiday. I didn't realise it would be such a shock——"

I caught hold of her then. "You little fool!" I snapped. almost shaking her. "You come here for the truth. I give it you and you don't believe me."

"Please, Mr. Farrell." She took hold of my hands gently and pulled them away from her shoulders. "Why not lie down for a bit? I don't think you should be out here on the balcony. The glare——"

I started to say something, but she stopped me. "You mustn't excite yourself any more." Her eyes looked at me sadly. "I'll let myself out." Then she turned and went through in to the room. I heard the door close. I was alone then with the knowledge that Sansevino was here in Naples.

I dressed quickly, packed my things and checked out of the hotel. Thank God Zina had suggested visiting this villa. I could forget things so easily with Zina. And they'd never find me there. I got a taxi and drove straight out to the Villa Carlotta.

Zina's big, cream-coloured Fiat was waiting at the door as I drove up. Roberto was in the driver's seat, lounging over the steering wheel. He didn't smile at me. His eyes looked black and sullen and I had a sudden feeling that he hated me. The good-looking youth in the bathing trunks seemed to have become coarsened into a surly peasant.

I was shown into the room where I'd met her before. The powder-blue walls and furnishings seemed colder, more artificial. The view from the balcony was bleak and grey and the air was heavy so that my shirt stuck to my body. On a table in a corner was a photograph in a heavy silver frame—Zina in a white wedding dress, her hand resting on the arm of a tall, uniformed man with a drawn, leathery face. The door opened as I was putting the photograph back on the table. "You like my husband?"

I swung round. Zina, in a pale green silk frock covered with scarlet tigers, was smiling at me from the doorway. I didn't know what to say. The man looked more than twice her age.

She gave me a quick, angry shrug. "What does it matter? He is already a part of the past." She smiled. "Shall we go?"

I realised then that it had never occurred to her that I should not come.

"You look tired," she said as she took my hand. Her fingers were very cool.

"It's nothing," I answered. "Just the heat. What's wrong with Roberto this morning?"

"Roberto?" An amused smile flickered across her lips. "I think perhaps he is a little jealous."

"Jealous?" I stared at her.

For a moment she seemed about to burst out laughing. Then she said quickly, "Roberto is employed by my husband. He think he is my watch-dog and he does not approve of my taking hand-some young Englishmen out to Santo Francisco." She held the door open for me. "Come," she said gaily. "I have arranged every-thing. We will have lunch at Portici and then we have an appoint-ment to keep with your American friend at Pompei. Remember?" She wrinkled her nose at me. "I think it will be very dull. I ask him only because you are so stupid with me yesterday. But it does not matter. We have all the night."

Outside Roberto was just putting my suitcases in the boot. He went round to the door and held it open. Zina paused as she was getting in and said something to him in Italian. She spoke softly and very fast. His eyes flicked to my face and then he grinned at her rather sheepishly. He was like a small urchin that has been promised a sweet.

"What did you say to Roberto?" I asked as I subsided into the cream upholstery beside her.

She glanced at me quickly. "I say he will have the whole afternoon to sit in a café and drink and slap the waitress's bottom." She laughed at the expression on my face. "Now I have shock you. You are so very, very English, you know." She slipped her hand under my arm and snuggled down into the leather. "Relax now, please. And remember, this is Italy. Do you think I do not know what a boy like Roberto wants? You forget I am born in the slums of Napoli."

I didn't say anything and the car slid out through the big wrought-iron lacework of the gates and swung south down the Via Posillipo towards Naples. It was wonderful to feel the cool air on my face. Heavy clouds were banked up across the sky. It was oppressively close and the ash-heap of Vesuvius stood out almost white against the louring black of the sky. "Did you see Vesuvius last night?" I asked her.

She nodded. "For three nights it has been like that. From Santo Francisco we shall see it much more clearly." She sighed. "Perhaps it is because of Vesuvio that the women of Napoli are like they are."

"How do you mean?" I asked.

She looked at me from under arched eyebrows. "Our passions are like that volcano," she said huskily.

I stared at the mountain rising so quiet and serene above the sea. "Do you think it will erupt again?" I asked.

"I do not know. You must talk to the scientists at osservatore. But I do not think they know very much. When you have seen Pompei, you will understand how powerful that mountain is. It is unpredictable and terrible—like a woman with a love she must destroy in order to hold."

We had lunch in a restaurant that had once been a private house. The tall, scrolled rooms were almost Regency in architecture. It was just near Herculaneum, that other Roman town that had been buried in the ash of Vesuvius.

After lunch we turned inland from Portici, through narrow, dusty streets where naked babies sucked their mothers' breasts and old men lay like bundles of rags asleep in the dust. Then we were out on the autostrada roaring southwards with Vesuvius towering higher and higher above us to the left. Zina looked back several times and then ordered Roberto to stop. As we pulled in to the side of the road a big American car flashed by. I caught a glimpse of two people seated in the back of it, a man and a girl, and though they did not glance at us I had a feeling they were conscious of us. I turned to Zina. She was looking at me out of the corners of her eyes.

The by-roads connecting the villages pass either over or under the autostrada and not until Torre Annunziata is there a side road branching off the autostrada. There is a petrol station at the fork and the American car was there. I looked back as we shot past and saw it nosing out on to the autostrada.

Five minutes later we were in Pompei. Hacket was waiting for us near the entrance to the ruins, his tiny hired Fiat almost lost in the crowd of coaches and souvenir stalls. Zina asked for the *Ruggiero* and we were passed straight through the turnstiles. But when we got to his office we found he was in Naples, lecturing at the University, so Zina showed us round herself.

Our progress was slow, for Hacket was continually pausing to refer to his guide-book or to take a photograph. It was oppressively hot and my leg began to ache the way it often does in England before it rains.

It was the sunken streets that made it so hot. Most of them are still just twenty-foot deep cuttings lined with the stone façades of shops and villas exactly as they were two thousand years ago. Zina showed us all the important things and as we followed her round she told us story after story, building up in our minds a picture of a voluptuous, orgy-ridden life in a Roman seaside resort in the days before Christ was born. But though I saw the forum and the baths, the various theatres and the brothel with the penis sign outside and the indelicate pleasure murals above the cubicles, and the villa with the revolting picture at the entrance and the murals in the love room, it was the little things I remembered afterwards —the deep ruts worn in the stone-paved streets by the wheels of the chariots, the shop counters with the pots in which olive oil and other household necessities had been stored; the small bones still lying in the room where a child had been caught by the hot ash. It was an overall impression of a town suddenly halted in mid-flow of activity.

Walking through those narrow, rutted streets, the phallic symbol of good luck still clearly marked on the paving stones, the initials of lovers and of men in the cells of the prison still as clear as when they had been cut, it seemed as though only yesterday the Romans in their togas had been here in place of this motley crowd of camera-slung tourists speaking a dozen different languages.

But in the Terme Stabiane all these impressions were swept aside. After seeing the hot bath Zina took us back to the entrance to look at a mozaic. And it was there that we came face to face with Maxwell and Hilda Tuček. They didn't seem to notice me as they went straight through into the dim cavern of the baths. But I knew then who the occupants of the big American car had been.

Zina turned to me. "Do you tell your friends to follow us?" She was white with anger.

"Of course not," I said.

"Then why are they here? Why do they follow us from Portici?"

"I don't know."

She stared at me. I could see she didn't believe me. Then she shrugged her shoulders. "I think we go now. I do not like to be followed about. Is that girl in love with you?"

"No."

She gave a quick sneering laugh. "You do not know very much about women, eh?" We went out and turned left towards the forum.

As we went back down the narrow, sloping street with the chariot ruts, she slipped her hand through my arm. "Do not worry about it, Dick. Roberto will get rid of them for us. My car is very fast and he is a good driver." She seemed to have recovered her spirits for she chatted gaily about the scene in Pompei when Vesuvius erupted. She seemed to have an almost frighteningly morbid interest in the scene and I remember the way she laughed as she said, "It happens so suddenly that men and women were caught in bed together and when they excavate they find them still like that. Can you imagine yourself in bed with a girl and then suddenly the room is full of hot sifting ash, you are suffocated, and there you are, in the same position, when a digger uncover your love couch two thousand years later? That is immortality, eh?"

As we went out through the gates I looked back. There was nothing to be seen of Pompei except the burnt grass of what looked like a rabbit warren. It was all below the level of the ground. Behind and above it the ash slopes of Vesuvius had a grey sheen and at the very summit a little puff of vapour showed, like a miniature atomic explosion.

Hacket was also looking up at Vesuvius. "Must be a fine sight out here at night," he said. "Guess I'll drive out and have a look after it's dark."

Roberto drove up and Zina held out her hand. "Good-bye, Mr. Hacket. Now you have seen Pompei I think perhaps you respect our little volcano, eh?"

"Believe me, Countess, I've immense respect for it—and for you, too," he said with a slow smile. "I certainly appreciate your kindness in showing me around. Good-bye, Mr. Farrell. Be sure to take it easy now."

As we drove away he was rummaging in his bulging pockets for candy to give to a ragged, importunate urchin. Zina was very silent on the drive back to the autostrada. As we approached the turning to Torre Annunziata she looked back and then spoke rapidly in Italian to Roberto. He nodded and put his foot down on the accelerator. Behind us I saw the black and chromium of Maxwell's car. I felt angry then. It was ridiculous to be followed like this as though I were some sort of a criminal.

We turned left and swept down towards the leaden mirror of Naples Bay. Roberto knew his way and we roared and slithered through the narrow streets, in and out between the trams, syren blaring and children scattering. Then we were climbing out of Torre Annunziata, across the railway line, over the bridge that spans the autostrada and along the dusty road to Boscotrecase with the bulk of Vesuvius hanging right over us.

Just beyond Boscotrecase Roberto stopped the car. We sat and waited. Two carts, one drawn by a white buffalo and the other by a horse whose bones pierced his hide, passed us. But no car. Zina gave an order to Roberto and we drove on.

"We go as far as Terzigno and then we turn left," Zina said. "Santo Francisco is the village above Avin. The villa we are going to is just off the road between the two villages."

The road was narrow and the sides of it were coated in a film of white dust. Dust rose behind us in a white cloud. The country on either side was flat, with vines and oranges. Away to the right the ugly tower of Pompei's modern church thrust its needle-like top over the trees. It reminded me of the campanili of the Lombardy Plain.

It was past five when we reached the villa by a dusty track that ran dead straight through flat, almost white earth planted with bush vines. The villa itself was perched on a sudden rise where some long-forgotten lava flow had abruptly ceased. It was the usual white stucco building with flat roof and balconies and some red tiling to relieve the monotony of the design. It was built with its shoulder to the mountain so that it faced straight out across the hard-baked flatness of the vineyards to the distant gleam of the sea and a glimpse of Capri. As the car stopped the heat closed in on us. There was no sun, but the air was heavy and stifling as though the sirocco were blowing in from the Sahara. I began to wish I hadn't come.

Zina laughed at me and took my hand. "Wait till you have tasted the vino. You will not look so glum then." She glanced up at the mountain, which from where we were standing seemed crouched right over the villa. "To-night I think it will look as though you can light your cigarette from the glow of her."

We went in then. It was very cool inside. Venetian blinds screened the windows from the sunless glare. It was like going into a cave. All the servants seemed there to greet us—an old man and an old woman with gnarled, wrinkled faces, a young man who smiled vacantly and a little girl who peeped at us shyly from around a door and pulled at her skirt which was much too short for her. I was shown to a room on the first floor. The old man brought up my bags. He pulled up the Venetian blinds and I found myself looking up to the summit of Vesuvius. A little circle of black vapour appeared for an instant, writhed upwards and then slowly dissolved, and as it dissolved another black puff appeared to replace it. "*Le piace il Lachrima Christi, signore?*" the old man asked. He had a soft, whining voice.

I nodded.

He gave me a toothless smile and hurried out. He had surprising agility and he moved quickly as though expecting to be kicked out. In a few minutes he returned with a carafe of vino and a glass. "What's your name?" I asked him in Italian.

"*Augustino, signore.*" He gave me a smile that was as fawning as a spaniel.

Zina had been right about the wine. It was the sort of wine you never find in the trattorias. It was the wine reserved for the grower, the pick of the vintage.

A brief exploration along the passage revealed a bathroom, beautifully tiled and complete with foot-bath and bidet. I had a bath, shaved and changed. Then I went downstairs. Augustino was laying the table in one of the rooms. I asked him where the Contessa was. "She is having her bath, signore," he answered.

I nodded and went outside. Some little distance away from the villa was a huddle of farm buildings. There was a large ugly house with a reddish plaster front that seemed to house several families as well as a good deal of livestock. A girl was drawing water from a well. She wore a black cotton frock that showed the backs of her knees and by the way her body moved under the dress I knew it was all the clothing she wore. She turned and looked at me, a flash of white teeth in a dirty brown face. Near a stone building which presumably contained the wine presses an old woman was milking a buffalo. The buffalo stood quite still working its jaws very slowly.

I turned and went back to the villa wondering why in the world Zina had suggested coming out to this little peasant backwater.

4*

But I was glad it was so secluded. And then I started to wonder why Maxwell had tried to follow us. What the devil was it he thought I knew?

As I approached the villa I heard the sound of a piano and a voice singing the jewel song from Gounod's *Faust*. I went up the steps and into the room on the left. The shutters were pulled and the lights were on, and Zina was seated at the piano in a plain white evening gown with a blood red ruby at her throat and a white flower in her hair. She smiled at me and went on singing.

When she had finished she swung round on the stool. "Phew! It is so hot. Get me a drink. It is over there." She nodded to the corner.

"What will you have?" I asked.

"Is there some ice?" I nodded. "Then I will have a White Lady." She gave a little grimace to stop me making the obvious crack.

I mixed the drink and as I handed it to her I said, "Why exactly did you suggest coming out here?"

She looked up at me. Then her lips curved in a slow smile and she caressed the keys of the piano with one hand. "Don't you know?" Her eyebrows arched. "Here I can do as I please and there is nobody to tell my husband that he is a cuckold." She suddenly threw back her head and gave a brazen laugh. "You fool, Dick! You know nothing about Italy, do you? You are here for two years during the war and you know nothing—nothing." She banged the keys of the piano with sudden violence. Then she finished her drink and began to play again.

I stood there, listening to her, feeling awkward and somehow shy. She was so different from any woman I'd ever met before. I wanted her. And yet something stood in the way—native reserve, my damned leg; I don't know. The music swelled to a passionate note of urgency and she began to sing. Then Augustino came in to announce dinner and the spell was broken.

I can't remember what we had to eat, but I do remember the wine—lovely, soft, golden wine, smooth as silk with a rich, heady bouquet. And after the meal there were nuts and fruit and Aleatica, that heavy wine from the Island of Elba. Zina kept my glass constantly filled. It was almost as though she wanted to get me drunk. The smooth mounds of her breasts seemed to rise up out of the shoulderless dress, the ruby blazed red at her throat and her eyes were large and very green. I began to feel muzzy. The pulsing of my blood became merged with the gentle putter of the electric light plant outside in the stillness of the night.

Coffee and liqueurs were served in the other room. Zina played to me for a bit, but she seemed restless, switching from one tune to another and from mood to mood. Her eyes kept glancing towards me. They were bright, almost greedy. Suddenly she slammed her hands on to the keys with a murderous cacophony of sound and got to her feet. She poured herself another drink and then came and sat beside me on the couch and let me touch her. Her lips when I kissed them were warm and open, but there was a tenseness about her body as it lay against me. Once she murmured, "I wish you were not such a nice person, Dick." She said it very softly and when I asked her what she meant, she smiled and stroked my hair. But a moment later the madonna look was gone. She was listening and there was a hungry look in her eyes that I didn't understand.

It was then that I heard the aircraft. It was flying very low, its engines just ticking over. I jerked upright, listening, waiting for the crash. It seemed to pass right over the villa, so low that I thought I could hear the sound of the slip-stream. The engines were throttled right back and after a moment's silence they roared into life and then stuttered to a stop. "I believe it's landed," I said. I had half-risen to my feet, but she pulled me back. "They often pass over here like that," she said. "It is the plane from Messina."

I rubbed my hand over my eyes. I started to tell her that the plane from Messina wouldn't be flying from east to west, but somehow it didn't seem to matter. I was too drunk to care.

Roberto came in then. He didn't knock. He just walked straight in and stood there, staring at me with an angry, sullen, animal look. Zina pushed me away from her and got to her feet. They talked together for a moment in low voices. Roberto was looking at her now, his features heavy and coarse with desire. I wasn't so drunk I didn't know what the look on his face meant. They reminded me of King Shahryar's Queen and the blackamoor and I began to laugh. Zina turned at the sound of my laughter. The blood drained from her face so that her eyes were big and dark and angry. She dismissed Roberto and then came towards me. "Why do you laugh?" Her voice was tight with rage.

I couldn't stop myself. I suppose it was the drink. It seemed so damned funny. She was leaning over me now, her face white. "Stop it. Do you hear? Stop it." I think she knew why I was laughing, for she suddenly hit me across the face. "Stop it, I tell you," she screamed at me. Whether it was her voice, which was not pleasant, or the blow, I don't know, but I stopped laughing.

She was leaning over me still and I thought for a moment she was going to hit me again. Her face was twisted with passion.

"Because I tell you I am born in the slums of Napoli——" She stopped herself and turned quickly to the drink table. She came back with cognac in a balloon glass. "Drink that," she said. "Then you must go to bed."

I didn't want the cognac. I'd sobered up a little and I was beginning to feel uneasy. "Why did you bring me out here?" I asked. My voice sounded slurred and I couldn't get her properly into focus.

She sank down on to the couch beside me. "I am sorry, Dick. I do not want to hit you like that. Something get into me, I think. It is the heat."

"Whose villa is this?"

She pulled my head down on to her breast. "You ask so many questions. Why are you not content to take things as they come?" Her hand was stroking my hair again, her fingers caressing my temples. It was very soothing. "Close your eyes now and I will sing to you." She chose a soft Neapolitan lullaby. My eyes felt heavy with sleep. Somehow I found the glass in my hand and I drank. Her voice came and went, the drowsy murmur of a bee, the soft lilt of water. I closed my eyes for the room was pulsing to the sound of her voice.

Then I was being helped up the stairs to bed. I heard her say in Italian, "He will sleep now." Her voice sounded very far away. It was Roberto's voice that answered her. He just said, "*Bene.*"

Some sixth sense told me I mustn't become unconscious. I fought to get control of my reeling brain. Then I was lying on a bed in complete darkness. No breath of air stirred in the room. It was suffocatingly hot and I felt sick. I rolled out of bed and felt my way to the farther wall. I found the basin just in time. I broke into a cold sweat then, but I felt better and my head was clear. I cursed myself for a fool. To come out to a lonely villa with a girl like Zina and then get so drunk that I had to be put to bed!

I stood there leaning on the basin and wiping the sweat from my forehead with a towel. The villa was very still. The gentle putter of the electric light plant had ceased and I could hear no sound of voices. I glanced at my watch. The luminous face of it shone bright in the utter darkness. It was just after one.

I was feeling much better now. I rinsed out the basin and had a wash. As I dried my face I was wondering why Zina had given me so much wine to drink. Had she wanted to get me drunk? Was that the way she liked her men? Maybe she'd been in the room with me. Then I remembered the expression on Roberto's face and her sudden blaze of anger. And I began to feel uneasy again.

I put the towel down and turned to feel my way towards the

door. Her room would be somewhere along the passage. I was feeling fine now. Half-way across the room I remembered there was a torch in my suitcase which was on the window seat. I found the case and was just slipping back the clasps when I noticed a vertical red line where the shutters were swung across the window. I lifted the securing bar and pulled the shutters back.

I stood quite still then, staring in amazement at the sight that met my eyes. Framed in the window was the dark bulk of Vesuvius outlined against an incredible, lurid glow. On either side of the summit two great streaks of red snaked down towards the villa. They were like a finger and thumb of fire crooked to clutch at something on the slopes. The hand and shaft of the wrist were formed by a ruddy column that flamed from the crater, reflecting itself on great billowing masses of gas that rolled upwards, filling the sky and blocking out the stars.

I turned slowly and faced the room. It was full of a demon red glare. I got my torch and moved towards the door. As I did so the head and shoulders of a man moved to meet me. It was my own shadow thrown on the further wall by that ghastly volcanic glare.

I reached the door and turned the handle. But nothing happened. I turned the knob in the opposite direction, but the door would not budge. I was suddenly very wide awake. I jerked furiously at the door in the grip of a sudden panic fear of being trapped. With the horrid glare of the mountain behind me I became desperate to reach the safety of the passage outside. But I couldn't shift it and at last I realised that I was locked in. For a moment I was terrified. The mountain was in eruption and I had been left here to die under the ash. I was on the point of shouting for help when some instinct kept my mouth shut. I turned quickly back to the window and stood gazing up at the flaming mass of the volcano.

My heart was still pounding against my ribs, but my brain was clearer now. The mountain wasn't in eruption—not yet. It was worse than it had been last night, but it wasn't in eruption—not in the way it had been when Pompei had been destroyed. A lot more gas was escaping, but the glow was mainly from the lava outflows. The villa wasn't in any imminent danger. And if the villa wasn't in danger then there was no call for me to panic because the door of my room had been locked. Perhaps it was just jammed.

I went back and tried it again. But it was locked all right. And then I remembered the nightmare of that night in my room at the Excelsiore in Milan. I felt the sweat breaking out on my forehead again. I told myself there couldn't be any connection. But why had the door been locked? Why had Zina gone out of her way to fill me up with wine till I was so drunk I couldn't stand? Whose villa was this?

I remembered then what Maxwell had said—*But somehow you're a part of it whether you like it or not.* And the man who called himself Shirer—Hilda had said he was in Naples. I flashed my torch round the room. The hard white beam of it seemed somehow solid and friendly. I lit a cigarette. My hand trembled as I held the match to it. But at least I was forewarned. I glanced up at Vesuvius. The whole night sky seemed on fire like a scene from *Paradise Lost*. The headlights of a car stabbed the lurid country-side on the road to Avin. It slowed and stopped. Then the head-lights went out. A door closed in the stillness of the villa below me. Involuntarily my muscles tensed. I thought I heard the creak of a stair board, and suddenly I knew someone was coming up the stairs, coming to my room.

I swung the shutters to and moved towards the door. The palms of my hands were sweating and the chromium of the torch I held felt slippery. But the weight of it was comforting. I stood with my head pressed close to the panelling of the door, listening. There was somebody outside now. I couldn't hear him, but I sensed him there. Very quietly the key was turned in the lock. I stiffened and then stepped back, so that I should be behind the door when it opened.

I couldn't see it, but I felt the handle turning. Then my hand, which was touching the woodwork of the door, was pressed back as the door was opened. I grasped the heavy torch, raising it ready to strike out. But before I could hit him the man was past me and moving towards the bed. I slipped out into the passage then, the sound of my movement lost in the deep pile of the carpet. A faint red glow showed through an unshuttered window at the far end of the corridor. I reached the dark shaft of the stairs and hesitated. The villa was all silent, an alert stillness that seemed to be listening for the sound of my footfall.

And as I stood there, hesitating, there was a sudden shout from my room. "Roberto! Augustino!"

The lavatory was right opposite the head of the stairs. The door was ajar and I stepped back into the shadows as footsteps came running out of my room. A torch flashed in the corridor. "Roberto! Augustino!" Somebody went hurtling past and flung himself down the stairs. I had a brief glimpse of a short, angry figure. Then a door opened along the corridor, near the red glow of the window. I peered out and saw the silhouette of a man hurrying down the corridor towards me. As he passed me he switched on a torch and in the reflected light from the walls I saw it was Roberto. His black hair was tousled and his features coarse and puffed with sleep. He wore a singlet and was buttoning on his trousers. He left behind him a faint smell of sweat mingled with the scent of a perfume that I recognised as Zina's.

He went to the door of my room, peered inside and then came quickly back and ran down the stairs. I left the shelter of the lavatory then and went along the corridor. I think I knew in my heart who it was that had entered my room. But I had to know the truth. Zina had brought me here. She'd filled me up with liquor so that I couldn't stand. I suddenly felt utterly callous and quite sure of myself. This was the end of it all, here in this villa. And if I had to throttle the little bitch, I'd get the truth out of her.

I reached the door from which Roberto had emerged and I went in. The shutters were closed. It was quite dark and very hot and airless. My breath was coming in quick pants. But it was excitement, not fear. Below, the silence of the villa was torn by running feet. I closed the door of the room behind me, shutting out the sounds. There was a key in the lock and I turned it. A voice murmured sleepily, "*Che è capitato*'" It was Zina all right. I switched on my torch and swung the beam to the big double bed.

She sensed something was wrong, for she sat up, clutching the bedclothes to her in an effort to hide her nakedness. Her hair looked damp and straggly and her mouth was thicker. "*Chi è?*" she whispered.

"Farrell," I answered and wondered why I'd ever thought her attractive. "Get some clothes on. I want to talk to you." My voice showed my disgust. "Make a noise and I'll hit you. The door's locked."

"What do you want?" She tried to give me an alluring smile, but her voice was hoarse with uneasiness and her smile was fixed and brassy like a prostitute's.

Her dressing-gown was lying in the middle of the floor. I picked it up. It smelt faintly of the perfume I'd smelt on Roberto. "Put this round you," I said and tossed it over to her.

She flung it over her shoulders and pulled it round her under the bedclothes. I went over to her then and sat down on the bed. I kept the beam of the torch full on her. "Now then. Whose villa is this?"

She didn't answer, but lay back, shielding her eyes from the glare of the torch. I leaned forward and pulled her arm roughly away from her face. "Whose villa is it?" I repeated. She lay quite still, staring up at me. My disgust had turned to anger—anger at myself for being such a damned fool. I caught hold of her arm and twisted it. She gave a gasp of pain. Perhaps she sensed the violence of my anger for she said, "Please. You do not have to break my arm. It is the villa of someone you know. You meet him with me in Milano."

"Shirer?" I asked.

"*Si, si, Signor Shirer.*"

So I'd been right and I had walked straight into the trap. I suddenly wanted to hit her. I got up quickly and went over to the window, flinging back the heavy shutters. I heard a gasp from the bed as the lurid glare of Vesuvius invaded the room. I stared out across the balcony to the flat land below that showed quite clear and saffron-tinted, part moonlight, part glare of the mountain. It was like the sunset glow on snow. I saw figures moving by the outhouses. They were searching for me down there. I turned back to the bed. I had control of myself now. "Did he ask you to bring me here?"

"Yes." Her voice was scarcely audible. Her eyes were very large as they stared up at me out of the pallor of her face.

"And you were to get me drunk?"

"Yes. Please, Dick. I couldn't help——"

"I thought you hated the man?"

"I do. I do. But——"

"Why did he want me here? Was he going to kill me? Was he afraid I knew——"

"No, no. He was not going to hurt you. It was only that he wanted something."

"Wanted something?" I had caught hold of her arm again. "What did he want?"

"I do not know."

I shook her angrily. "What did he want?"

"I tell you, I do not know what he want."

I remembered something then—something that suddenly had significance. "When we went to Casamicciola that day—why were you so worried about my leg?" She didn't answer and I repeated the question. "You wanted to get my leg away from me. Did he ask you to do that?"

She nodded.

"Why?"

"Please. I do not know. He ask me to take it. That is all I know."

"He was there, at Casamicciola?"

"*Si.*"

The thing took shape then. I remembered how my leg had stood propped beside me that night I'd lain drunk on my bed at the hotel in Pilsen. I heard myself laughing, laughing at myself. What a bloody fool!

"Why do you laugh like that?" Her voice sounded scared.

"Because now I know what it's all about." I stood looking down at her, wondering why she'd trapped me like this. "Are you in love with this man?" I asked her. It seemed to me the only possible reason.

She sat up then, regardless of the way her dressing-gown gaped. "I tell you once before—I hate him. He is—he is a cretin." She spat the words at me.

"Then why do you do what he tells you?"

"Because otherwise he will ruin me." She lay back again, pulling the dressing-gown round her. "He knows things about me and he will tell my husband if I do not do what he ask."

"Because of Roberto?"

"No. Not because of Roberto." She dropped her eyes. "It is because—because he has something I need." The sound of voices came through the open window. She listened for a moment. Then she said, "I think you should go now."

But I paid no attention. I was thinking of Walter Shirer. He'd been tough. But he wouldn't have blackmailed a girl, whatever she was. And he wouldn't have got involved in the Tuček business. Reason confirmed now what instinct had already told me. I knew beyond any doubt who it was searching for me in the grounds of the villa. "His name is Sansevino, isn't it?"

She stared at me. "Please. I do not understand."

"His real name," I said impatiently. "It's Sansevino, isn't it?" But the name apparently meant nothing to her. "All right," I said. "It doesn't matter. But I'd keep clear of him in future. His name's Doctor Sansevino, and he's a murderer."

"Doctor Sansevino." She frowned. "You say he is a doctor?" Then she nodded her head slowly. "Yes, I think perhaps he is a doctor."

Il dottore. My hands clenched. If I could only get hold of him! I thought of Hilda Tuček then, frantic over the disappearance of her father. Had he killed him? Or was he just torturing the poor devil? "Where is Jan Tuček?" I asked her.

She shook her head. "I do not know where is Tuček. I never hear of this man Tuček." She lay back on the pillows. "Go now, please. I think it is not safe for you to stay any longer."

I hesitated. But I couldn't force her to talk, and it was quite possible she knew nothing about Tuček. Sansevino wouldn't have told her more than he had to. I went over to the window. The world outside was very still in the red mantle of the volcano.

Nothing stirred. The search must have moved to the back of the villa. If so, perhaps I could get out by the front. I went over to the door and quietly unlocked it. The walls of the corridor outside were faintly tinged with the red glow from the window and there were deep shadows. The house was very quiet.

"Dick!"

I swung round at the sound of movement by the bed. Zina was sitting up fumbling in her handbag. "Do not do anything foolish. I think this place is very dangerous for you now."

I didn't answer, but as I turned to leave the room, she hissed, "*Un momento*. Wait."

She slipped out of bed and came towards me in her bare feet. She held something in her hand. "Take this," she whispered. I felt the cold touch of metal against my hand and my fingers closed over the butt of a small automatic. Her hand touched my arm. It was almost a caress. "You think me very bad, yes? But remember, please, we come from two different worlds. Leave the villa now and do not come back. Get a plane very quick and go back to England where life is so easy and so secure." Her fingers squeezed my arm. Then she turned and went back to bed.

I went out into the corridor and closed the door behind me. The villa was deathly quiet. It was so quiet that it seemed to be full of sound. And then I realised that the sound was the sound of gases escaping from the crater vent high up on the summit of Vesuvius. It was a steady hissing sound that seemed to invade the place like an air-lock in the water system.

I went to the head of the stairs and started down. The stairs were of bare tile and it was difficult for me to manœuvre my leg so that it made no sound. Below, it was pitch-black, for the shutters were still drawn over the windows. I didn't dare use my torch in case they had come in from their search of the grounds, but the weight of it in my hand was comforting and I kept a tight hold of the little automatic Zina had given me.

There were two courses open to me—either to wait for Sansevino or to try and escape. *Leave the villa now and do not come back.* That was what Zina had said and I knew that it was the sensible thing to do. My courage was ebbing away in the dark stillness. Once I had got away I could contact Maxwell and tell him the whole thing. The proof was on me, strapped to my body in the shaft of my artificial limb. I was certain of that.

I felt my way to the front door. It was locked, and the key was not in the lock. The darkness all round me seemed suddenly alive. I had to get out. I couldn't fight him alone here in the darkness. If he got hold of me.... I shuddered at the thought of the touch of his hands on my body. I turned in a panic and groped my way to the hall window. It was shuttered and the iron bar that secured the shutters was padlocked. I tried the dining-room. There, too, the shutters were padlocked. Again I had that feeling of being trapped, a nightmare sense of claustrophobia. I went back into the hall and there I hesitated. I was considering trying to get out through the servants' quarters when I noticed a slight glow from the half-open door of the room where Zina had played to me earlier that evening. I crossed the hall and pushed open the door. Then I breathed a sigh of relief. A rectangle of red light showed opposite the door. The room was full of shadows. But I didn't mind. All that mattered was that there were no shutters across the window. I went straight over to it and slipped the catch.

And then something about the stillness of the room made me turn. Was it my imagination or was there a figure seated at the piano? I stood there for a moment, quite still and rigid, the blood pumping against my eardrums. Nothing stirred. The room glowed faintly. I reached again for the window and pushed it open. The night air was cool on my face. The vineyards below the terrace were bathed in a macabre light. "You finding it hot to-night, Farrell?"

I swung round, my heart thudding. The voice had come from behind me, from the direction of the piano.

"I couldn't sleep either." The voice was almost American, but in the darkness I detected an unpleasant sibilance. The piano came to life, whispering the old Yankee tune *Marching through Georgia*. Shirer had whistled that tune, whistled it endlessly through his teeth to keep himself from crying out at the pain of his gas blisters. I switched on my torch. The beam cut across the glossy surface of the baby grand to the face above the keyboard—Shirer's face; only not quite Shirer's.

The man's name was on the tip of my tongue—his real name. But I stopped myself in time. Maybe I could bluff it out. If I could make him think... "God! You scared me," I said quickly. "What are you doing here? I thought you were in Milan."

"I live here. Do you mind switching that torch off. It's a bit dazzling."

For an instant I hesitated. If I kept the beam on his face maybe I could get Zina's automatic out of my pocket without him seeing. But I might miss and then—— The trouble was I couldn't see his hands. But he wouldn't have sat there waiting for me to be attracted to the open windows without having a gun. Somehow I had got to convince him that I'd no idea anything out of the ordinary had happened. I switched the torch off. The sudden darkness made me wish I'd chanced a shot.

"Couldn't you sleep?"

"I slept for a bit," I told him. "Then I felt ill. I'm afraid I had too much to drink."

"Where've you been—for a walk round the grounds?"

"No. I tell you, I felt ill. Somebody was calling for Roberto and Augustino. Was that you?"

"Yeah. That was me. Where exactly have you been? When I heard you were here I went up to your room to say Hullo, but you weren't there. Where were you?"

"I tell you, I felt ill. I was in the lavatory."

"In the lavatory?" He suddenly laughed. I think he was convinced then that I wasn't suspicious. "Well, what do you think of the local firework display?" he asked. "Quite a sight, isn't it? There's tourists rubber-necking on the road between here and Avin."

"It's incredible," I murmured. "Do you think it will get serious?"

"Can't say. Never seen anything like this in the two years I've had this place. The mountain's always been quiet as a mouse."

"Are you the owner of this villa?" I asked him.

"Yeah. Didn't Zina tell you?"

"No." And then I added, "I'm sorry. I wouldn't have come if I'd known."

"Maybe that's why Zina didn't tell you. Zina's an old friend of mine. If she wanted to bring you out here, that's okay by me."

I was getting accustomed to the weird light now and I could see that his eyes were watching me closely all the time. I think if I hadn't been so wrought-up I'd have found the situation funny. There was I with whatever it was he wanted in the hollow of my artificial leg and he didn't know how to get it out of me. "I think I'll go back to bed now," I said.

He nodded and got to his feet. "Me, too. But first I'm going to have a drink. What will you have?"

"Nothing, thank you."

"Oh, come on now. You're not going to make me drink alone, are you?"

"I've had too much to-night already," I reminded him.

"Nonsense. I insist." He was over at the drink table. I couldn't see what he was doing, but I heard the clink of glass. I started towards the door, but he stopped me. "Here you are, Farrell. A straight cognac. Just the thing you need."

"No, really—I'd rather not." I was edging towards the door all the time.

"Damn it, man, it won't bite you." His voice had sharpened. The light caught his eyes and they glowed like two coals in the half-dark. He'd almost certainly drugged it, but if I didn't take it I was afraid he'd try some other method of getting what he wanted.

"All right," I said. I took the glass.

"Well, up she goes."

"Cheers," I said and raised the glass to my lips. It was cognac all right. I tipped it up and let it spill down inside my jacket. I thought he couldn't possibly see in the dark, but he did.

"Why do you do that?"

I'd slipped up and I knew it, for he'd spoken softly, almost menacingly. And there was no pretence of an American accent. It was Dr. Sansevino speaking in English.

I didn't say anything and we faced each other. There was a sudden void in the pit of my stomach and the hairs crawled along my scalp. We were no longer play acting now. We were face to face—I knowing who he was, and he knowing that I knew. I slid my hand to my jacket pocket. It was a mistake. He saw the movement and knew that I was armed. He dived for the piano. Propped against the music rest I caught the dull gleam of metal. As he picked it up my hand tightened on the butt of the automatic.

And in that moment the rectangular space of the window blossomed in a monstrous flower of flame that went roaring out across the sky. With it came a noise that seemed to fill the heavens with sound. It was like fifty thousand express trains thundering through a tunnel. It was like a tornado sweeping over the open gates of Hell. It was a lion's roar magnified until it shook the earth. The villa trembled to its foundations. The ground on which it was built rocked. It was as though the world were splitting open under the impact of another planet.

I saw Sansevino standing with the revolver in his hand staring at the window as though transfixed. His features shone with sweat in the ruddy glare. I followed the direction of his gaze and saw that the whole summit of Vesuvius was on fire. Two great fire gashes streaked the mountainside and from the crater a great column rose, red at the base with the reflected glow, but darkening to a hellish black as it opened out, writhing and twisting as though in agony. And where it blackened and spilled outwards across the sky it was criss-crossed with vivid flashes of forked lightning.

The noise went on and on, prolonging itself unbelievably. It was the noise of an angry mountain—a mountain breaking wind from the distended bowels of its rock stomach. Its gases and lava-excreta were being sprayed out of its crater orifice—thousands on thousands of feet upwards.

I stood absolutely motionless, unable to move, the sight was so staggering, the noise so terrifying. In a mental flash I saw Pompei, buried under its millions of tons of hot ash, men and women caught and held in the midst of their daily life to be exhibited to tourists two thousand years later. Was this the same? Was this noise the roof of the mountain being blown to airborne fragments? Were we to be buried here for the benefit of archæologists years hence?

All these thoughts and half my life poured through my mind as I stared up at that ghastly sight, the noise dinning in my ears so that it seemed as though there never could be any other sound in all the world.

Then, as suddenly as it had started, it ceased. The abrupt stillness seemed somehow more frightening than the noise. The noise had died to a faint, whistling sigh high up in the black sky. It was as though it had never been and all living things were dead and silent. Through the rectangular frame of the window the world looked just the same, the vineyards and orange groves serene and tranquil. But the light had changed. The scene was no longer saffron-tinted. It was red—red as Hell itself. The moon had been blotted out. The scene was lit only by the red glow of the mountain.

And then slowly the fires died down. The light seemed to go out of the scene, as though I were watching the sunset glow and the rim of the sun was sinking below the horizon. I looked up towards the mountain. The red streaks of the lava flow were gradually fading. A curtain was being drawn over the mountain, veiling the terrible red anger of it. In a moment it was black as the pit. And as the glow vanished all the world went black. I could see nothing—no sign of the vineyards or the orange trees, not even the shape of the window outlined against the night outside.

And then the gentle hissing sound of something falling—continuously and relentlessly. It was like the sound of hail. But it wasn't hail. It had a heavy, sulphurous smell. It was ash raining down from the mountain above.

I knew then what to expect. This was it—the rain of ash that had buried Pompei. The history of the mountain was repeating itself. I felt suddenly calm, almost detached. There is a moment after you have been badly frightened when you accept death as the inevitable, logical conclusion. That was how I felt as I stared at the black, sulphurous night with its sifting sound of falling ash. I accepted it, and once having accepted it I didn't mind so much.

And now I became conscious of other sounds. A woman was screaming. A door banged and footsteps ran along the corridor overhead. The villa seemed suddenly to have come to life. It was like the relief of the jungle after it has been frozen to stillness by the hunting roar of a lion. Sansevino came to life, too. He turned and ran to the door. As he passed me he cried, "The cars. *Presto! Presto!*"

I turned and followed him. A torch was bobbing towards me down the stairs. The beam showed a grey curtain of ash sifting down from the top of the villa. The tiny particles gleamed and danced in the light. The torch flashed on my face and Zina's voice said, "*Che dobbiamo fare? Che dobbiamo fare?*"

I could hear Sansevino shouting for Roberto. "They've gone for the cars," I told her.

"We must get away from here. Where is Roberto? Roberto! Roberto!" Her voice was a scream. "We must get to the car. We must drive away quick before the roads are blocked."

I thought of the cabriolet's canvas hood. Hot ash would burn through it. Anyway, how could anyone drive through it? It'd be worse then driving through a sandstorm. The ash would be like a solid wall reflecting the light of the headlights. "Better to stay here," I said.

"Stay here!" she screamed at me. "Do you know what it is like to be buried alive? Did you not see what happen to Pompei? *Madonna mia!* I wish to God I never come 'ere. Albanese of the osservatore tell me something will happen. But I have to come. I have to come." She was literally wringing her hands. I'd heard of people doing it, but I'd never actually seen it before. Her hands were locked together, her fingers twisting and twining so tightly that she seemed to be trying to squeeze the flesh out from between the bones. "We must get away. *Dio ci salvi!* We must get away."

She was on the edge of hysteria. I caught hold of her shoulders and shook her. "Pull yourself together," I said. "We'll get out of it somehow."

She shook my hands off. "Let go of me. *Idiota!* Do you think I am a peasant and am going to scream? It's only that I need——" She didn't finish, but in the light of my torch I saw that her eyes had a feverish, starved look.

There was something about her face that was quite frightening. She looked as though she were in hell. "What do you need?" I asked her.

"Nothing." Her voice was high and harsh. "We must get to the car. Hurry!" She pushed past me and flung herself at the front door. When she found it was locked she turned like an animal in a trap. Then she darted towards the servants' quarters. A candle glimmered in the darkness of the passage. "Augustino!" It was Sansevino's voice.

The candle halted. "*Si, signore?*"

"Get upstairs and shut all the windows." Sansevino came through into the hall. "It's hopeless," he said. "Thick as hell."

"We must get to the cars." Zina started to push past him, but he caught hold of her arm. "I tell you, it's hopeless. You'll only get lost if you go out. I've told Roberto to start the light plant. We'll have to stay here till the ash lets up a bit."

Zina sagged against the wall as though all the stuffing had been knocked out of her. Augustino's wife had joined us now, passive as a buffalo, one hand holding a candle and the other fingering the beads of her rosary. Her lips moved as she reiterated again and again, endlessly, "*Mamma mia! Mamma mia!*" as though that in itself would keep the ash at bay. The little girl I'd seen when we arrived clung to her skirts, her eyes enormous in her white, frightened face.

The bulbs in the chandelier glowed into life, flickered and then brightened. We stood blinking at each other in the sudden brilliance. Sansevino was almost unrecognisable, he was so caked in ash. The air was thick with dust. A white film covered everything. We might have been in a building that had just been hit by a bomb.

Roberto came in then from the servants' quarters. His hair and face were powder-grey and pellets of cinder slid from the shoulders of the leather jerkin he'd flung on over his singlet. Zina clutched at him. "We must get the car, Roberto. If we can reach the autostrada we——"

But he threw her off. "*Impossibile,*" he grunted.

"But it must be possible," she blazed at him. "It must be." She caught his arm and shook it. "Will you stand there and let us all be buried here alive?"

He shrugged his shoulders, dragging down the corners of his mouth and spreading his hands in that inevitable Italian gesture of resignation.

"Go and get the car!" she ordered him.

He stood there, staring at her.

"Go and get the car!" she shouted. "Do you hear? I want my car." Then as he didn't move: "You are a coward. You are afraid to——"

"If you want the car, go and get it," he said sullenly.

She stared at him as though he'd struck her. Then she turned to Sansevino who was standing by the table, his fingers stroking his upper lip. "If the car is no good, there is still the *aeroplano*. Where is Ercole?"

"He went into Napoli in the jeep," Sansevino replied. "It's no good, Zina. We've just got to stay here."

I thought for a moment she was going to break down. Instead she went towards him and in a quick whisper said, "Then give me some *morfina*."

"Later," he said quickly. "Later." His eyes had glanced in my direction.

She began to plead. Her voice was an abject whine and now I knew what that feverish, starved look in her eyes meant. He had started to move towards the stairs when suddenly there was a violent banging on the front door. Somebody was calling out, asking us to open.

It was Sansevino who opened it. A man staggered in with a blast of hot air and a rolling cloud of choking dust. He had his arm flung up to guard his face. He was white with ash, and cinders as big as peas rolled off the shoulders of his overcoat. As Sansevino flung the door to I had a momentary glimpse of a world that was black like a pit, a world that stirred and moved and was alive with an ugly hissing, sifting, drifting sound. The man shook himself like a dog. "I sure am glad I found your house," he said to Sansevino. And as the ash fell away from him I saw who it was. "You've had a lucky escape, Mr. Hacket," I said.

He stared at me. And then his face creased in a smile. "Well, if it isn't Mr. Farrell. Well, well—we just don't seem to be able to keep away from each other, do we? And the Countess. Wonderful!" He was coughing and beaming at us at the same time. I introduced him to Sansevino. "A fellow countryman of yours," I added and tried hard not to sound sarcastic.

"Glad to meet you, sir." He wrung Sansevino's hand. "I motored up to Santo Francisco. They told me it was the best place to see Vesuvius at night. Well, I certainly seen something. The folks at home will never believe me when I tell them. I was right there in Santo Francisco when it started." He shook his head in wonderment. "Stupendous! Just stupendous! I've never seen anything like it in my life. No, sir! And I've been down to see the volcanoes in Mexico."

"Is it possible to get away by car?" Zina asked him.

He shook his head. "Not a chance, lady. Countess, I mean. When it started all the villagers came out into the streets. At first I thought they were rubber-necking, same as me. But then they started loading up their carts and I only just got out before the road was blocked with screaming horses and bullocks and humans. I'd got the idea by that time that it was going to be dangerous and I started to drive back down towards the autostrada. Then the ash began to fall. Couldn't see a damn thing. Not a damn thing. It was like trying to drive along a pit shaft just after they've blown the coal face. Black as hell!" He turned to me. "Remember those two people we saw at Pompei—a man and a girl?"

I nodded.

"They were out there. I ran slap into the back of their convertible."

I glanced at Zina. She was looking at Sansevino. "What were they doing?" she asked.

"Just looking at the mountain, I guess. They were parked outside the gates to your place. They told me there was a villa up here so I came along. Didn't fancy the hood of my little beetle-car would last long if the ash got hot."

"Who are these people, Zina?" Sansevino asked.

"Remember John Maxwell?" I asked him.

His eyes flicked to my face. They were narrowed and wary. He didn't say anything, but he nodded. "If it is the two people we met at Pompei this afternoon," I added, "it will be John Maxwell and a girl called Hilda Tuček."

"Hilda Tuček!" His voice had a sudden note of surprise. "No—I don't think I know her. But I remember Maxwell, of course." The speed with which he covered up was amazing. "Well, since we can't do anything we'd better have a drink." He opened the door of the room where we'd faced each other only a few minutes ago.

But Zina caught hold of his arm. "Walter! Are you going to do nothing? Do you wish to be buried here in your villa?" The urgent, panicky note was back in her voice.

Sansevino shrugged his shoulders. "Tell me what I ought to do and I'll do it. In the meantime you'd better have a drink to steady you." He had caught hold of her arm. But she flung herself free. "You want me to die. That is it." Her eyes were blazing. "You think I know too——"

"Shut up!" His eyes slid to my face.

"I tell you, you cannot do this to me. I do not wish to die. I will——"

He had hold of her arm again and she cried out as his fingers dug into her flesh. "Shut up—do you hear? What you need is one of your injections." He turned quickly to the drink table and poured her a stiff cognac. "Drink that and get a hold on yourself. What about you, Mr. Hacket? Cognac?"

The other nodded. "So you're an American, Mr. Shirer?"

"Italian by birth, American by nationality," Sansevino answered, handing him his drink. "After the war I bought this place and settled down to producing wine. Would you care for another cognac, Farrell?"

"Yes," I said.

"And what part of America do you come from?" Hacket asked him.

"Pittsburgh."

"You don't say. Well, isn't that a coincidence! I'm from Pittsburgh myself. Do you know that little eating-house off Dravo Street—Morielli's?"

"Can't say I do."

"Well, you go right over to Morielli's when you're next in Pittsburgh. Wonderful hamburgers. I thought all Italians knew Morielli's. And that other place. What's its name? Pugliani's. Just inside the Triangle near Gulf Building. You remember Pugliani's?"

"Seltz?"

"Er—yes, make it a long one, will you. Of course, Pugliani's has changed hands now. They've put a dance floor in and——"

"How deep was the ash when you came up to the villa, Mr. Hacket?"

"The ash? Oh, about three or four inches, I guess. It must have been that because I got some inside my shoes." He took a pull at his drink. "Do you reckon it's going to be like it was the time Pompei was destroyed? About three foot of ash fell at first and then there was a breathing space. That's why most of the inhabitants were able to escape. It was only those that came back later who got buried. If it lets up at all I reckon we ought to get out while the going's good, eh?" He shook his head, "Incredible what this mountain can do!"

There was a sudden pounding on the front door. Hacket turned at the sound and then said, "That's probably the rest of the party. I told them if I didn't come back it would mean I'd found the villa. They said they'd follow me if it got worse."

Shirer sent Roberto to open the door. A moment later two dusty figures were shown into the room. It was Maxwell and Hilda Tuček all right, but they were barely recognisable under the film of ash that covered them. The lines on Maxwell's forehead were etched deep where ash and sweat had caked. For a moment they stood quite still in the entrance, their eyes searching the room. The contrast between Hilda and Zina was very marked. Zina was still clean, but she was trembling and her eyes bulged like a startled rabbit. Hilda, on the other hand, was quite calm. It was as though Vesuvius and the falling ash were nothing to her.

Sansevino went forward, his hand outstretched. "It's John Maxwell, isn't it? My name's Walter Shirer."

Maxwell nodded. He was looking across the room towards me. The white mask of his face looked old and very tired.

"You remember, we met at Foggia—before Farrell dropped me over Tazzola?"

Maxwell nodded. "Yes, I remember."

"Come on in and have a drink. Guess I wouldn't have known you in that make-up if Hacket here hadn't told me you were coming up. Cognac?"

"Thank you." Maxwell introduced Hilda Tuček and then Sansevino turned to me. "Perhaps you'd get them a drink, Farrell?"

It was clear he wasn't going to give me a chance of talking to Maxwell alone. I hesitated, on the point of blurting out the truth—that the man they thought was Shirer was Sansevino and that I had what they all wanted tucked away inside my leg. Sansevino was standing slightly apart from the others so that he could command the whole room. One hand was thrust into the pocket of his jacket and I knew he had a gun there, the gun he'd taken up from the piano. The atmosphere of the room suddenly seemed strained and on the edge of violence. I went over to the drink table and in the sudden burst of conversation that followed my movement I sensed relief.

"Tell you who came to see me the other day—Alec Reece. You remember Alec Reece, Maxwell? He was with us...." Sansevino was talking to ease the tension—talking too fast, and he shouldn't have called Maxwell by his full name. He'd been Max to everybody on the station at Foggis.

I got the drinks and then Hacket was talking—talking about the mountain again. "It's incredible to think what that mountain can do. Why in the eruption of 1631 heavy stones were thrown a distance of 15 miles and one weighing 25 tons fell on the village of Somma. And only a hundred years before the volcano was dormant with woods and bushes growing on the slopes and cattle actually grazing in the crater. There was one eruption in the early eighteenth century which lasted from May to August and covered Naples...."

He went on and on about Vesuvius. He was chock-full of guide-book statistics. It got on my nerves. But it was Zina who suddenly screamed at him—"For God's sake, can you not speak of nothing but your damn mountain?"

Hacket stared at her open-mouthed. "I'm sorry," he said. "Guess I didn't realise."

"You do not realise because for the moment you are safe inside this villa and cannot see what is happening outside." Zina's eyes blazed with anger—anger at her own fear. "Now, please shut up, will you. Everything that you have described may happen to us at any moment." She turned to Roberto. "Go and see what it is like outside, please. As soon as the ash ceases to fall we must get away from here quick."

Roberto left the room. He was back a moment later, coughing and wiping his face with a dirty rag. "Well?" Zina asked him.

He shook his head. "It is still falling."

Sansevino had been watching her all the time. Now he said, "Zina. Suppose you play to us. Play something gay—something from *Il Berbiere*."

She hesitated. Then she went over to the piano. She began to play the scandal song. Shirer looked at Maxwell. "You like Rossini?"

Maxwell shrugged his shoulders indifferently. Hacket moved over towards Sansevino. "I suppose you were pretty fond of opera, even as a kid?"

Sansevino nodded abstractedly. "Trouble is I didn't get much of a chance to hear it."

"Why not?"

"Good God, man—I was a miner, until 1936. Then I got a job with the Union and moved to New York."

"But the miners had their own operatic company." Hacket was looking at him with a puzzled frown. "They gave shows free."

"Well, I never went. I was too busy."

Sansevino took my empty glass and went across to the drink table. I could see Hacket watching him. "That's queer," he murmured.

"How do you mean?" Maxwell asked him.

"The opera company was sponsored by the Union." He shrugged his shoulders. "Funny how some people never know what's going on in their own home town."

Maxwell was watching Sansevino and as he came back with another brandy for me, Maxwell said, "By the way, Shirer, you remember that message I gave you for Ferrario at Tazzola?"

The other shook his head. "I don't remember much about that mission. I was suffering from loss of memory by the time I reached the Swiss frontier. My memory is very patchy."

"But you remember me?"

"I tell you my memory is patchy. Another cognac?"

"I still have some, thanks." Maxwell was swilling his drink round in the bottom of the glass. He didn't look at the other and his voice was casual as he said, "Remember the fellow who was with you the night they arrested you at Polinago?"

"Mantani?"

"Yes. I always meant to ask you this if ever I met you again. Did he take you to Ragello's trattoria or did you take him? When I interrogated him, he swore that he'd warned you Ragello was a Fascist and that you'd just laughed at him. Did he warn you?"

"He did not. I think it was I who told him it was dangerous. Miss Tuček—another drink?"

She nodded and he took her glass.

Maxwell was standing right beside me and quite softly he said, "You were right, Dick."

"How do you mean?" I asked.

"The man who owned the trattoria where they were picked up was called Basani, not Ragello," he answered.

I didn't say anything, but Vesuvius seemed suddenly remote. The volcano was right here in this room and at any moment someone would touch the spark that would send it off. My hand slipped to my jacket pocket, folding round the cold, smooth metal of Zina's automatic. Only Hacket was outside it all. He was still the tourist with his mind on Vesuvius. But the others—they were all tied together with invisible threads: Hilda and Maxwell searching for Tuček, Sansevino searching for what rested in the shaft of my leg. And all the time Zina played—played Rossini, flatly, without any life, so that the music had the quality of tragedy. And over by the door Roberto stood watching her. I felt my nerves tightening in that electric atmosphere so that I wanted to shout out that I'd got what Sansevino wanted—anything to break the tension which was growing all the time. And all I could do was wait—wait for the moment when it would reach snapping point and break.

VI

IT was Zina who expressed the mood of that room. She suddenly switched to the *Damnation of Faust* and the angry, violent music throbbed through the room. No one was talking now. We were all watching her. Her eyes were fixed on her hands and her hands expressed all the bitterness and hate that was in her and us.

I shall always remember her sitting there, playing that damned piano. Her face was white and shiny with sweat and there were lines on it I hadn't noticed before. Her hair was damp and sweat marks began to show at her armpits, and still she went on playing and playing. She was playing the same piece over and over again as though condemned to play it for the rest of her life, and she was playing it as though her very life depended upon it, as though if she stopped she was doomed.

"I think your Contessa is going to break soon," Maxwell whispered to me.

I didn't say anything. I couldn't take my eyes off her. It was as though the music had mesmerised me. It seemed to clutch at my nerves, stretching them, yet holding them at the same time.

Then suddenly it happened. She looked up. For a moment she was staring straight at me. Then her eyes roamed the circle of our faces while the notes of the music died under her fingers. "Why do you all stare at me?" she whispered. And when none of us answered she crashed her hands on to the keys and through the thunder of the chords she screamed out, "Why do you stare at me?" She bowed her head over the piano then and her shoulders shook to the violent gust of passion that swept through her.

Sansevino started towards her and then stopped, glancing over at me. I could see his dilemma. He wanted to quieten her and the only way he could do that was to give her the drug her nerves were screaming out for. At the same time he didn't dare leave me alone in the room with Maxwell.

And then, as though he had been waiting for his cue, Augustino came in. He stood blinking in the doorway, his old peasant face beaming and his eyes alight as though he'd seen a vision of the Blessed Virgin. "Well, what is it?" Sansevino snapped at him.

"The ash, signore. It is finished. We are saved. *La Madonna, ci ha salvato!*"

Sansevino went over to the window at the far end of the room and swung back the shutters. Augustino was right. The ash had stopped falling and now we could see Vesuvius again. A great glow burned in the crater top, igniting a pillar of gas that writhed up over the mountain and spread in a black cloud across the sky. And down the slopes ran three wide bands of fire. The hot glare of the lava flow invaded the room with a lurid light.

Sansevino turned to face us. "Maxwell—you and Miss Tuček better get back to your car right away. You, too, Mr. Hacket. The sooner we're out of here the better."

"It sounds like good advice, Mr. Shirer." Hacket was already moving towards the door.

I glanced at Maxwell. He hadn't moved. He was watching Sansevino. "I'll come with you," I told him.

Hilda Tuček moved close to me. Her hand gripped my arm. "Please, Mr. Farrell—is he up here?" Her eyes were fixed on the horrid glare of the mountain slopes. "I must know." I could feel her trembling and I began to think of Tuček. Was it possible that he was here in this villa?

But before I could decide what to do Zina had rushed forward. "Quick!" she said clutching hold of my hand. "We must get out of here. Roberto! Roberto, where are you?" Her voice had risen to a note of hysteria. "Get the car. *Presto, Roberto—presto!*"

Her fear seemed to paralyse the others. They stood rooted to the spot, staring at her. I could see her breasts heaving at the thin silk of her dress, smell the sweat of her fear through the strong scent of her perfume. Her eyes were bulging as she tugged frantically at my hand. She swung round on Roberto who was standing quite still, staring at us, his face sullen and passionate. "Don't stand there," she screamed at him. "The car, you fool! The car!"

Sansevino moved then. He moved very quickly. "Control yourself," he hissed at her in Italian. Then he was at the door. "There is no hurry. We can make an orderly evacuation. Maxwell, will you take Miss Tuček to your car. Hacket, you go with them, too."

But Zina's terror was too great to stomach any delay. She dragged at my hand, screaming at Roberto to get her car. And I went with her for my one desire was to get out of the villa where I could talk to Maxwell alone. Roberto was moving towards the door now. The three of us were converging on the door and Sansevino stood there with his hand on the handle, his eyes narrowed to two angry slits that seemed to bore into me as though he were saying—"*You will have no anæsthetic. First the knife, then the saw....*" I felt the blood hammering in my ears. And I knew suddenly that this was the moment that all that night had been leading up to.

Sansevino shut the door in our faces. "Pull yourself together, Zina." He took her by the shoulders and shook her. Then he whispered something to her. I heard the word *morfina*. She seemed suddenly to relax and I felt her fingers slide out of my hand. His eyes were staring into her face, willing her to be calm, hypnotising her into a state of relaxation. "Now," he said, "go and get the car, Roberto. You can go with him, Zina." He had the door open and I was about to follow Zina when he stopped me. "You will come with me, Farrell."

All my fear of the man returned as I stood there staring into his eyes.

"No," I said, and I could hear the tremor in my voice. "No, I'll go with Zina. I think she needs——"

"I am the best judge of what she needs," he snapped. "Kindly stay here."

But Zina had turned and caught hold of my hand. "Come quickly, Dick," she said.

Sansevino caught hold of her hand and with a twist forced her fingers to release their hold on me. "Go to the car, Zina," he ordered. "Farrell comes with me."

"No, no," she cried. "I know what you are going to do. But I will not——"

"Shut up!"

"Then let him come with me. You want him to stay with you so that——"

"Shut up—do you hear?"

"I will not go without him. I will not let you——"

He caught hold of her and pushed her roughly back into the room. "Very well, then. Stay here until our guests have gone. Hacket. Will you please go now. And you, Maxwell. I am afraid the Contessa is not herself."

I saw her face set hard. "You cannot do this thing. Do you understand? I will not be responsible——"

"You are not responsible for anything. You can stay here with him, since that's the way you want it."

Her eyes widened in sudden fear at his tone. "I know what you are going to do," she screamed at him. "You will let us all be buried alive up here. You can do that to the two you have at Santo Francisco. I do not care about them. But you cannot do that to——"

"Shut up—damn you!"

Zina stamped her foot. Her mood had slid from fear to anger. "I tell you you cannot do this to me. I do not wish to die. I will tell these——"

Sansevino hit her then, hit her across the mouth with the back of his hand. "Shut up, will you," he hissed. His ring left a streak of blood across the pallor of her right cheek.

There was a sudden, stunned silence. I felt my fist clench. A desire to smash his face to pulp, to hammer him to bloody pulp welled up inside me.

But before I could move Roberto had hit him. He hit him with all the force of pent-up passion. His face was bestial with the desire to kill. It wasn't human. It was something primitive and violent. I heard the crack of bone breaking as Roberto's fist smashed into the centre of the man's face. The force of the blow

A.M.-5.

flung Sansevino across the room. He stumbled against Hacket and fell sprawling on the floor.

For a moment he lay there, staring across at Roberto. The young Italian was breathing heavily and licking his bloody knuckles. Then he began to move in on Sansevino. He came forward deliberately and with relish, his face coarsened by some urge that was akin to lust. Sansevino saw him coming and reached into his jacket pocket. His hand came away with a glint of metal. There was a spurt of flame, an earsplitting crash and Roberto checked as though he'd been stopped by a blow in the stomach. His mouth fell open and a look of surprise crossed his face. Then with a little choking cough his knees folded under him and he crumpled up on the floor, his eyes open and staring.

Zina started forward, but I caught her by the arm. Sansevino was on his feet again now and the muzzle of the gun was pointed at her, a thin twist of smoke coming from the end of it. His eyes had a murderous look. " *Mascalzone! Sporco schifoso mascalzone!* " Zina poured her hate of him out in a spate of Italian. And then suddenly she was crying. "Why did you have to do that? It wasn't necessary. There was no need. I would have stopped him from hurting you. Why did you do it?"

It was at this moment that Hacket intervened. He cleared his throat as though about to address a meeting. "This as a very terrible thing you have done, Mr. Shirer. I don't know how you stand in Italian law, but in America at best you'd be guilty of third degree murder. Better hand over that weapon before anything else happens." I saw Sansevino trying to collect his wits as Hacket came towards him. Then suddenly he had him covered. "Stand back!" he ordered.

"Come, Mr. Shirer. Be sensible. You're a fellow countryman of mine and I wouldn't want anything bad to happen to you." Hacket walked straight up to him. There was something impressive about his complete fearlessness. For a moment he dominated the room with his quiet, almost suburban matter-of-factness. Sansevino hesitated and in that moment Hacket had reached him and had taken the gun out of his hand. Sansevino stood there with a dazed look on his face, rubbing his twisted wrist. Hacket glanced at the weapon curiously and then with the calmness of a man who did this every day of his life, he pointed it at a corner of the room and cleared it by firing. The room shook with the sound of the gun. It seemed to go on and on. Then suddenly there was silence and all we could hear was the sound of gases escaping from high up on the flaring top of the mountain. Hacket tossed the empty gun into the corner and walked over to where Roberto lay, a smudge

130

of blood staining his singlet. He knelt down and lifted the man's head. Then he got to his feet, wiping his hands. "I guess we'd better have a drink now," he said. "Maybe it will help us to decide what ought to be done." He went over to the table and began to pour drinks.

"Well, you certainly are a cool customer." Maxwell's voice seemed part of the easing of tension.

Hacket took a large cognac over to Sansevino. "Better knock that back." He was like a doctor handling a difficult patient and I suddenly felt as though I wanted to laugh. "A guy as hot-tempered as you shouldn't go around with a gun in his pocket." He got out a silk handkerchief and mopped his brow. "Guess this mountain has a lot to answer for."

He turned back to the drink table and in the silence I became conscious of a dry sobbing sound. It was Zina. She was sitting crouched on the floor and she had Roberto's head in her lap and was crooning over it, stroking the damp hair with her fingers as she rocked back and forth with the tears streaming down her face.

"So. Roberto was your lover, eh?" Sansevino spoke in Italian and his voice was a mixture of contempt and anger. "Pity you didn't explain. I would have acted differently if I'd known." He wiped the blood from his nose.

She looked across at him. "There was no need to kill him. I would not have let him hurt you." Her voice was sad. And then suddenly she flung Roberto's head out of her lap as though she were throwing away a doll that had been broken. "I will make you pay for this," she spat at him.

Hacket handed her a brandy. "Drink this. It'll do you good."

"I do not want to be done good."

"A drink always helps."

"No."

"Listen, lady. A drink will——"

She smashed the glass out of his hand. "I do not want your damn' drink." She turned and pulled at Roberto's belt. Then she got to her feet in one smooth, lithe movement. She had a knife in her hand and she moved towards Sansevino. Nobody spoke. Nobody moved. It was as though we were a group of spectators standing watching a scene from Grand Guignol.

Sansevino retreated towards the window as she advanced slowly and deliberately. She had forgotten her fear of the mountain. She had forgotten everything in her hatred of the man. And he was afraid. I saw it and the knowledge sang through my body like a lovely song. She was going to murder him. It was there in every slow languorous movement of her limbs. She was going to kill

131

him—not with one blow, but with slash after slash of the knife. And she was going to love every minute of it. "Remember how you gave me my first cigarette, here in this room?" Her voice was soft as a caress. "Remember? You said it would help me to forget my husband's beastliness. You said you had been a doctor and that you knew what was good for me. You made me drunk and then you gave me that cigarette. And after that there were more cigarettes. And then injections. You drugged me till I was your slave. Well, I am not your slave any more. I will kill you and then——" She was literally purring. She was like a tigress.

Sansevino had backed until he was brought up by the wall. He moved along it, his eyes wide with fear. Then he was in the corner and could retreat no farther. "Don't let her do it," he screamed. And when nobody moved he started to bargain with her. "If you kill me you will get no more of the drugs. Listen, Zina—think what happiness it gives you. Think what it will be like when your nerves are screaming out for——"

"*Animale!*" She darted at him and then away again and I saw the knife was bloodied. His shoulder was ripped and the white of his jacket stained crimson. I was staring fascinated at a macabre ballet played in real life.

It was Maxwell who stopped it. He went behind her and twisted the knife out of her hand. She turned on him, her face distorted with rage and her fingers clawed at him. He flung her off. "Get hold of her, Hacket, and make her have that drink. I want to talk with this fellow."

Hacket caught her by the arm. She struggled for a moment, and then suddenly she went slack. He half-carried her to the sofa. She was sobbing again, dry, racking sobs that seemed to fill the room. Through them I heard Maxwell say, "Now then—suppose you tell me first who you really are."

"You know who I am." Sansevino's eyes were wide, but I could see he was getting control of himself again.

"I know who you're not," Maxwell snapped. "You're not Shirer."

"Then who am I?" His eyes were looking past Maxwell, searching the room, trying to seek out some chance of escape.

I couldn't help it. I suddenly began to laugh. It seemed to well up inside me and burst from my lips uncontrollably. It was relief to nerves stretched too taut—it was rage and bitterness and mental exhaustion all wound up tight and uncoiling in this horrible sound. I seemed to be standing outside myself, listening to that wretched laughter, wanting to strike myself, do something to stop it. But I couldn't and gradually it subsided of its own accord and I was suddenly silent and very weak. They were all staring at me.

Maxwell came over to me. "Why did you laugh like that?" he asked.

"His name is Sansevino. Il dottore Giovanni Sansevino. He's the man who did the operations on my leg in the Villa d'Este."

Hacket left Zina on the couch. "I just don't understand," he said. "This place belongs to a man named Shirer. I know, because I asked in the village. If this guy isn't——"

"Keep quiet, can't you?" Maxwell cut him short. "Now, Dick. If this is your Doctor Sansevino, what happened to Shirer?"

"I found him the morning after the escape slumped over Sansevino's desk, dressed in his uniform with no moustache and wearing dark glasses. I thought it——" My voice trailed away. I had an almost uncontrollable desire to start laughing again. It was the thought that I'd been looking at Walter Shirer that morning.

"Then it was Sansevino who escaped with Reece that night?"

I nodded.

"And when you met this man in Milan you recognised him?" It was Hilda who put the question to me.

"No," I said. "I didn't recognise him. I just kept on seeing him as the doctor, that was all. They were very much alike, except for the moustache and the glasses."

"And that is why you left Milan?"

I nodded. My eyes seemed held by hers, for I sensed sympathy there and I clung to it. Anything to stop myself laughing. "I was scared," I said. "I thought I was seeing things—going out of my mind."

The room was suddenly lit by a brighter glow. We all glanced involuntarily towards Vesuvius. The whole top of the mountain flamed as great gobs of molten rock were hurled out of the crater and up into the column of black gas. And through the window, quite clearly in the still, oppressive heat of the night came the creak of wagons and the shouts of people urging cattle along the road to Avin.

"We must hurry, Max," Hilda said. "I am so afraid he is somewhere up there." She turned to Zina. "What was it you said about two men up at Santo Francisco?"

But Zina seemed to have fallen into a coma. She didn't answer. "I'll have to get it out of this little swine then," Maxwell said. He turned to Sansevino. "Where is Tuček?" The man didn't answer and I saw Maxwell hit him. "You picked him up at Milan Airport. Tuček and Lenlim. You were after what he was bringing out of Czechoslovakia, the same as you were with the other poor devils. Well, where is he?" There was a scream of pain.

133

Then Hacket had Maxwell by the shoulder. "Because the guy's killed someone, it doesn't entitle you to third degree him."

"You keep out of this," Maxwell said sharply.

"Then leave the guy alone."

"This isn't the first man he's murdered. You heard what Farrell said."

"I've heard a lot of nonsense about doctors and assumed identity and I've heard the man who made that accusation laughing like a maniac. Now you just leave the guy alone and I'll telephone the carabiniere. It's their responsibility."

"Listen, Hacket. This man has kidnapped Hilda Tuček's father."

"I don't believe it."

"I don't care whether you believe it or not. Go out and telephone the carabiniere. Meanwhile——"

It was at this moment that the lights dipped. They did it twice and then they faded away. For a moment we could see the filaments in the candle bulbs of the chandelier glowing faintly and then they vanished and the room was a red glare full of moving shadows. "The plant must have run out of gas," Hacket said. At the same moment Maxwell shouted. A figure slid by me. The door opened and slammed shut. Maxwell dashed past me, had it open in a flash and disappeared into the darkness of the hall. I got my torch out and followed him.

The front door was still bolted. "Through the servant's quarters," I said.

We dived into a passage. It led to the kitchen. Beyond were outhouses and here we found a door hanging open. We went out, sinking to our ankles in soft ash. We could see his footsteps in the ash leading out of the shadow of the villa into the red glare towards some outhouses. As we ran over the sifting surface of the ground there was the roar of a motor and Zina's cream cabriolet came slithering round the corner of the house, the back wheels sending up twin sprays of ash that caught the light so that they looked like firemen's hoses in the glow of a fire.

I had a brief glimpse of Sansevino at the wheel, then the big car was charging straight at us and we were jumping for our lives. He just missed us and I heard him change gear as he rounded the corner of the villa. "Quick! See which way he goes." I followed Maxwell as fast as I could to the front of the building. The car's headlights cut a swathe through the red night as it hurtled down the track through the vineyards. We could see carts and people straggling along the road to Avin and Maxwell's car shrouded in ash standing by the open gateway. With blaring sirens Sansevino nosed out on to the refugee-strewn road and turned right. "He's going up to Santo Francisco. Come on! We've got to follow."

Hacket and Hilda had joined us now and as we started off down the track to where the cars were parked, Zina came flying after us. "Don't leave me," she whimpered, clutching hold of my arm, "Please don't leave me. I'll show you where they are."

Maxwell heard her and turned. "You know where Tuček is?" he asked her.

"I do not know anything about Tuček," she replied. "But I know where he kept the others you speak about. It is in the old monastery of Santo Francisco."

"Come on then."

By the time I caught up with them Max had the car turned and he was waiting for me with the door open and the engine running. The stream of refugees seemed already to be thinning. Most of those who had fled on foot had already passed. Only those who had stopped to salvage some of their belongings were still on the road. We passed bullock cart after bullock cart piled to a crazy height with furniture, bedding, children and livestock. As we forced them off the road, with the blare of our horn the loads canted over at a crazy angle.

Zina was in the front beside Max. I could see the shape of her head against the white swathe of the headlights and the glare of the lava streams. "Hurry. Hurry, please." She was getting scared again. It was hardly to be wondered at. The scene was like something out of the Bible—the bullock carts and the terror-stricken people fleeing from the wrath of the Lord. And then I caught a glimpse of the village of Santo Francisco, a black huddle of ancient houses outlined against the blazing wrath of Vesuvius. The red glare of the lava streams was ahead of us and on either side of us. Santo Francisco was doomed and I thought of the fire and brimstone that had put an end to the towns of Sodom and Gomorrah. It must have been very like this.

"Pray God we're not too late." It was Hilda who had spoken and I realised suddenly that she was clutching my hand.

On the far side of the back seat Hacket said, "This is the craziest thing I've ever been mixed up in." He leaned towards me across Hilda. "Farrell. Do you mind telling me what it's all about?"

Hilda answered for me. "It's my father. This man Sansevino has shut him up somewhere in Santo Francisco." I think she wanted to talk, for she went on, telling him about her father's escape from Czechoslovakia. I looked at my watch. It was just after four. In little over an hour it would be light. A great shower of sparks rose out of the crater glare and lifted to the black cloud above that was shot with intermittent stabs of forked lightning.

"Any moment that damned mountain's gonna blow its top," Hacket muttered. His voice trembled slightly. But it wasn't fear. It was because he was excited. He had come all the way from America to see this volcano and I think he was as near to being happy as he'd ever been.

We were entering the village now. The crimsoned stucco fronts of the houses closed in on us, throwing back the roar of the car's engine and blocking out the sight of Vesuvius. The streets were quite deserted. The last of the refugees had left. There wasn't a cat or a dog, not even a chicken, to be seen. It was as though we were entering a lost town.

We passed a shop where a candle still guttered on the counter and vegetables piled the shelves. The doors of the houses gaped open. In a small piazza a cart stood forlornly, abandoned because one of the wheels had broken under the strain of the furniture heaped on top of it. By the village pump a small child sucked its thumb and stared at us with big, frightened eyes.

"Did you see that kid?" Hacket asked as we swept by. "We mustn't forget him when we leave. The poor little beggar must have been deserted by his parents."

"*Ecco!*" Zina was pointing to a big stone archway. The gates were open and we drove into a stone-paved courtyard. And there was the cabriolet. "Thank God!" Hilda breathed.

Maxwell slammed on the brakes and we piled out. "Where now?" he asked.

"Through here," Zina cried. She made for a low stone doorway. A gleam of metal showed in Maxwell's hand. At least he was armed. But I hung back. I was thinking what I'd do if I were Sansevino. If he could blot us out—all of us—he'd be safe then. The lava would obliterate Santo Francisco and there'd be no trace of us. I caught Hilda's hand. "Wait," I said.

She wrenched herself free. "What are you afraid of?"

The contempt in her voice stung me. I caught her arm and twisted her round. "Max told you my story, did he?"

"Yes. Let me go. I must get to my——"

"You won't reach your father any quicker than Maxwell," I said. "And if we go in a bunch we may walk straight into it."

"Into what? Let me go, please."

"Have some sense," I snapped at her. "Sansevino got here ahead of us. He knew we'd follow him. And if he could kill us all——"

"He would not dare. He is afraid now."

"He's as cunning as the devil," I said. "And cruel. He'll use your father as a bait."

She was trembling again now as she realised all the possibilities. "Perhaps he has come up here to kill him," she breathed.

"I don't think so," I said. "So long as we're alive he may need your father in order to bargain with us."

"Bargain with us?"

I nodded. "I have something that he wants. You see that doorway over there?" I pointed to an opening in the stone wall on the far side of the courtyard. "Go and wait for me there." I turned to the Fiat. As I lifted the bonnet I heard her crunching through the ash of the courtyard. I removed the rotor arm and closed the bonnet again. I immobilised Maxwell's Buick in the same way. Then I joined Hilda in the doorway. "If the others are success-ful——" I shrugged my shoulders. "If not, then we've still got a chance."

The courtyard was full of vague shadows that seemed to move with the varying intensity of the glare. It was an incredible scene, like a stage setting of the sunset glow on Dunsinane. "Do you still think me a coward?" I asked her.

I could see her face against the red glare of the upper half of the monastery buildings. It was like a cameo—the firm set of the jaw, the little tip-tilted nose. She hadn't moved. She was watching the doorway through which the others had disappeared. Then her hand found mine and gripped it as she had done in the car coming up. It seemed an age that we stood there, waiting and watching that doorway.

"Will they never come?" The words seemed forced out of her and her grip on my hand had tightened.

There was nothing I could say. I just held her hand and stood there in the shadow of the doorway, knowing what hell she was going through and unable to do anything to help her. At last she said, "I think you are right. Something has happened."

I looked at my watch. It was nearly half-past four. They had been gone well over a quarter of an hour. Why hadn't Sansevino come out to the car? But I knew why. He was watching, waiting for us to make the first move. "I'm afraid it is going to be a cat-and-mouse game."

She turned her head. "How do you mean—cat-and-mouse game?"

"Whoever moves first must give away his position."

The glare in the courtyard suddenly deepened as though Hell's flames had been banked up. Shadows moved and flickered. "I do not think we have too much time," Hilda said.

I nodded. I wished I could see what the lava was doing. "I think we must go in search of the others," I said. The blood was hammering in my head and my foot and my hands felt cold. I was quite convinced now that Sansevino was watching that courtyard just as we were watching it. I gripped her hand, nerving myself for the dash to the doorway, for the groping along endless corridors and through huge, silent rooms expecting every shadow to materialise into that damnable doctor. I had that void in the very core of me that I'd had on my first solo, on my first combat flight.

And then Hilda said, "Listen!"

Somewhere out in the unnatural stillness of the village was a murmur of sliding stones. It was like a coal truck being tipped and it went on and on. Then suddenly everything was still again—unnaturally still. It was as though the whole village, all the living stone of it, held its breath, waiting for the thing it dreaded. "There it is again," Hilda whispered. It was like clinker falling in a huge grate. And then there was a crumbling sound. A shower of sparks flew up beyond the monastery towards the billowing column in the sky that marked Vesuvius. "What is it?"

I hesitated. Some instinct told me what it was and I didn't want to tell her. But she'd have to know soon. A haze of rubble dust was rising, the particles reflecting the flickering gleam of flames below. "The lava is entering the village," I told her. She was so close to me that I felt the tremor that ran through her body. The heat was becoming intense. It hung over us like the heat from the open door of a furnace. "We must do something." Her voice was on the edge of panic.

"Yes," I said.

I was just about to tell her to run for the doorway through which the others had gone when she cried out, "Look!" She was pointing to the roof of the monastery buildings opposite. For an instant I saw the figure of a man outlined against another shower of sparks. He was running along the roof. "Is that him?" she asked.

"Yes," I said. "The lava's scared him. He's coming for the car." I got out the little automatic Zina had given me, loaded it and stood there waiting.

He wasn't long. He flung out through the doorway and jumped into the Fiat. I heard the starter buzz. Then the sound was drowned in the crumbling roar of another building going down. The dust rose as the sound died. Sansevino was still pressing the starter button. Then he abandoned it and dived into the Buick. Again the buzz of a starter. I could see his face in the dashboard light. The eyes glittered with panic and I suddenly wanted to laugh. I'd have stood in the very path of a thousand streams of lava to see fear so stamped on the man's face.

When he realised it wouldn't start he got out and went back to the Fiat. He tried the starter again. Then he opened the bonnet. It didn't take him long to realise what the trouble was. He straightened up, looking about him as though sensing our presence. For an instant he stared at the doorway where we were standing. His hand reached to his pocket and he began to come towards us.

At that moment a great vomit of fire sprawled into the sky. He turned and glanced upwards, his body crouched as though to ward off a blow. He stayed like that as though petrified while the arch of flame spread over the under-belly of the black, billowing gases that covered the sky and the roar of the mountain shook the ground under our feet. There was a whistling sound and something fell with a thud into the courtyard sending up a little puff of ash. Then he straightened up and at the same moment a rain of stones descended on the courtyard, hot stones that smouldered where they fell. They clattered against the stone of the monastery building and rolled to our feet, smouldering and stinking of sulphur.

Sansevino was running now, slithering and stumbling on the loose ash. In the ruddy glare I could see his face twisted with terror. He almost made the main gateway, but then suddenly he was struck down. It seemed to catch him by the shoulder and send him sprawling in the ash. Above the sound of the mountain and the thump of falling stones I heard his squeal of fear. He twisted over and over, his body contorted, and then he was up again, limping painfully and making for the archway. He reached it and disappeared into the shadows.

The fall of stones ceased as abruptly as it had begun. I gave Hilda one of the rotor arms. "See if you can find the others," I told her. "I'm going after him."

"Why not let him go?"

"No," I said. "He may be the only one who can lead us to your father. I must try and stop him. You get the others."

I left the shelter of the archway then and crossed the courtyard. "Please be careful," she called after me. I floundered in the sifting surface of ash. It made my leg very difficult to handle. The sound of my feet on the clear paving stones of the main archway seemed unnaturally loud. Then I was out in the street. I could see the piazza with its pump and the cart lying drunkenly on its broken wheel. The ash was pitted by the fall of stones as though there had been a brief shower of heavy rain. Not a living thing moved in all that street. It was as though a grey desert had moved in and destroyed all life.

I turned then and looked back up the narrow rise of the street. Sansevino was standing in the middle of the road, quite still, his back towards me. He was staring up the street and I saw why he'd stopped. It was a truly terrifying sight. The road was narrow like a cutting between the sheer walls of the houses. But instead of going up out of the village into the open vineyards of the mountain slopes, that street ceased abruptly in a great wall that towered as high as the houses. In the lurid glow the narrow cut seemed choked with an enormous coke pile.

There was a sudden shifting sound as the coke spilled forward and as it spilled a white molten glare filled the end of the street. The house fronts flickered with light, their faces seeming to be twisted in agony as they saw their doom, and a blast of furnace-hot air ran down the shaft of the street, blistering hot and chokingly sulphurous. Then the light died as the outer surface of the lava-spill cooled.

Sansevino turned and started down towards me. I was so astonished by the sight of the lava that I did nothing. I just stood there in the middle of the street and watched him trying to run towards me, his right side twisted with pain. He didn't see me for a moment. When he did he stopped. He had the startled, frightened look of a thing trapped. He gave one glance over his shoulder at the spilling face of the lava and dived into the open doorway of a house.

If he'd had a gun he could have shot me down from the shelter of that doorway. But he hadn't got a gun. His gun was lying in the villa, one bullet in Roberto's body, the others embedded in the floorboards. As I followed him through the doorway where he'd disappeared there was a crumbling sound and I saw one of the houses at the end of the street topple into the lava stream in a cloud of mortar dust.

The building was very dark after the glare of the street. It smelt of garbage and earth closets. Dusty windows gave the shadows a reddish gleam. I listened. I could hear no sound but the distant gaseous hiss of the crater. He wasn't climbing the stairs. Either he was waiting in the shadows for me or else he had gone straight through the building. I switched on my torch. The beam showed stone steps leading upwards. A passageway led past these to the back of the house. The stone floor was worn smooth and deep by the footsteps of many generations. It led to a back room. There was a big double bed with huge Birmingham brass knobs, an old chest of drawers and a table supported at one corner by a packing case. The place was littered with household things all mixed up with straw on which animals had been bedded. The door on the other side stood open.

It led to a small patch of ground backed by a low wall and then more houses. And in the ash that covered the garden I saw the track of a man's feet. I followed them, over the stone wall, to the back of the next row of houses. They ended at the steps to a balcony. The balcony was arched with pillars of stone. Stone steps led upwards from one corner and down the funnel of the stairs I heard the sound of footsteps climbing.

I followed. At each floor there was a balcony with stone arches and as I climbed higher the arches became blacker as they stood out against the lava glow. At each balcony I caught a glimpse of rooms that had suddenly been vacated. The panic litter of clothes and household things bore dumb witness to the haste with which the occupants had fled. At last I reached the top floor. A wooden ladder ascended to the roof. I switched my torch off and went cautiously up, gripping the tiny automatic in my hand.

The roof when I reached it looked red hot. It was quite flat and as my head emerged through the trap-door I saw Sansevino not fifty feet away, his body a black silhouette against a huge flow of lava that ringed Santo Francisco to the west. He was climbing the low balustrade to the next house. I followed him, running as best I could on the treacherous surface of loose ash. I glanced up to my right and saw the mountain leaning over me. The great welts of the lava flow streamed down towards the village. There were four flows—one reaching down to the houses, one to the west and two to the east. And over it all was the red, roaring mass of the crater column of gas like an oil gusher that has been fired. Looking up at the incredible sight I trod on a stone and fell with my face in the ash. I think it was the ash that saved me from hurting myself. I spat it out of my mouth and got to my feet, rubbing my eyes.

Sansevino had reached the end of the block now. I saw him hesitate at the edge and turn back. Then he disappeared into a doorway. The stump of my leg was beginning to ache and a piece of ash had got into my left eye, hurting damnably. The filthy stuff was in my mouth, too, and as I clenched my teeth against the pain of my eye they gritted unpleasantly.

I reached the doorway where Sansevino had disappeared and stumbled through. There was a ladder like the one I'd come up. And then I was descending through stone arched balconies, hearing Sansevino's footsteps clattering ahead of me. I nearly slipped on a patch of oil—olive oil spilled from a big pottery jar that someone had dropped on the steps.

At the bottom we came out into a garden full of stunted orange trees, the fruit glowing like little Chinese lanterns. I followed his footsteps to another row of houses, taller this time and in bad repair with the plaster hanging in great mouldering slabs. Here were big rooms littered with beds of bare wooden boards. Many people had slept and lived and kept their livestock in those over-crowded, dirty rooms. An old stone archway led in from the shadow of a narrow street that smelt of rotting garbage and in the far corner of one of the rooms I found a narrow ramp running up to the floor above. It was cobbled and ridged with stone. I could hear Sansevino climbing above me and I followed.

The ramp was slippery with manure and smelt of horses. With the beam of my torch lighting the way I struggled up to the floor above and then to the next. Here a gaunt, big-boned mule stared at me with rolling, frightened eyes and wisps of straw hanging from its sulky mouth. It twitched its long ears in the light of the torch, laid them back and looked as wicked as hell.

The ramp finished there, but stone steps led on upwards. I was beginning to feel very tired—a combination of nervous exhaustion, lack of sleep and the ache in the stump of my leg. I stumbled and the tin of my leg clanked against the stone where the treads had been worn into two deep little hollows. I thought of all the people who had climbed up and down those stairs every day of their lives. Generation after generation of them. Parts of these old houses had probably been in constant occupation for well over a thousand years, and in a few hours they would be wiped off the face of the earth.

The room above was less dirty. There were family pictures on the walls and a little shrine stood in one corner. I went on up. Another floor with a broken bicycle and a small blacksmith's forge and a smell of charcoal. Would I never get to the top? I felt pretty well at the end of my tether. I seemed to be stumbling on and on, up never-ending flights of worn stone.

Then suddenly I was out again in the eruption glare. There was a breath of sulphurous heat on my face and I had a glimpse of a building, black against the red glow of lava, toppling slowly, toppling and crumbling as it crashed downwards. Then something smashed against the side of my head and I was falling, like the building had done, falling in a shower of sparks to a red, eyeball-searing glow.

I felt something wrenched out of my hand and then I was struggling back to consciousness with a voice I knew saying, "I hope I do not hurt you." The voice was the voice I'd heard on the operating table and I screamed.

"Ah! So now you are frightened, eh?"

I opened my eyes to find the face of Il dottore wavering over me. The cruel lips were drawn back in a thin smile. I could see the tongue flicking over them and the pointed, tobacco-stained teeth. His eyes gleamed like red coals.

"Don't operate again," I heard myself say. "Please don't operate any more."

He was laughing at me now and suddenly I saw that he had no moustache. The face dissolved into Shirer's face. But the red, sadistic excitement of the eyes remained.

Then my head cleared and I knew where I was. I was in Santo Francisco and Sansevino was bending over me. A torch was switched on and his face vanished in the blinding light of it. He had my automatic in his hand and he was laughing, a horrible, tensed-up, tittering sound. "Now, my friend, perhaps you will be good enough to let me have a look at your lovely new leg."

His hands were tearing at my trousers. I jerked upright at his touch. He hit me in the face with the torch then, knocking me back into the grit of the ash that covered the roof-top. I felt the blood trickling down from a cut above my right eye. It reached my mouth. I licked at it with my tongue. It was salt and full of grit. He had pulled my trousers clear of my thigh now and his hands were working at the straps of my leg. Involuntarily I flinched. He gave a soft snicker. "Do not be afraid," he said. "I do not have to operate this time to remove your leg. See, it is only held by straps—leather straps; the living tissues have gone." I could hear his tongue savouring the relish of his words. And all the time I was thinking there was something I had to do. Fear clutched at me at the touch of his hands. I fought it, struggling to clear my brain, to think what had to be done. I couldn't think with those bloody fingers moving over the flesh of my thigh, touching the cringing skin of my stomach.

Then suddenly he had my leg free. "There. You see. It is quite painless, this operation."

I sat up. He stepped back quickly. The metal of my leg gleamed a dull red. It looked absurdly horrible as he held it in his hands—like looking at my own leg, severed from my body in one lump and bathed in blood. He had switched off the torch now and he was smiling at me. "You can do what you wish now, Mr. Farrell. You're not very mobile." It was Shirer's voice. But almost in the same instant he had reverted to Il dottore. "I make a nice job of that leg, eh? The stump has healed well."

I cursed him then, mouthing obscenities in an effort to drown my fear. But he only laughed, his teeth a red, pointed gleam. Then

143

he had ripped the pad out of the artificial limb and turned the contraption upside down. He gave a little cry of satisfaction as a chamois leather bag and a roll of oilskin fell into the ash. He picked the bag up, tearing excitedly at the cord that bound it, his eyes gleaming with greed.

"So!" He peered into the mouth of the bag, crooning to himself. "Tuček told the truth. *Bene! Bene!*"

"What have you done with him?" I cried.

He looked at me. Then he smiled. It was a wicked, devilish smile. "You need not worry about him. I have not hurt him—very much. He is quite safe. So is Maxwell and the lovely Contessa. The stupid American is safe too." He laughed. "He come all the way from Pittsburgh—where I come from, eh?—to see Vesuvius in eruption. Well, now he has a grandstand view. I hope he likes it," he added venomously.

"What have you done with them?" I demanded, anger suddenly getting the better of my fear.

"Nothing, my friend. Nothing at all. I give them a good view of the eruption, that is all. Would you also like to see how a village can disappear under a mountain? You see all these houses?" His hand indicated the roof tops of Santo Francisco. "This village is built in the days when Rome is a great power. And in a few hours it will be gone. And you will go with it, my friend." He re-tied the mouth of the leather bag and slipped it into his pocket. Then he stooped and picked up the oilskin package.

He was coming towards me now and suddenly I knew what it was I had to do. I fumbled in the pocket of my jacket, found the rotor arm and showed it to him. "This is what you want, isn't it?" I said.

"Ah, you think to barter, eh?"

"No," I said. "I don't barter with a murderous swine like you. You can try and get out on foot." I struggled up on one elbow and flung the little bakelite and metal arm as far as I could. He ran after it. But it fell clear of the roof. He stopped at the edge, staring down into the black pit into which it had fallen. Then he came back, his face livid with rage. He lashed out at me with his foot, kicking at the bare stump of my leg, mouthing curses at me in Italian. I felt grit searing the flesh and the pain of his kicks ran up the left side of my body and struck like hammer blows on the nerves of my brain. Then suddenly he turned, picked up my artificial leg and flung it after the rotor arm. I watched it fall with a red gleam of metal beyond the edge of the roof and a sickening feeling of fear took hold of me. It was silly to be frightened by the loss of an ugly metal attachment. But without it I was helpless and he knew it.

"Now try to get out of Santo Francisco on your bare stump," he snarled.

The black vault of the night flared redder as the mountain blew off again. He glanced up to the glare. I could see the sweat shining in drops on his face. He turned to me, lashed out at my pelvis with all the frustrated violence of a man who is scared of death. I rolled over involuntarily and caught the kick on my thigh. He didn't kick me again, but bent down, searching through the pockets of my coat and trousers. "What have you done with it?" he screamed at me.

"Done with what?" I asked.

He drove his fist into my face. "The other rotor arm, you fool."

"I haven't got it," I mumbled through my broken lips. "Maxwell has it." I thought the lie might send him back to them and give them another chance.

He beat at my face with his clenched fist until the mountain flamed again. Then he dived for the door of the roof and disappeared. I heard bolts being shot home and then I was alone in the red glare of the mountain.

I wasn't frightened—not then. I was too relieved at his departure. Fear came later with the dawn and the lava eating at the buildings across the street and the heat of it withering my body.

After he'd gone I crawled to the shelter of the door and lay there for a while recovering my breath and trying to sort things out. Stones fell clattering against the stonework, throwing dust in my face. Huddled close to the door they missed me and when the shower of *rapilli* had ended I started on a painful tour of my roof-top prison.

It was about fifty feet by thirty, surrounded by a stone balustrade a foot high. On one side was a drop to a street and on the opposite side, where I'd thrown the rotor arm, the house dropped to a garden carpeted in ash. In the middle of it I could see the faint metallic glimmer of my tin leg. The house was one of a row, but it was separated on either side from the neighbouring houses by a narrow alley, a sheer crevice about five feet across. There was no hope of crossing the gap and there was no way into the house from the roof other than by the door. If there'd been a clothesline, even an old piece of wood to act as a crutch I would have felt less helpless. But there was nothing, just the flat expanse of the roof, covered in ash, the foot-high balustrade, and in the middle the stone-built rabbit hutch with the door that led to the floor below. I hadn't even a knife or any implement with which to set to work on the door.

I felt utterly helpless. My only hope was that Hilda would find the others and that they would come to look for me. At least I could call out to them, signal to them. I had the freedom of that roof-top. I could see what was happening. I wasn't locked away in some evil-smelling room waiting for death to come suddenly in a fall of masonry. I could move about and watch what happened, and that did more than anything to sustain my courage in the hours that followed.

The stones that had fallen were pumice and hard and sharp. And since the door was my only hope of escape and the stones my only tools, I set to work to rub away the wood. I think I knew it was hopeless from the start. But I had to do something to keep my mind off the red glow of the lava flow piling into the village.

The streams on either side seemed to move faster, flowing down through the open country and curving round below Santo Francisco like two columns mounting a pincer attack on the village of Avin two miles lower down the slopes. The flow coming into Santo Francisco was narrower and slower. But it ate steadily into the village and I could mark its progress by the sound of crumbling buildings and the shower of sparks it set up as it ground over the ruins. I worked it out that it was destroying a house every ten minutes which meant roughly that it would reach my own house in approximately one and a quarter hours. It was then a quarter to six. I had until seven.

I suppose I worked away at that door for half an hour. Then I stopped. I was completely exhausted and dripping with sweat. The heat was already beginning to prick at my skin and my flesh felt tight and shrivelled. I had scraped about a quarter of an inch of wood away on a strip little more than a foot long. It was quite hopeless. The door was of tough, seasoned wood and a good inch thick. I hadn't a hope of getting through it in time.

Dawn was beginning to break. I brushed the sweat from my eyes and slithered away from the door so that I could look at the mountain. The glow of the crater was fading and in the faint, cold light I could see the dense pall that covered the sky—a writhing, billowing cloud of utter blackness. The lava flow no longer showed as a fiery streak. It was a huge black band coming out of the side of the mountain near the top of the ash slope. It came down like a thick wrist, broadened out into a palm and then split into four fingers. Smoke rose from it in a lazy cloud and the mountain behind it trembled in the heat.

The stump of my leg hurt abominably where Sansevino had kicked at it. My head ached and my lips were swollen and blubbery. I pulled up the leg of my trousers. The flesh where it was drawn tight over the bone was bleeding and coated in grit. Sitting there in the ash I did my best to clean it and then bound it up with a strip torn from my shirt and tied it with my handkerchief. I could have done with some water, not only to cleanse it, but to drink, for my throat was parched with the heat and the acrid sulphur fumes. But it didn't seem to matter much. The lava was very near now. Buildings were crumbling continuously all along the wide front of its advance into the village and the sound of their falling seemed so close that more than once I looked to see whether the next house had gone.

Then the sun came up. It was an orange disc barely visible through the haze of gas and ash that filled the sky. And as it rose higher it got fainter. I thought of the mountains up there on the back of Italy. The villages would be basking in clear, warm sunlight. And beyond would lie the blue of the Adriatic. And yet here I was under a cloud of ash, faced with a stinking, suffocating end. Something glittered in the ash. It was Zina's pistol. Sansevino had dropped it in the blindness of his anger. I slipped it into my pocket—if I couldn't face the lava, then...

I don't think I was frightened so much as bitter. I could so easily have not been here. If I hadn't gone out to that villa—if I hadn't arranged my trip so that I went from Czechoslovakia to Milan. But what was the good of saying If. If I'd been born a Polynesian instead of an Englishman I wouldn't have lost my leg in three operations that made me sweat to think about. I folded my empty trouser leg up over the stump of my leg and tied it there with my tie. Then I crawled across the roof to the side nearest the lava.

It was full daylight now, or as near to daylight as it would be. I could see the black band of the lava flow broadening out as it piled up against the village. It was only three houses away and as I watched the third house crumbled into mortar dust and disappeared. Only two more houses away now. *Three little nigger boys sitting in a row....* The damned bit of doggerel ran in my brain until the second house went. *And then there was one.* Away to the right I caught a glimpse of the front of the lava choking a narrow street and spilling steadily forward. It was black like clinker and as it spilled down along the street, little rivulets of molten rock flowed red.

The air was full of the dust of broken buildings now. My mouth and throat were dry and gritty with it and the air shimmered with intense heat. I could no longer hear the roar of gases escaping from Vesuvius. Instead my world was full of a hissing and sifting—it was a steady, unrelentiug background of sound to the intermittent crash of stone and the crumbling roar of falling plaster and masonry.

Then the next building began to go. I watched, fascinated, as a crack opened across the roof. There was a tumbling roar of sound, the crack widened, splitting the very stone itself, and then the farther end of the building vanished in a cloud of dust. There was a ghastly pause as the lava consolidated, eating up the pile of rubble below. Then cracks ran splitting across the remains of the roof not five yards away from me. The cracks widened, spreading like little fast-moving rivers, and then suddenly the whole roof seemed to sink, vanishing away below me in a great rumble of sound and disappearing into the dust of its own fall.

And as the dust settled I found myself staring at the lava face itself. It was a sight that took my breath away. I wanted to cry out, to run from it—but instead I remained on my hands and one knee staring at it, unable to move, speechless, held in the shock of seeing the pitiless force of Nature angered.

I have seen villages and towns bombed and smashed to rubble by shell-fire. But Cassino, Berlin—they were nothing to this. Bombing or shelling at least leaves the torn shells and smashed rubble of buildings to indicate what was once there. The lava left nothing. Of the half of Santo Francisco that it had overrun there was no trace. Before me stretched a black cinder embankment, quite flat and smoking with heat. It was impossible to think of a village ever having existed there. It had left no trace and I could scarcely believe that only a few minutes before there had been buildings between me and the lava and that I'd seen them toppling, buildings that had been occupied for hundreds of years. Only away to the left the dome of a church stood up out of the black plain. And even as I noticed it the beautifully symmetrical dome cracked open like a flower, fell in a cloud of dust and was swallowed completely.

In my fascination I leaned forward and peered over the balcony. I had a brief glimpse of a great wall of cinders and rivulets of white-hot rock spilling forward across the rubble remains of the house that had just vanished, spilling across the narrow alley and piling up against the house on which I stood. Then the heat was singeing my eyebrows and I was slithering back to the far end of the roof in the grip of a sudden and uncontrollable terror.

To be wiped out like that, obliterated utterly and all because of a wooden door. I heard myself screaming—screaming and screaming for help through grit-sore throat. Once I thought I heard an answering call, but it didn't stop me. I went on screaming till suddenly a crack ran splintering across the roof, splitting it in two.

The sudden realisation of the inevitability of death gripped me then, stifling my screams, stiffening my nerves to meet the end.

148

I knelt down in the soft ash of the roof and prayed—prayed as I used to pray before those damned operations, praying that I'd not give way to fear, that I'd face what had to be without flinching.

And as the crack widened out I felt suddenly calm. If only the end would come quickly. That was all I prayed for. I didn't want to be buried alive in the rubble and wait half-suffocated for the lava to roll over me.

The crack widened steadily—a foot, two feet. Then the farther half of the roof split into fragments and folded inwards, sinking down towards the lava in a heat blast of dust. And as it fell I saw the stone housing of the doorway disintegrate.

I scrambled towards it. It was a chance in a million. Through the choking dust I saw the wooden stairs intact leading down to the room below. I hesitated. I think any one would rather die in the open than be caught like a rat in a trap inside a building. But it was still a chance and I took it. I swung myself over the edge, dropped on to one foot and jumped the whole length of the stairs. I landed in a heap on the boards of the room below. The farther wall was missing and through it I could see the heat curling up from the top of the lava.

The stone staircase, thank God, was behind me. I scrambled to the top and slithered down. On the second flight I almost broke my arm as I fell against the side of the archway at the bottom. I could feel the building trembling now and the room I was in was full of a vicious, suffocating heat.

As I picked myself up I saw through the choking dust clouds a long face with ears twitching and eyes rolling. It was the poor wretched mule, lashing out with its legs as it strained at the halter that held it. A long-bladed butcher's knife lay on the floor. I grabbed it, hopped over to the animal and slashed it free. I had a childish fear that if I let the creature die, I should die too.

God knows why I did it. Some pilot's instinct, I suppose, to have a mascot. But the mule was nearly the death of me. It leapt free and ran careering and screaming round the room, hoofs lashing and teeth grinding in its fear. Then it found the ramp and went thundering down, slithering the last part on its haunches. I was so close behind it that I saw the sparks kicked up by its hooves as it pawed itself to its feet at the bottom.

Those ramps were easier than the stone stairs. They were slimy with dung and I slithered down them, lying on my back and thrusting myself forward with my hands. I could feel the building rocking as I descended and at each floor I could see the burning face of the lava where the farther wall had once been. As I reached the ground floor there was a series of splintering crashes and I knew the house was disintegrating above my head. The way to the street, the way the cattle had been brought in, was gone and in the ragged gap I saw the white heat of the lava face and felt the scorching breath of it singe my hair.

The mule had gone out by a window, crashing through it and taking the whole frame with it in its terror. I followed and as I fell to the ground I realised I was in the garden of the house and there lying almost beside me was my leg.

It was one of those strokes of luck that fate is kind enough to offer once in a while and looking back on it I can't help having an instinctive feeling that it was all because I paused to free the mule. I know it sounds stupid. But there it is. We had odder beliefs than that when we were flying night after night over Germany.

I picked up the dented limb, hopped to the wall and scrambled over. And as I fell into the next garden, the house I'd been imprisoned in disintegrated, filling the narrow space between the houses with noise and dust. I got through the next house and came out into a narrow street that was blocked at one end by the lava. The place was a cul-de-sac, and there was my mule, standing at the end of it with his face to the lava and whinnying.

I dropped my trousers and strapped the leg in place. The lava grit embedded in the stump of my leg hurt like hell when I put my weight on it. But I didn't care. It was such a relief to be able to stand upright like a human being again. It's a horrible feeling to have only one leg and to be forced to crawl around like the lower order of creatures. To stand upright again and move normally gave me a sudden surge of confidence and for the first time that morning I felt I might win out in the end.

I went down the street towards the mule. He stood quite still, watching me. His ears were laid back, but the whites of his eyes weren't showing and there was nothing vicious about his expression. He was standing by a door leading into one of the houses. I opened it and went in. The mule followed me. And when he followed me like that I wouldn't have parted with that mule for anything. I swear the animal seemed almost human. It was probably just that he'd lived all his life close to people and was used to going in and out of houses. But at the time I didn't bother to try and explain it. I just knew that his presence gave me courage like the presence of another human being.

The door led to a stables and on the far side daylight showed through the cracks of big wooden doors. I slid back the securing bar and we passed out into a track. The mule turned right. I hesitated. I was completely lost. I hadn't an idea where the monastery was. In the end I followed the mule. The track was narrow and flanked by the tall backs of houses with here and there the open doors of stables. It swung away to the right and then I saw it was blocked by the lava.

The mule turned. Pain was shooting up my leg from the grit that was being ground into the flesh. Big stones jutted out from the wall of the building I had stopped beside and this gave me an idea. I caught hold of the halter of the mule and it stopped at once. I got it close to the stones, climbed up and so on to the animal's back. A moment later I was trotting comfortably back along the track. The animal seemed quite placid now.

The track led out into a wider street. I tugged on the halter and the mule stopped. "Where now, old fellow?" I asked. Its long ears twitched. The monastery was up towards the lava so I turned left, kicked the animal's ribs and started off at a trot. I passed a trattoria where an overturned cask dribbled wine into the grey ash that covered the floor. The little wooden tables looked grey and derelict. Close by on the wall of a building was a life-size statue of the Virgin Mary. It was surrounded by tinsel and coloured lights, and at the foot were jam jars full of flowers that had been killed by the sulphurous air. Nearby a rude figure of Christ hung from a wooden cross. This, too, had jam jars of dead flowers and there were one or two sprays of artificial blooms under a cracked glass globe.

The street swung to the right. The tall houses seemed to close in on it as it climbed. And then it ended abruptly in a wall of black cinder nearly as high as the buildings. I had a sudden sense of being trapped. Every street seemed to lead up to the lava. It was like being in a partially excavated Pompei. All I could see was the façade of the houses flanking the street and the abrupt, unnatural end of it.

The mule had turned of its own accord and we trotted back the way we had come, past the decorated figure of the Virgin Mary, past the trattoria. And then I heard my name called. "Dick! Dick!" I pulled up and looked back. It was Hilda. She had come out of the house next to the trattoria and was running towards me, her dress all torn, her hair flying. "Thank God you're safe," she gasped as she reached me. "I thought I heard somebody scream-ing for help. I was afraid——" She didn't finish. She was staring at my face. Then her eyes dropped to my clothes. "Are you hurt?"

I shook my head. "I'm all right," I said. "What about the others? Where are they?"

"I couldn't find them." Her eyes were frantic with worry. "I went all through the monastery—they weren't there. What do you think has happened to them?" And then in a rush. "We must find them. The lava's almost reached the monastery. I called and called, but they didn't answer. Do you think——" She didn't finish. She didn't want to put her thought into words.

"Where is the monastery?" I asked her.

"Through this building." She nodded to the house next to the trattoria. I turned the mule and slid off at the door. The smell of the trattoria made me realise how parched I was. "Just a minute," I said and dived inside. There were bottles behind the counter. I reached over and took one, knocking the top off against the counter edge. The wine was warm and rather sharp. But it cleared the grit from my throat. I passed the bottle to Hilda. "You look as though you could do with some."

"We haven't time to——"

"Drink it," I said. She did as I told her. When she'd finished I threw the bottle away. "Now, let's get to the monastery."

She led me through the open doorway of the next house. Broken wooden stairs climbed to the floor above. "I was at the top of this house when I thought I heard you call," she said. We passed the foot of the stairs and along a stone-flagged passage. There was a clatter of hooves behind us. "What's that?" She turned, her eyes wide and startled. I realised then how near to breaking she was.

"It's only George."

"Oh—the mule. Why do you call him George?"

We were out of the house now and crossing a dusty patch of garden. Why had the name George come automatically to my mind? My mascot, of course. "George was the name of my mascot," I said. It had been a little shaggy horse Alice had given me. It had gone all through the Battle of Britain and then flown all over France and Germany. Some bloody Itye had pinched it just before that last flight.

We were in the next row of houses now. "Funny the way he follows us through the house." She was talking to keep control of herself.

"George is used to houses," I said. "He's lived all his life in a house, in the same room as the family."

We were out in the street now, and there was the piazza with the cart leaning drunkenly on its broken wheel. In the instant of recognition I glanced to the left. The lava had moved a long way down the street since I'd last seen it. The twenty-foot wall of black, heat-ridden cinder was not a dozen yards from the main archway of the monastery. I stood there, staring at it, realising that in half an hour the face of it would be about where I was standing and the monastery of St. Francis would have disappeared. "Hurry! Please. We must hurry."

I caught her arm as she turned impatiently towards the main archway. "Steady," I said. "We must decide what we're going to do. You say you've searched the monastery?"

"Yes."

"Every room?"

"I do not know. I cannot be quite sure. You see it is very confusing inside."

I hesitated. "Did you go round the outside of the buildings?"

She shook her head. "Why should I? I was searching——"

"Most of the rooms will have windows, or at least gratings. They will have hung something out to attract attention."

She stared at me, her face suddenly lighting up with hope. "Oh, why did I not think of that for myself. Quick. There is a way through to the back by the entrance they went in."

I limped after her, the mule following at my heels. But the clip-clop of his hooves ceased just before we reached the archway. I looked back. He was standing in the middle of the road, his ears laid back, sniffing at the smoking cinder-heap of the lava. "You stay there, George," I said. "We'll be back later."

Hilda was running across the courtyard as I passed under the arch of the entrance. The stone square of the courtyard was beautifully cool after the heat of the lava-blocked streets. I glanced up at the windows. They were sightless eyes staring down at me unwinking. No sign of a scarf or handkerchief or anything to show that the others were in any of those rooms.

I entered the monastery buildings. It was almost dark inside and full of the damp coolness of stone. I felt suddenly fresh and full of vigour. Hilda called to me. I crossed a big refectory room with high windows and a long table laid for breakfast. Then I was in a wide stone passage and the walls were echoing the limp of my leg. Hilda was calling to me to hurry and a moment later I passed through a heavy, iron-studded door into the monastery grounds. There was a small flower garden and then vineyards flanked with orange-laden trees. I joined Hilda who was staring up at the monastery.

Parts of the building were very old, especially the section away to our left where a great rounded tower was falling into ruins. The building had been added to at various periods and though it was all constructed of tuftstone it presented a scattered, haphazard appearance which was enhanced by the fact that the stone varied in colour according to the extent to which it was worn. There was a chapel with some fine stained glass and a line of outhouses ran out in a long arm. Smoke still curled up from one of the chimneys here and even in the sulphurous atmosphere I could detect a smell of burnt bread. Evidently the eruption had started whilst they were in the middle of baking.

"I bet Hacket has the full guide-book history of the place." I said. I had to say something to cover my disappointment, for the windows were all as blank as those in the courtyard. "Better try the side nearest the lava." I was just turning away when Hilda caught my arm.

"What is that?" She was pointing towards the great rounded tower. There were no windows in this ruined keep, only narrow slits. And from the topmost slit something hung limp. In that unnatural twilight it was impossible to see what it was. It looked like a piece of old rag.

"Did you have a look at that tower when you searched the monastery buildings?" I asked her.

She shook her head. "No. I did not find it."

I pushed my way through some azaleas, skirted a sewage pond and reached the base of the tower by a footpath that ran through coarse grass. There was a garbage heap there and the flies buzzed and crawled amongst broken bottles, rotting casks and all the refuse thrown out by the monks. Looking up I could just see that the piece of rag was clean and new and bright blue. I remembered then that Hacket had been wearing a blue silk shirt. I cupped my hands round my mouth and called up, "Max! Max! Zina! Hacket!" I called all their names. But when I stood listening, all I could hear was the sifting, spilling sound of the lava, punctuated by the rumbling crash of falling buildings.

"Can you hear anything?" Hilda shook her head.

I called again. In the silence that followed my shouts I could hear the lava move nearer. I glanced back across the huge, buzzing pile of the rubbish heap to the brown line of the outhouses. Reared up above them was the advancing wall of the lava.

Hilda suddenly gripped my arm. "Look!" She was pointing upwards to the slit. The piece of cloth was moving. It waved gently to and fro and then suddenly seemed to take on life as though the end of it were being violently shaken. Sleeves fell out towards us. "It is Hacket's shirt," I cried. Then cupping my hands I shouted up, "How do we get to you?"

The shirt waved. I thought I heard somebody shouting. but the noise of the lava drowned it and I couldn't be sure. Hilda tightened her grip on my arm, tugging at me. "Quick! We must find a way to reach them." I loosened her grip on my arm. "Wait," I said. "Max will try to get a message down to us."

I was staring up towards the slit. There was a great, rumbling crash and I heard Hilda say, "Oh, my God!" I glanced down at her and saw she was gazing towards the outhouses—or rather where the outhouses had been, for they were gone completely. A rising cloud of dust marked the spot where they had stood and in their place was the shifting, red-shot face of the lava.

Something struck my arm and fluttered to the ground. It was part of the silk lining of a coat, one corner of it weighted. I picked it up and untied the corner. The weight was a silver cigarette case and inside the case was a note. *We're all here. To reach tower enter by arch in courtyard, turn right in refectory room and follow passage to chapel. There is a flagstone with a ring bolt in robing room to right of altar. This leads to passage connecting Chapel to tower. We are in the top cell. Door is wood and can be burned down. Spare can of petrol in my car. Bless you, Max.*

I glanced up. The shirt was no longer hanging from the slit. But there was something there that shone dully and I realised that it was a mirror being held out on the end of a piece of wood. They couldn't look down at us from the slit, but they were watching us through a primitive periscope. I waved my hand in acknowledgment and then turned back along the path. "Run and get the can of petrol," I told Hilda. "I'll go straight to the chapel."

She nodded and with one terrified glance at the lava front ran back into the monastery. There wasn't even a dust haze now to mark where the outhouses had been and the frightful slag heap had slithered half across the flower garden where we'd stood, blistering the trees with its heat and withering the flowers. The first section of the main monastery building was crumbling as I dived into the coolness of the interior.

I found the passage leading off the refectory room and reached the chapel. There was no difficulty in finding the robing room or the flagstone with the ring bolt. I had lifted it up and thrown it back by the time Hilda arrived with the jerrican. Stone steps led down into a dank, cold passage. I switched on my torch. The walls were solid lava rock, black and metallic-looking. We passed right through the foundations of the Chapel and then we were climbing stone steps worn by the tread of men who'd come this way centuries past.

The tower was clearly a ruin. The wood of the big iron-studded doors was powdery with worm. One we passed had almost no wood at all and was just a lacing of wrought-iron and studs. I shone my torch in as I passed and caught a glimpse of mouldering floorboards and rusty iron chains secured to the wall and what looked like a rack standing beside some rotted iron implements of torture. The tower had evidently been a religious prison.

At last we reached the top of the spiral staircase and my torch showed a new door of plain oak. Beyond it a builder's ladder led to a square of dim light that was the roof. Here the smell of sulphur was strong again and ash had sifted down on to the stone platform outside the door. I pounded on the wood. "Are you there, Max?"

"Yes." His voice was muffled by the door, but quite audible. "We're all here."

"My father?" Hilda murmured. She couldn't nerve herself to voice the question aloud. I think she feared the answer might be No.

I had taken the can of petrol from her and was forcing back the cap. "Is Tuček there?" I called through the door.

"Yes. He's here."

I heard Hilda give a gasp of relief.

"Get up the ladder to the roof," I said sharply. I was afraid she was going to faint. "Stand back now," I called. "I'm sprinkling the door with petrol." I had tipped the can up and as the petrol ran out I flicked it with my hand on to the woodwork of the door. I put about half a gallon on and around the door. Then I hauled the can up the ladder and passed it through the gap to Hilda. "Are you well back from the door?" I called.

"Yes, you can light the bonfire," came the answer.

I climbed out on to the roof. "Pull the ladder up, will you, Hilda," I said. I tipped the can of petrol up, soaking a strip of cloth in the stuff. Then holding one corner of it, I leaned down through the opening, struck a match and lit it. As the handkerchief blazed I tossed it down into the darkness below. There was a whoof of searing flame, a blast of hot blinding air and I flung myself backwards on to the roof of the tower.

"Are you hurt?" I felt Hilda's hands grip my shoulders, lifting me up. I wiped my hand across my face. It smelt of petrol and burned hair. "The damned stuff had vaporised," I mumbled. My face felt raw and scorched. Flames were licking out of the square hole in the roof. I crawled to the edge of the roof and leaned over the crumbling battlement above the slit. "Are you all right down there?" I shouted. I was scared I'd put too much of the stuff on the door.

It was Hacket who answered. "We're fine, thanks." His voice was faint and muffled. "Quite a fire you started."

I stood up then and looked down on the stone roof of the monastery. Half the building had gone already. Beyond lay a flat, black plain of lava slanted gently upwards and thinning out to a dark gash in the mountainside. Above the gash the conical top of Vesuvius belched oil-black smoke shot with red lumps of the molten core of the earth which rose and fell, rose and fell like flaming yoyos in the crater mouth. Higher still, faint streaks of forked lightning cut the billowing underbelly of the cloud that hid the sun and blotted out the light of day. Hilda gripped my hand. She, too, was staring up at the mountain and I saw she was scared. "Oh, God! Do you think we shall ever get out?"

"We'll get out all right," I said, but my assurance sounded false and hollow. The lava seemed to be advancing faster. Already it had obliterated the flower garden where we'd stood and was pouring across the vineyards beyond in a slow, inevitable wave. Another section of the monastery fell with a crash and an up-thrust blast of dust. Soon it would reach the chapel. We must get out before then or...

I went forward to the opening that led into the tower. The flames had died down now and in the light of my torch I saw the door was charred but still solid. "We need more petrol," I said. I didn't dare pour it down. I needed some sort of a container. Hilda still had her handbag looped over her arm. "Give me that," I said. I opened the bag, filled it with petrol and tossed it down through the opening. There was a sound like an explosion and flames leapt up through the square again.

I stood watching them, praying that the fire would soon burn through the door. Another section of the monastery fell in a blaze of sparks. I glanced across to where I had been imprisoned on that other roof. I could gauge the spot by the position of the monastery. There was nothing there, just the flat desolation of the lava. "*Childe Rolande to the Dark Tower came.*"

"What do you say?"

I realised then that I had spoken aloud.

She must have read my thoughts for she said, "What happened over there, before I found you? Did you catch that man?"

"No. He caught me."

"What happened? You looked terribly hurt."

"Nothing happened," I said. She wanted to talk—anything to take her mind off the waiting. But I couldn't tell her what happened. It was too close to our present situation.

At last the flames died down again. I went to the battlements and called down, "Can you break your way out now?"

I could not hear their answer. It was lost in the sound of the lava. "They are kicking at the door now," Hilda called. She was leaning over the hole. A shower of sparks shot up and she flung back, coughing, her face black with smuts, "I think it breaks down now."

There was a sudden shout, the sound of splintering wood and more sparks. Then Max's voice called up: "We're almost out now." More sparks and then a crash. "Where are you?"

"Up here," I answered.

Hilda and I pushed the ladder through the smoking gap. "Go on down the stairs," I shouted. "We'll follow."

The light of a torch flashed in the opening. Then I heard footsteps on the stone stairway. "Quick!" I said to Hilda. "Down you go."

She stepped into the smoking gap and scrambled down. As I stood there holding the end of the ladder the last section of the monastery before the chapel fell in. The lava was right across the monks' vineyards now, slithering in towards the base of the tower. I glanced behind me, towards Avin and the way out to safety, and my heart stood still. The lava streams that had swung past Santo Francisco on either side were curving in like pincers. I remembered how I'd seen this pincer movement from that other roof. But now it had developed. The two ends of the pincer were curved in towards Avin. One arm was already eating into the village. The other was only just outside it, following the slope of a valley.

"Dick! Hurry, please."

I realised suddenly I was sweating with fear. "I'm coming." I called. I swung myself on to the ladder. The air was choked with smoke, and wood still blazed at the foot of the ladder. I heard someone coughing below me, then my eyes were streaming and I fell suddenly into the charred wood. I put my hand out to break my fall and felt a searing burn on the palm. Then I was clear of the charred debris and on the stairway.

"What happened?"

"One of the rungs had burned through," I told her. I had my torch on now and we hurried after the others. We caught them up in the passage leading to the chapel. It was with a sense of wonderful relief that I climbed out of the passage into the robing room. I had had an awful feeling of claustrophobia there, picturing the lava slithering over us and imprisoning us for all time underground.

We went through into the dim light of the chapel just as Max came out of the archway leading to the refectory room, his arm upraised and his eyes showing white in his blackened face. "No good," he gasped. We stood there for a moment staring at him in a daze. I was dimly aware of Zina, her clothes torn and charred, and Hacket with his chest naked under his jacket and matted with singed hair. He was supporting two other figures, whose bodies drooped. Hilda ran forward, clutching one of them and called hysterically, *"Co se stalo, tati"'* It was Jan Tuček. I barely recognised him.

I think Hacket and I moved forward at the same moment. We came together in the doorway and stopped there, holding our arms up to shield us from the heat and staring in blank hopelessness. There was no passage any longer, no refectory room—no courtyard, no main archway. There was nothing there but a pile of broken stone and beyond it the lava heaped twenty, maybe thirty feet above us.

"The abbot's room." Max shouted suddenly. "There's a window there."

We scrambled back to the robing room in a body, choking the doorway. The window was high up, narrow, and of stained glass, leaded and barred. Hacket seized hold of a crozier. I saw Zina's mouth open in horror at the sacrilege. But it was just the thing we wanted and Hacket was essentially a practical man. Max and I dragged chairs in from the chapel and piled them up while the American smashed the glass in. The lead was thin and bent easily. He smashed at the crossbar. The iron gave and broke under his blows. "Up you go, Countess. And you, Miss Tuček."

They scrambled up. "Feet first," Max called. Zina was halfway through when she looked down. Then she cried out something and clung frantically to the stone frame of the window. "Jump!" Hacket shouted at her.

"I can't," she screamed. "It's a long——" Her voice died in a fluttering scream as Hilda, who had seen more of the lava and realised the urgency, pushed her through. Tuček and Lemlin we got up that crazy scaffolding of chairs somehow. They seemed weak and in pain. Hacket went up with them and helped them through. "They're drugged," Max explained. "And the bloody swine had them chained."

"Chained to the wall?" I asked.

He nodded. "Imprisoned in the fetters they used for heretics. Fortunately they were rusty and we were able to smash some of the links. You go on Hacket,," he called. "Now you, Dick." I hesitated. "Go on, man. I'll give you a hand up, if it's your leg that's worrying you."

I scrambled up, caught hold of the stone of the window and slid my legs through. Max was right behind me. It happened as I clung there, steadying myself for the drop, getting my tin leg under me. There was a crumbling roar. I caught a glimpse of the roof cracking and falling and then I let go. I fell on my good leg and rolled sideways, conscious of a horrible jar on the stump of my left leg and hearing a thin scream that for a second I thought was myself screaming with pain.

But it wasn't I who had screamed. It was Maxwell. He had his head half out of the window and his face was contorted to a frightening mask of pain. Above the window rose the dust cloud I'd seen so often in the past few hours. We were looking at a wall with nothing behind it. I shouted up to Maxwell. He didn't say anything. Blood was running down his chin where he was biting through his lower lip as he heaved at the rest of his body. "It's got my legs," he hissed down.

"Try and pull 'em clear," Hacket shouted. "We'll catch you." He signalled to me to join him under the window. "Easy does it, fellow. Come on now. Get out of that and we'll soon have you safely tucked up and comfortable."

There was a sudden shifting of masonry and a cloud of dust swirled through the broken gap where Maxwell's head was. "I've got one leg free," he hissed. "The other one's broken, but I think I'll——" He screamed then and suddenly slumped over the sill of the window, his face running with sweat that dripped down on to us. It was only a momentary black-out for a second later he was hauling himself forward.

He fell head first on top of us, tumbling us in a heap. We scrambled up and dragged him clear of the wall. "We must get him to the car," Zina said.

We were on a path and I could see gates wide open leading to the street. "I'll get the car," I said. "Hilda. Give me the rotor arm."

She stared at me. Then her mouth fell open. "It—it was in my bag. I put it in my bag—the one you filled with petrol."

I stared at her blankly. I felt dazed and sick with tiredness and the reaction.

"You don't need to worry about the cars," Hacket said. "There aren't any cars. Come on. Help me get him up. We got to get away from the lava."

"No cars?" Zina exclaimed. "But we've two cars here. We parked them——" Then her eyes widened as she realised that the courtyard was now buried under the lava. She began to cry. "Get me out of here. Get me out of here can't you. You brought me here. You made me come. Get me out——" Hilda slapped her twice across the face with the flat of her hand. "You're alive and you're not hurt," she snapped. "Pull yourself together."

Zina gulped and then her face suddenly seemed to smooth out. "Thank you—for doing that. I'm not frightened. It's just my nerves. I'm a—a drug addict, and I haven't——" She turned away quickly. She was crying again.

"Only a nurse would have known what to do, Miss Tuček," Hacket said. "You have been a nurse, haven't you?"

Hilda turned to him, "Yes. During the war."

"Then see what you can do for this poor fellow." He nodded to Maxwell, who lay writhing in agony on the ground. "We'll get him down to the street, clear of the lava first. Then you go to work on him while we rig up some sort of a stretcher."

We got Maxwell and the other two to the street and went down as far as the piazza. We were safe there for the time being. There was a pile of bedding on the broken cart and we laid Maxwell on a mattress and covered him with some blankets and a quilt. Hilda said she thought she could set the leg temporarily at any rate. "What we need is some sort of a conveyance," Hacket said to me. "There's those other two guys can't walk far and we can't carry Maxwell, let alone them. You look about all in and I'm not feeling so fresh myself."

I told him about the other lava streams then and how they threatened our line of retreat through Avin. He nodded "We'll have to hustle."

I suddenly remembered. "George!" I said. "George may get us clear in time." I looked about the piazza. There was no sign of a living thing. "I wonder where he's got to?"

"Who's George?"

"My mascot. A mule I rescued from a building. I let him go just outside the monastery."

"He's probably bolted out into the country by now. Come on. We got to find something."

"No," I said. "I don't think he'll have bolted. He's the sort of animal that likes the company of humans. I don't think he'd go out of the village." I began calling.

"How do you expect him to recognise a name you've only just given him?" Hacket said irritably. "Come on. We've got to do something practical."

But I was feeling obstinate. Perhaps it was because I was so darned tired. But I had a feeling that I'd saved that animal to meet just such an emergency. "He's probably in a grocery store somewhere," Hacket said sarcastically.

"A greengrocers." I snapped my fingers. "Zina," I called. "Where's the nearest greengrocers'?"

"Greengrocers? What is?"

"Where they sell vegetables."

"Oh. *Fruttivendolo*. There's one just down that street there."

161

She pointed past the pump to a narrow, dirty-looking thorough-fare. "The others have all gone I think."

I crossed the piazza. The fruiterers' was the third shop on the left and there, sticking out of the doorway, was the bony rump of my mule. I called to him and he backed out and stood looking at me, some green stuff hanging from his mouth. I went to the shop. It was asparagus he'd been eating. I filled a basket with the neatly tied bundles and he followed me back towards the piazza nuzzling at it. The last house in the street had big doors gaping wide and the smell of manure. It was a stables and inside I found collar and traces.

Hacket stared at us as we crossed the piazza. Then he began to laugh. "What's so funny?" I snapped at him.

"Nothing. I was only thinking. . . ." He stopped laughing and shook his head. "Guess I thought the mule wasn't real, that's all. Now all we've got to do is clear this cart, hack the back part off and we've got a buggy."

We set to with a will. The need for haste drove me and gave me strength. We pushed the pile of furniture overboard and then got to work with axe and saw which we got from a nearby shop. This was the first opportunity I'd had of questioning any of the others and I asked Hacket what had happened after they had entered the monastery.

"We were had for suckers," he said. "That's about all there is to it. We ought to have known considering the door wasn't locked. But seeing those two poor devils chained to the wall—well, we just forgot everything else. And the next we knew the door had closed and the key was grating in the lock. The doctor fellow must have been waiting for us on the roof. The son-of-a-bitch had the nerve to wish us *bon voyage*. If I ever get my hands on the bastard. . ." He swung the axe viciously.

It didn't take long to smash the back half off the cart. The wood was old and rotten. Then we harnessed George and backed him in. By the time we'd finished, Hilda had set Max's leg. "I've done the best I can for him," she said.

"How is he?" I asked.

"Not good. He says much that I do not understand, but he knows what is happening."

We lifted him on to the cart. Then we got the others on. "Can you drive?" I asked Hacket.

"I don't know. Maybe I've forgotten how. But I was an artilleryman in the first war."

"You carry on then," I said. "I never held a pair of reins in my life."

He nodded. "Okay, then. Here we go." He clicked his tongue and flicked George's back with the reins. The mule started forward at a walk. Hacket slapped the reins. Still the animal ambled. I could have walked faster myself and I thought, *My God, we'll never get through Avin before the lava streams cut us off.*

I think Zina had the same thought for she called out to Hacket, "Swear at him in Italian. He requires many curses to make him go fast."

"*Via!*" Hacket shouted. "*Via!*"

"Oh, you do not understand what I mean by curses." She moved over to him and took the reins. She jerked at them and then she began to scream curses at the wretched animal. She screamed them at the top of her voice, using gutter language, many of the words quite unrecognisable to me. George laid his ears back and then suddenly he had broken into a trot. "*Ecco!* Now we move."

We must have presented an extraordinary spectacle if there'd been anyone to see us, the cart swaying and slithering on the shifting surface of the ash and Zina standing there balancing herself to the swing of it like a charioteer, her black hair streaming in the wind. Behind us the mountain belched a red glare of farewell.

"I think he has been very kind," Hilda said to me.

"Who?" I asked.

"Vesuvius. We have had no more falls of hot stones."

I nodded. "But pretty near everything else has happened."

She smiled and put her hand over mine. "Now tell me what happen when you go off after that—that man?"

We were past the last of the houses now and in open country, forlorn-looking under its mantle of ash. I looked back at the remains of Santo Francisco and I knew I'd never in my life be so glad to be out of a place. Then I told her all that had happened on the roof of that house, and as I was talking I was looking at Jan Tuček. He was barely recognisable. He looked like an old man and he met my gaze with eyes that were dull and lifeless as though he had suffered too much. His companion—Lemlin—a big man with a round baldish head and china-blue eyes was the same.

When I had finished Hilda said, "You have been lucky, Dick."

I nodded. "The devil of it is that swine got away with your father's things."

"What does that matter?" she said sharply. "You are alive. That is what matters. And I do not think he will get far—not now."

"Have you found out what happened to your father?" I asked her.

Her eyes clouded. "Yes—a little. He will not tell me all. He and the general letectva landed at Milan as arranged. They were met by this man Sansevino and another man. They have pistols and they tie Lemlin and my father up and then they fly to the villa where we find you this evening. They land in a vineyard of very young bushes. The next night my father is brought up to the monastery, chained to the wall in that terrible tower like a convict and then tortured. When this Sansevino learn that my father has not what he wants and that you have it, then he leave. An old man called Augustino bring them food every day. That is all. They see no one else until Maxwell and the Contessa arrive." The grip of her fingers tightened on my hand. "I think he will wish me to say he is sorry to have involve you in this business. He will tell you himself when he is recovered."

"It doesn't matter," I said. "I'm only sorry——"

"Do not reproach yourself please. And I am sorry I was so stupid that time in Milan and again in Naples. I did not realise then . . . ." Her voice trailed away and she dropped her eyes. "You have been wonderful, Dick."

"You don't understand," I said. "I was scared stiff. That man who posed as Shirer——"

"I do understand. Max told me all about what happened to you at the Villa d'Este."

"I see."

"You do not see," she said angrily. "It makes what you have done——" She shrugged her shoulders. "I cannot put it into words."

The blood was suddenly singing in my veins. She believed in me. She wasn't like Alice. She believed in me. She offered hope for the future. I gripped her hand. The grey eyes that stared up at me were suddenly full of tears. She looked away quickly and where the dust had been rubbed from her skin I saw the freckles reaching to the neat shape of her ears. I looked past her to the gaunt remains of Santo Francisco and the mountain behind it with the great belching column of smoke and the broad bands of the lava and I was glad I'd been there. It was as though I'd been cleansed by fire, as though the anger of the mountain had burned all the fear out of me and left me sure of myself again.

"Stop! Stop!" It was Hacket and he was shouting at Zina. She tugged on the reins and the American jumped down. . . . He ran back up the road and picked up something lying in the ash at the side.

"It's the little boy," Hilda said.

"What little boy?" I asked.

"The little boy who was sucking his thumb by the fountain when we drove into Santo Francisco."

Hacket handed the small bundle up to Hilda. She took the little fellow in her arms. His brown eyes opened wide in sudden fear, then he smiled and closed them again, snuggling close to her breast.

"He's probably lousy," Hacket said. "But you can get cleaned up later."

He climbed in and we started off again. I caught Maxwell's eyes looking up at me. His lower lip was in shreds where he'd bitten it. "How much farther?" he asked. I scarcely recognised his voice.

I looked past Zina's skirt along the road ahead. I could see the entrance to the villa now and beyond it, down the straight, tree-lined ribbon of the road I caught a glimpse of Avin lying in a huddle under a cloud of dust. "Not far," I said. I didn't tell him a great sea of black lava was reaching into the village. Away to the left, beyond the villa, the air shimmered with the heat of the other lava flow. It ran past the back of the villa and on down towards Avin. On either side of us was lava—nothing but lava. "How's the leg?" I asked.

"Pretty bad."

The dust and sweat on his face had caked into a mask that split and cracked as he moved his lips.

"I wish we had some morphia," Hilda whispered to me.

I glanced up at Zina. "There's some at the villa," I said.

Maxwell must have heard, for he said, "No time. Must get through before we're trapped by the lava. I'll last out all right." The cart jolted violently in a rut and the beginnings of a scream was jerked out of his throat. He clutched at Hilda, catching hold of her knee. She took his hand and held it as the cart rocked and swayed and he writhed and bit at his lip in pain.

Then we were entering Avin and suddenly it was hot and the air was full of dust. A smell of sulphur hung over the village. It was as though we had returned to Santo Francisco.

The cart came to a halt. I heard Zina say, "What do we do now?" and I looked past her at the narrow village street that had been full of children and carts when we'd come through the previous day. It was utterly deserted now and it finished abruptly in a wall of lava. I don't remember feeling any sense of surprise at finding our way out blocked. I think I'd known all along we'd find it like this. There'd been such a narrow gap when I'd looked towards Avin from the top of that tower. I heard Zina sobbing with vexation and Hacket saying, "Well, we'll just have to find a way round, that's all." And I sat there with a sense of complete resignation.

"Come on, Farrell. We got to find a way round." Hacket was shaking me.

"I don't think there is a way round," I said. "Remember what I told you back in Santo Francisco? The two streams have converged."

"Come on, man. Pull yourself together. We can't just sit here."

I nodded and got out of the cart. The stump of my leg was very painful when I put my weight on it. The lacerated skin seemed to have stiffened and as I moved I could feel the grit working into the flesh again. "What do you want me to do?" I asked. All I wanted to do was to sit still and wait for the end. I felt resigned and at peace. Hilda believed in me. It wouldn't be so bad going like that with someone believing in me. I was very, very tired.

"This lava flow is coming in from the right." Hacket's voice seemed far away, almost unreal. "We'll just have to work along the flank of it until we can find a way round."

I rubbed my hand over my face. "There isn't a way round," I said wearily.

He caught hold of my shoulders and shook me. "Pull yourself together," he snapped. "If we don't find a way round we've had it. That lava flow behind us will push its way through Santo Francisco. Then we'll find ourselves driven into a smaller and smaller area. We'll be slowly burned up. We got to find a way through."

"All right," I said.

"That's better." He turned to the others, still huddled on the cart. "You wait here. We'll be back soon." They looked like refugees, a cartload of derelict humanity fleeing before the wreck of war. How many times had I seen them—on the roads in France, in Germany, here in Italy? Only they weren't fleeing from war. I glanced back again at the dim, smoking ruins of Santo Francisco and the mountain hanging over it, spilling death out of its sides, belching it into the sunless air, and I found myself thinking again of the end of Sodom and Gomorrah.

"Come on," Hacket said.

Hilda smiled at me. "Good luck!" she said.

I turned then with sudden, violent determination. I had to find a way through. There just had to be a way. Seeing her sitting there, calm and confident in me, the little bambino asleep in her arms, I felt there had to be a future. I couldn't let her die up here in this world of utter desolation. If I had to tear a way through the lava with my bare hands I'd got to break a way through into the future for her and her father.

We went down towards the lava, found a track that ran to the left and started along it. Then Hacket stopped and I saw there was a man coming towards us. He wore no jacket and his shirt and trousers were burnt and torn. "You speak Italian, don't you?" Hacket said. "Find out whether there's a way through."

I limped forward. "Can we get through?" I asked him.

The man stopped. He stood staring at me for a moment and then came running towards us. Something about the stockiness of his build and the square set of his ash-caked jaw seemed familiar. "It's Farrell, isn't it?" he asked in English.

"Yes, but——" And then I knew who it was. "Reece!"

He nodded. "Where's Maxwell?" He was panting as he stopped in front of us and his eyes looked wild.

"Back on the road," I said. "He's hurt. Is there a way through?"

He brushed his hand through his matted hair. "No. We're completely cut off."

VII

MEETING Reece like that, all the serenity and confidence seemed drained out of me. The sight of him brought back the memory of Milan and my fear and that brief meeting with Alice. "How did you get here?" I asked him.

He ignored my question. "Who's this?" he asked, staring at Hacket.

"An American. Mr. Hacket." I turned to my companion. "This is Reece, a friend of Maxwell's."

"Pleased to meet you," Hacket said. It was ridiculous, standing there, cut off by the lava and yet maintaining the formalities of a way of living that lay beyond the lava.

"You're quite certain there's no way through?" I asked.

His blue eyes looked at me coldly. "Why the hell do you think I've got myself in this mess? There's a lava flow coming in from back there. It must have joined up with this flow about half an hour ago. There's a twenty-foot high band of lava hemming us in. I've been up to the top of one of the houses. There's absolutely no way through. It's hundreds of yards wide and it encloses us completely."

"Well, there's more coming down from Santo Francisco," Hacket said. "If we're not out by nightfall, I guess we'll have had it."

"A fine lookout." Reece turned to Hacket, ignoring me. "Is Maxwell badly hurt?"

"Pretty bad. His leg's smashed. We'd better go back and have a council of war." Reece nodded and they moved back along the track to the road. I followed. "How did you come to get caught?" Hacket asked him.

"I got into Naples last night," Reece answered. "Maxwell had left a message for me to meet him out here. I got a taxi and drove out. That was about four-thirty this morning. The eruption was in full blast by then. We got held up by refugees and then when some stones fell my driver refused to go any farther. I came on on foot. The villa was deserted except for the body of an Italian. I walked up as far as the outskirts of Santo Francisco. Then I came back. I was just too late to get out."

"Tough luck."

We were back in the street now. The others were just as we'd left them, all huddled in a bunch on the cart. Hilda and Zina stared at us. I think they knew by the expression on our faces that we were trapped. Zina picked up the reins and screamed at the mule. She got the cart round and called to us to get on. "Where are you going?" Hacket asked her.

"Back to the villa," she said, "It is comfortable there and——" She didn't finish but I knew by the starved look on her face and the feverish light in her eyes that she was thinking there were drugs there.

I think Hacket understood, too, for he nodded. "All right," he said. "Jump on, Mr. Reece."

Hilda had been staring at Reece and now she said, "Why didn't you go while you could?"

He told her what had happened. Her face looked drawn and wretched. "I'm sorry," she said. "I feel it is my fault. It was I who asked Max to leave that note. I was so anxious about my father and I thought maybe you'd have some news from Milan."

"Don't worry," he said. "It's not your fault." He looked at me. "It's you who've got us all into this mess, Farrell," he accused.

I felt suddenly sick with tiredness. I hadn't the energy to argue with him, to tell him I hadn't known what it was all about until last night. I just stood there staring at him dumbly, unable to meet the anger and contempt in his eyes.

It was Hilda who answered for me. "That's not true," she told him.

"It is true," he answered. "If he hadn't been so scared—if he'd done what we asked him in Milan——"

"He's done everything a man could do. He's been——"

"Have it your own way." He shrugged his shoulders. He looked at me and suddenly laughed. "It's just as it was before. You've trapped the two of us."

"How do you mean—the two of you?" I asked.

"Walter Shirer and myself."

I stared at him.

"Please—get on. All of you. I wish to go back to the villa." Zina was standing up, holding the reins ready.

"Okay," Hacket said. "I guess she's right. We may as well be comfortable." He climbed on to the cart. I followed.

"Wait!" Reece called out. "There's another of us to come."

"Who?" Zina asked.

"I told you. Walter Shirer."

"Walter Shirer!" Her eyes widened in a blaze of violence.

"Do you mean the guy that owns that villa?" Hacket demanded, and his voice was thick with anger.

"Yes."

I began to laugh. I couldn't help it. It was so damned funny.

"What the hell are you laughing at?" Reece demanded angrily. His eyes glanced uncertainly round the ring of faces. "What's the matter with you all?"

A voice called from back down the street. Reece turned. "Ah! Here he is. Did you find a way through, Shirer?" he called out.

"No. It's all round us."

He came up the street, running, his eyes wild. "You have not found a way through?" Reece shook his head. "What about those peasants. Perhaps they——"

He stopped then and his mouth fell open. I think it was Zina he'd recognised. He stared at her, then slowly, reluctantly his eyes turned first to Hacket, then to me. We didn't speak. We were quite motionless, watching and—yes, I'll admit it—enjoying the way the truth dawned on him and fear spread across his face.

"What the devil's the matter, Shirer?" Reece demanded.

The man gulped and then turned and bolted.

"Shirer!" Reece called. "Shirer! Come back! What's the matter?"

The man twisted into the track we'd just left and disappeared. Reece turned and looked at the set anger of our faces. "What's the matter?" he asked. "What's happened?" He was bewildered, suddenly unsure of himself.

"Ask Dick," Hilda said suddenly. "He will tell you."

169

Reece turned to me. "What is it?" he asked. Then suddenly threatening he came towards me. "Come on, damn you, what's the mystery?"

"That isn't Shirer," I said.

"Who is it then?"

"Doctor Sansevino."

"Sansevino? Of the Villa d'Este?" He suddenly laughed. "What story have you been telling these people?" He caught hold of my arm and shook me. "What's the game, Farrell? Sansevino shot himself. I checked up afterwards. Anyway, I'd know Shirer anywhere. Didn't I escape with him?"

"You escaped with Dr. Sansevino," I said.

"Don't lie."

"It's the truth. Ask any of these people."

"But I've been through his villa. I know it's Shirer. And he talked to me about our escape. Nobody but Shirer could have ——"

"You escaped with Dr. Sansevino," I said.

He swung round on Hacket. "Would you mind telling me what this man's talking about? That was Shirer, wasn't it?" His voice trailed away again as he met the set expression of Hacket's face.

"I don't know who the guy is and I don't care," Hacket said. "All I know is if I get my hands on the bastard's throat I'll kill him."

There was a movement in the bottom of the cart. Maxwell had half-levered himself up, "Alec. Is that you?" His voice was a dry croak. "Dick's right. That man was Sansevino. Get hold of him. There's a——" He slumped back, his head falling with a hollow thud on the boards of the cart.

"What was he going to say?" Hacket asked.

"I don't know," Hilda answered. "He's fainted. If we could get to the villa——"

"Yes." Hacket called to us to get on to the cart. "The sooner he's made comfortable the better. And there's some drink there. I could do with a drink myself."

We clambered on. Zina swore at the mule and we started back along the road. Reece sat quite still, a dazed, almost horrified look on his face. I sensed what was happening behind the blankness of his eyes. He was remembering the night he'd escaped, how Shirer had gone first and then he'd followed half an hour later, remembering how they'd met at the ambulance and how they'd driven away together. He was remembering all the little details, seeing them in a new light, realising for the first time that the man he'd escaped with was the man who'd killed his friend.

"Forget about it," I said. "We've enough to worry about without that."

He stared at me. I think he was hating me like hell at that moment for having revealed the truth to him. He didn't say anything. He just sat and stared at me for a moment and then looked away towards the black shimmering horizon of the lava.

Nobody talked as we drove back to the villa. The only human sound was the crying of the little fellow Hilda was nursing. He seemed to have sensed that something was wrong. He didn't stop crying till we reached the villa. We got Max on to the couch in the room to the left of the door. It was queer going into that room again. It looked cold and unlived in in that queer half-light. Roberto's body still lay in a heap on the floor and there were unwashed glasses and ashtrays. By the time we'd got Tuček and Lemlin upstairs to bed, Hilda had found water and was busy cleaning Maxwell up.

"Let me do that," I said. "You get upstairs and see to your father."

She shook her head. "My father is all right. He is only drugged."

"Better for him if he stay drugged," Zina said. "Better for us all if we have drugs." She stared down at Maxwell. Hilda had cleaned the dirt off his face. The skin was very white and the lower lip horribly bitten through. "You want some morfina?"

Hilda glanced up. "Morphia?"

"*Si, si*. Morphia. I think I know where it is."

Hilda looked down again at Max and then nodded. "I think it might help—later when he becomes conscious again."

Zina went out. "Well, what do we do now?" Reece asked.

"Clean up, I guess," Hacket said. "We'll feel better when we've got rid of some of this ash."

"But there must be something we can do. There's a telephone here, isn't there?"

"I wouldn't be surprised. But what good is that? You can't just ring for a taxi."

"No, but I could ring Pomigliano. There's just a chance a plane could land here. There's a flat stretch beside the road leading up to the villa."

"It's a chance," Hacket murmured. "But I don't see any pilot risking being caught up in the mess we're in."

"Well, I'll have a try."

We followed him out to the hall. The telephone stood on a wall-bracket and we watched him as he lifted the receiver. For a moment we were buoyed up by the sudden possibility of hope.

Then he began to joggle the contact up and down and hope receded. At length he put the receiver back on the rest. "No good. It's probably an overhead line."

"It'd be the same if it were underground," Hacket said heavily. "The heat would simply melt the wires. Well I'm going to get cleaned up."

Through the open door I saw George standing forlornly in the shafts of the broken cart. They'd all forgotten about him. I went out and he whinnied at me. I stood there for a moment in the blazing twilight, rubbing the mule's velvet muzzle. It'd be nice I thought not to know what was going to happen. I unhooked the traces and took him round to the outhouses where he'd have some shelter if more stones began to fall. I left him with the basket of asparagus and went back into the villa for a drink.

Hilda was alone in the room with Maxwell. Someone had removed the dead body of Roberto. "How is he?" I asked.

"He became conscious for a moment. He try to tell me something. Then he fainted again. I think he is in great pain."

Maxwell's face was very white and blood was dripping on to the floor. "Can't you stop the bleeding?" I asked her.

She shook her head. "The leg is terribly torn right up to the thigh."

I turned away to the drink table and poured her a cognac. "Drink that," I said. "You look as though you could do with it."

She took the glass. "Thank you. I am so afraid I have fixed the leg wrong. I have no experience of setting legs and he is in terrible pain."

"Well, it's not your fault," I told her and poured myself a drink. I was thinking it didn't matter very much. The lava would come and that would be the end of it. We could fill him up with drugs. He'd be lucky then. He wouldn't know much about it. I knocked back the cognac and poured another. The best thing would be to get drunk. I took the bottle and filled Hilda's glass. She tried to stop me, but I said, "Don't be a fool. Drink it. Things won't matter so much if you keep drinking."

"Isn't there a chance——" She didn't finish but knelt there staring up at me with her large grey eyes.

I shook my head. "None. The lava might stop, but I don't think so."

"If only we could get a doctor."

"A doctor?"

"Yes. I would feel so much happier if I knew he was as comfortable as he could be."

I knocked back the rest of the drink. I was beginning to feel fine now. "You want a doctor?" I felt a gurgle of laughter welling up inside me. It would be so damned ironical. "Would it really make you feel happier if you had a doctor?"

"Yes, but——"

"All right. I'll get you a doctor." I poured myself another drink, knocked it straight back and then I turned to the door. "I'll get you one of the best surgeons in the country."

"I don't understand. Where are you going, Dick?"

"I'm going to find Dr. Sansevino."

"No. Please."

"Do you want a doctor or don't you?" I asked her.

She hesitated.

"Sansevino's a damn' good surgeon. I should know."

"Please, Dick—don't be bitter. I would rather anything than that." Then as she realised that I was waiting for the answer to my question, she nodded. "Yes. Get him if you can."

I got George out of the outhouse, clambered on to his back and we trotted off down the track to the road. I'd had nothing to eat that morning and I felt very light-headed. I think I sang part of the way. Then I reached the road and glanced along it towards Santo Francisco. The sight that met my eyes sobered me up. Santo Francisco was gone, all except a few houses on the outskirts. Where the village had been was nothing but a long wall of black lava. It seemed to be fanning out, filling the whole gap between the two streams that had swung down to join at Avin. I suddenly realised there wasn't much point in getting Sansevino.

I think I might have turned back then. I needed another drink. I needed to keep myself drunk. But when I glanced towards Avin I saw the figure of a man trudging up the road towards me. I turned George and cantered towards him.

It was Sansevino all right. I pulled Zina's little automatic out of my pocket. But I needn't have bothered. The man was too shaken with fear to try any tricks, and he was literally glad to see me. I think he'd been coming to the villa anyway. He needed company. I remembered how I'd felt alone on that roof watching the lava steadily encroaching. It wasn't nice to be alone while you're waiting for the lava to reach you.

I hauled him up in front of me and we trotted back to the villa. As we turned off the road on to the track through the vineyards he said, "Suppose I could show you a way to get out of here?"

"How do you mean?" I asked.

"I will make a bargain with you. If I tell you how we may be able to get away, will you all give me your word of honour as gentlemen that you will not say anything of what has happened?"

"I don't bargain with people like you," I snapped. "If you know a way out you'll tell us to save your own miserable hide."

He shrugged his shoulders. "Later perhaps, when the lava is close, we make a deal."

He had no trace of American accent now. He had dropped the personality of Shirer entirely. He was an Italian speaking English.

I didn't even bother to question him about his proposition. I knew there was no way out.

"Is Maxwell badly hurt?" he asked.

"Thanks to you—yes. One leg's crushed."

We had reached the villa now and I slid to the ground. I had the pistol ready and I was prepared to use it. I think he knew that, for he went straight into the villa. "Where is he?"

"The room on the left," I told him.

Hilda was still kneeling beside the couch. Hacket and Reece were there looking much cleaner. "Here's your doctor," I said to Hilda.

Hacket started forward at the sight of Sansevino. Then Reece brushed past him and seized Sansevino by the shoulder. "What happened to Shirer?" he hissed. "Did you kill him? What happened?"

"Let him go," I ordered. I could see Reece's fist clenched, ready to lash out. His chagrin at realising how he'd been duped was eating into him, destroying his reasoning. I hit him across the knuckles with my pistol. "Let go, damn you!" I shouted at him. "Haven't you any sense? The man's a doctor."

He stared at me, his expression a mixture of shocked surprise and anger. I pushed quickly between him and Sansevino. "There's your patient, doctor," I said. "Get that leg set properly. Make a slip and I'll start shooting."

He looked at me. "Please, Mr. Farrell. You do not have to threaten. I know the responsibilities of my profession."

"You can hardly expect me to take a remark like that very seriously," I answered.

He shrugged his shoulders. "I do what I think is necessary. I told you that before. However, I do not expect you to believe me. Do you mind if I wash?" As I followed him, he added, "You do not have to worry. I shall not run away."

As we returned to the room I heard the sound of the piano. Zina was sitting there, playing—her fingers drifting easily, lingeringly over the keys and a dreamy expression on her face. She stopped playing as she saw Sansevino. "So you have found it, eh?" he said. "You feel better now?"

"I feel marvellous, Walter. Wonderful." She glanced towards

the black, louring sky beyond the windows. "I do not care any more." Her fingers rippled along the keys.

Sansevino crossed to the couch, stripped the blankets off Maxwell's body and then began to cut away the clothing from his injured leg. "Get me some water, please. Warm water. Also sheets for bandages and some pieces of wood. The banisters from the stairs will do nicely. Zina! Get me the morphia and my hypodermic." It was extraordinary. He ceased to be the man who'd tried to murder us up there in Santo Francisco. He was just a doctor faced with a surgical problem.

He got the clothing cut away and stood for a moment looking at the bloody pulp of flesh. At one point the white of the bone was showing. He shook his head. "It is very bad." His tongue clicked against the roof of his mouth. Then he went over to a desk in the corner and opened the bottom drawer with a bunch of keys he'd taken from his pocket. He brought out a small roll of surgical instruments. "Go and tell Miss Tuček I also need some boiling water, please." I hesitated. Reece and Hacket were outside, knocking out the banisters. There was only Zina in the room. "Hurry, please. Go on, man. I shall not hurt him. What would be the point?"

I went out into the kitchen. Hilda had a bowl of warm water. I carried it in while she got some hot water for the instruments.

When I got back Hacket and Reece were standing over the doctor. As soon as Hilda had brought in the hot water and he had sterilised his instruments, he began work. He was deft and quick and he worked with complete concentration. I watched, fascinated, as the long sensitive fingers moved over Maxwell's flesh. It gave me a horrible, almost masochistic sense of pleasure. It was as though I could feel them on my own leg, only this time I knew there'd be no pain for me.

Gradually the broken limb took shape. Then suddenly he was bending over, straining at it, forcing the bone into place whilst a high, thin scream issued from Maxwell's mouth. He straightened up at last, wiping the sweat from his face with a towel. "It's all right. He will not know anything about it afterwards. He is drugged." After that, splints and bandages, and then he was pulling the blankets up and rinsing his hands in the bowl.

"He will be all right now," he said, wiping his hands on the towel. "Would you be good enough to give me a drink, please, Mr. Hacket?"

Hacket passed him a stiff cognac. I became conscious again of Zina playing and realised she had been playing all the time. Sansevino gulped noisily at the liquor. "You see, I have not lost my touch." He was smiling at me. There was no double meaning intended. He was genuinely pleased that he'd done a good job. "When we get back to Napoli we will have that leg in plaster and in a few months it will be as good as ever." He paused, searching our faces with his dark eyes. "I take it you do not wish to die here in the lava?"

"Just what are you getting at?" Hacket asked.

"I, too, do not wish to die, I have a proposition to make."

Reece took a step forward. "If you think——"

Hacket caught him by the arm. "Wait a minute. Let's hear what he's got to say."

"I think I can arrange it so that we all get out," Sansevino said. "But naturally I expect something in return."

"What?" Hacket asked.

"My liberty—that is all."

"All!" Reece exclaimed. "What has happened to Petkof and Vemeriche? And probably there are others."

"They are alive. You have my word for it. I do not kill unless I have to."

"You didn't need to kill Shirer."

"What else was I to do? The Germans make me do their dirty work for them. When they lose the war I know what will happen. I shall be arrested and sentenced to death by your Allied murder courts. I do not like to be killed. If it is a question of my life or someone else's——" He shrugged his shoulders.

"It was not a case of your life with Roberto. You did not need to kill Roberto." Zina had stopped playing and had come towards us.

Sansevino looked at her. "Roberto is a peasant," he said contemptuously. "What does it matter to you? You use him as an animal. There are plenty more animals." He turned to Hacket. "Well, now—what is it to be, signore? We can all die here together —or we can come to an arrangement."

"How do we know you can get us out?" Reece asked. "If you know how to get away, why haven't you gone already?"

"Because I cannot go without you. As for whether I know how we can get away—if I do not, it will not be necessary for you to keep your side of the bargain. Well?"

"All right," Hacket said.

Sansevino looked at Reece and myself. I glanced at Hilda. Then I nodded. Reece said, "All right. How do we get out?"

But Sansevino didn't trust us. He got a sheet of paper and made Reece write out a statement that we were convinced he was really Shirer, that he'd done everything possible to help us to locate

Tuček and Lemlin and that Roberto was shot when crazed with fear. It was so much a repetition of what had happened at the Villa d'Este that it seemed unbelievable that we weren't back again in that hospital ward.

"Very well." Sansevino pocketed the piece of paper. "And I have your word, gentlemen?" We nodded. "And yours, Miss Tuček? And you all agree to hold Maxwell and the other two to this promise?" Again we nodded. "Good. Then I think we had better start. There is a plane in the outhouses halfway towards the road."

"A plane?" Hacket echoed in astonishment.

Hilda had jumped up. "Oh, what a fool I am! Of course. That is what Max was trying to tell us when he was on the cart. We saw it land whilst we were waiting out there on the road." I remembered then Zina saying—*What about the aeroplano, Walter?* and Sansevino reply—*Ercole has gone to Naples in the jeep.*

"But who's to fly it?" Reece asked. "Maxwell can't. Have you got an antidote to the drugs you've given Tuček and Lemlin?"

Sansevino shook his head. "No. Mr. Farrell will fly us out."

"Me?" I stared at him, sudden panic gripping me.

"You are a flier," he said. "Didn't you land Reece and Shirer behind our lines?"

"Yes, but——" I wiped the sweat out of my eyes. "It's a long time ago now. I haven't flown for——" God, it was ages since I'd flown a plane. I couldn't remember the position of the instruments. I'd forgotten the feel of the stick. "Damn it," I cried, "I had two legs then. I haven't flown since——"

"Well, you're going to fly now," Reece said.

"I can't," I said. "It isn't possible. Do you want to crash? I'd never get her off the ground."

Hilda came over to me. She had hold of my arms, gripping them. "You've been one of the best pilots in Britain, Dick. When you get into the machine it will come back to you—you will see." She was looking up into my eyes, trying desperately to communicate her sense of confidence.

"I can't," I said. "It's too risky."

"It's either that or stay here till the lava wipes us out." Hacket said.

I glanced round at the ring of tight, set faces. They were all watching me, seeing my fear, blaming me now for not getting them out. I suddenly felt I hated them all. Why should I have to fly the damned plane to save their skins? "You must get Tuček to do it," I heard myself stammering. "You must wait till he comes out of——"

177

"That is not possible," Sansevino cut in.

Hacket stepped forward and patted my arm. I could see the level set of his dentures as he forced a smile. "Come on, now, Farrell. If we're prepared to risk it——"

Reece thrust him aside. "Are you going to let us all die here?" he said angrily.

"I can't fly the plane"—the words seemed to be forced out of me. "I daren't." I was half-sobbing.

"So we're all to die here like rabbits in a trap because you're scared. You rotten, yellow——"

"You've no right to say that." Hilda hauled him away from me. "How dare you?" she stormed. "He has done more than anyone. Ever since the eruption started he has been fighting to save us. Did you go to get Dr. Sansevino for Max? No. You were too busy getting the dust out of yourself. And you didn't go near the lava. Dick has faced death twice to-day. And you have the nerve to call him a coward. You have done nothing—nothing, I tell you."

She stopped then. She was breathing heavily and she wiped her hand across her hair. Then she took my arm. "Come. We will go and get clean. We shall feel better when we have had a wash."

I followed her upstairs to the bathroom in a sort of daze. I wanted to crawl into a corner and hide. I wished I was back on that roof top. I'd welcome the approach of the lava now. If only it would come. I wanted it to end—quickly. "I can't fly that plane," I told her.

She didn't answer and ran the tap of the bath. "Take your things off, Dick," she said. And as I hesitated, she stamped her foot angrily and said, "Oh, do not be so stupid. Do you think I don't know what a man looks like without his clothes. I have been a nurse, I tell you. Now get those filthy things off." I think she knew that it was my leg I didn't want her to see, for she left the room saying she'd find me some clean clothes. She flung them in while I was getting the dirt off in the bath. Then whilst I dressed she washed her face in the basin.

"Now do you feel fresher?" she asked as I did up the buttons of one of Sansevino's shirts. She was rubbing her face with a towel and she suddenly began to laugh. "Please, don't look so tragic. Look at yourself." She thrust a mirror in front of my face. "Now smile. That's better." She caught hold of my arms. "Dick. You're going to fly that plane out."

I felt an obstinate dumbness welling up inside me. "Please, Dick—for my sake." She stared at me. Then her face seemed to crumple up. "Don't I mean anything to you?"

I knew then what I'd known all day—knew that she meant all the world to me. "You know I love you," I murmured.

"Then, for heaven's sake." She was laughing at me through her tears. "How do you imagine I'm going to bear your children if I'm buried under twenty feet of lava?"

Suddenly, I don't know quite why, we were both laughing, and I had my arms round her and was kissing her. "I shall be right beside you all the time," she said. "You will make it. I know you will. And if you don't——" She shrugged her shoulders. "Then the end will be quick and we shall not mind."

"All right," I said. "I'll have a shot at it." But my heart sank as I committed myself to the nightmare of trying to fly again.

VIII

MY recollection of the journey down to the plane is confused and vague. My mood had changed from panic to intense excitement. It had changed the moment I'd returned to the room where Maxwell lay and Hilda had told them I'd agreed to fly them out. They had looked at me then with a new respect. From being an outcast I had become the leader. It was I who ordered them to fix up a stretcher for Maxwell, to hitch George to the cart again, to bring Tuček and Lemlin down. The sense of power gave me confidence. But with that sense of power came the realisation of the responsibility I had undertaken.

I had time to think about this as we crunched down the ash-strewn track to the vineyard. And the more I thought about it, the more appalled I became. The sudden mood of confidence seeped away, leaving me trembling and scared. It wasn't death I was scared of. I'm certain of that. It was myself. I was afraid because I didn't think I'd be capable of doing what I'd said I'd do. I was afraid that at the last moment I'd funk it. I was in a sweat lest when I sat in the pilot's seat with the controls under my hands I'd lose my nerve.

I think Hilda knew how I felt for she held my hand all the way, her fingers gripping mine with a tightness that seemed to be trying to give me strength.

We were a queer cartload. The mule moved very slowly, Hacket holding the reins. Maxwell was coming round and moaning with pain under his blankets. Lemlin was unconscious, but Tuček, propped against the side of the cart, had his eyes open. They stared vacantly in front of him, the pupils unnaturally large. The little Italian boy was playing with Zina's hair while she lolled like a courtesan against Reece, her skirt rucked up to show her naked thigh, a dreamy smile on her lips. It was insufferably hot and the sweat trickled down between my shoulder blades.

I remember as we left the villa a little mound of ash by the front door with a swarm of flies buzzing over it. I didn't have to ask what it was, for there was a hand sticking out of the ash. Roberto's grave started in my mind a picture of the twisted wreckage of a plane and the flies buzzing in clouds about our swollen bodies. It was all mixed up in my mind with the flies that had crawled in swarms over my smashed leg up there in the Futa Pass so long ago.

I felt my mind drifting over the edge of reality into fantasy. Hacket was swearing at the mule and I found myself identifying myself with the animal's reluctance to reach its destination. I wanted to go jolting on into infinity, just moving steadily on and never reaching the plane. And then I saw Sansevino watching me curiously. I could see him following the antics of my mind with a cold, professional interest. And then for a moment anger and hate blended in the sweat of the heat and I wanted to be transported in a flash to the cockpit of the plane and go roaring out over the lava with a wild shout of laughter as I proved to them I could do it.

We were down by the rows and rows of planted bush vines now and Hilda's fingers clutched more tightly at my hand. "Where shall we live, Dick?" Her voice sounded a long way away as though I was hearing her talking to me in a dream. "Can we have a house by the sea somewhere? I have always wanted to live by the sea. I think perhaps it is because my mother was a Venetian. The sea is in my blood. But the frontiers of Czechoslovakia are all land frontiers. It will be nice to live in a country that is surrounded by water. It is so safe. Dick. What sort of house shall we have? Can we have a little thatched house? I have seen pictures——"

So she went on, talking about her dream home, trying to fill my mind with thoughts that lay beyond the nightmare of the present. I remember I said, "First I shall have to get a job—a job in England."

"That will not be difficult," she answered. "My father plans to build a factory. He has patents, and the money for the factory ——" She stopped then. "What happened to the things that were in your leg?"

I remembered then and my mind seized with relief on something immediate and practical. I leaned forward and grabbed Sansevino by the arm. "You took something from my leg—up there on that roof. Give it to me." I saw cunning and hesitation in his eyes. "Give it to me." My voice was almost a scream.

He put his hand in his pocket and for one awful moment I thought he'd got a gun and I half rose to fling myself at him. But his hand came out with the little leather bag and I remembered he hadn't got a gun. He handed it across to me. It was quite light and as I shook it the contents rattled like a bag of dried peas. I undid the neck of it and poured the contents into Hilda's lap. Zina's eyes opened wide and she leaned forward with a hiss of excitement. It was like a stream of glittering fire as I poured it on to Hilda's dust-caked skirt. Diamonds and rubies, emeralds, sapphires. They lay there winking and glittering, all the wealth of the Tuček steelworks condensed into that little pile of precious stones.

I was angry then, angry because Tuček had committed me unwittingly to smuggle his wealth out of the country. He'd come to my room that night with the intention of asking me to help him, and when he'd found me drunk he'd seen my leg and slipped the little leather bag into the hollow shaft. He'd realised that if I didn't know what I carried I'd be more likely to get through. But he'd no right to do it without my permission. He'd committed me to a danger that I hadn't known about.

I stared at him angrily. But he met my stare with vacant eyes, his head rolling mindlessly with the jolting of the cart. Then I remembered the other package. I demanded it from Sansevino. And when he'd handed it to me I knew why Tuček had done it without asking me. The little oilskin roll contained a dozen small metal cylinders, light as feathers. I knew what they were at once. They were rolls of films—microfilms of blueprints. There in my hand were the details of new equipment, arms and machinery, in production at the Tuček works. He'd done exactly as he'd done in 1939. I understood then. I closed the package and passed it across to Hilda.

She stared at the tiny cylinders for a moment and I saw that she was crying. Then slowly she poured the pile of precious stones back into the leather bag, tied it up and handed me the bag and the oilskin package. "Keep them, please, Dick. Later you can give them to my father." It was a gesture of trust and I suddenly felt like crying too.

Sansevino was talking to Hacket now and the cart lurched off the track, dragging slowly through the vineyards towards a big corrugated iron barn half-buried in an orange grove. When we reached it Sansevino jumped down and he and Hacket and Reece slid back the doors. Inside was an old Dakota, its camouflage paint worn to bright metal in places by the constant impact of air. My heart sank at the sight of it. It had been dragged in tail-first by the tractor that was parked under the starboard wing.

I sat there staring at it, quite unable to move. I was conscious of them carrying Maxwell's stretcher off the cart, of Zina clapping her hands with joy at the sight of the plane, of the child sucking its thumb and staring in awe. Even when Tuček and Lemlin had been got off the cart I still sat there. My limbs seemed incapable of movement.

"Dick." Hilda was tugging at my arm. "Dick. Please."

My gaze shifted from the plane to the mountain behind. It seemed to lean right over the improvised hanger, the great, black column of gas surging up from its crater, billowing, swirling, rising till it spread like a hellish canopy across the sky. And between us and the mountain was a thick, sulphurous haze. "Dick!" Hilda's voice was suddenly urgent and my body shook as though I were possessed of some horrible devil. Memory stood at my side, the memory of the last plane I'd flown, a crumpled heap of burnt-out wreckage. "I can't," I whispered. Panic had seized me again and my voice came like a sigh from deep down inside me.

Her hands gripped my shoulders. "You see that haze? You know what it means?" I nodded. She twisted my shoulders round so that I was facing her. "Look at me." Then she took my hands and put them about her throat. "I can't face that lava, Dick. Either you fly that plane or you kill me—now."

I remember I stared at her in horror. Her throat was soft beneath my fingers. And then the softness of her flesh gave me strength. Or perhaps it was her grey eyes, staring straight into mine. I got to my feet. "All right," I said. I jumped to the ground. I stood there, trembling. But she followed, caught hold of my hand and led me towards the machine. "When you feel the controls—you will be all right then." She looked up at me and smiled. "Are you very tired, Dick?"

I bit on my lip and didn't say anything. We walked to the plane then. I remember my feet seemed a long way away, almost beyond my control. They had the door of the fuselage open and were getting Maxwell's stretcher in. It was Reece who pulled me up into the plane. He patted my shoulder and grinned. I stood there, staring at the familiar details in the half dark. It was just as it had been when it had carried parachutists to half the countries of

Europe—the canvas seats, the oxygen notices, the Mae Wests and collapsible dinghies.

A hand gripped mine. I stared at it and then at Reece. He was stammering, awkward. "I want to apologise, Dick. I didn't realise—what guts you'd got."

I think it was that more than anything else that helped me to get a grip on myself. I felt that here, in this plane, I was in some measure squaring my account with him and Shirer. Hilda was beside me and together we went forward to the crew's cabin. It was as though I'd stepped back into the war. Everything was familiar, ordinary. I climbed to the cockpit and sat down in the pilot's seat. A helmet hung over the control column, trailing its inter-com plug-in wire. I felt as though if I put it on I could talk to my navigator and the wireless operator.

Hilda had climbed into the second pilot's seat. Reece, who had followed us, said, "I'll let you know when we're all set."

I ran my hands over the controls, thrust at the rudder with my feet, testing the weight of it against my dummy leg. Then I got my handkerchief out and wiped the sweat from my face and hands. It was so damnably hot and I felt sleepy. God, I felt sleepy. I stared at the dials and they seemed to be trembling in the heat of the cabin. I felt sick then.

Hilda's hand came out and gripped mine. "Are you all right?"

I wasn't all right. I felt faint. But I said, "Yes, I'm all right." I said it violently as though to convince myself. She kept a tight hold of my hand. And then Reece was at my elbow, peering up at me, telling me they were all on board. "Do you want the motors turned over? There's starting equipment here."

"No. They'll be all right. They shouldn't need warming up in this heat."

"Shall I close the door then?"

"Yes. Close the door."

The moment had come now. I looked up from the controls, looking out through the windshield to the ash-covered vineyard that was to be our runway. And then I saw George. They'd moved him to one side and he stood there, a desolate little figure standing dejectedly between the shafts of the broken cart. A violent, uncontrollable wave of anger swept over me. "You swines," I shouted. "You bloody swines." I was out of my seat and down the fuselage in an instant. "Get him on board. Get him on to the plane."

They stared at me, Reece and Hacket standing by the door, the others sitting in the canvas seats.

"Who?" Hacket asked.

"The mule, you bastard!" I screamed at him. "Do you think I'm going without my mule?"

Reece came towards me. "Steady, Farrell," he said. "We can't take the mule."

"You'll bloody well take him or we don't go at all. You leave him there, trailing that cart——"

"All right. We'll cut him loose from the cart. But we can't——"

"You'll get him on board or I don't fly this plane out."

"Have some sense, man," Hacket said. "I'm very sympathetic about animals, but, damn it, there's a limit."

If I hadn't been so tensed-up maybe I'd have seen his point. But George was something more to me than just a mule. He'd got me out of Santo Francisco. Just as I wouldn't leave him in that building, so I wouldn't leave him now to be slowly burned up by the lava. I went down to the door, and wrenched it open And then Sansevino caught me by the arm. My flesh cringed at his touch. "You must not become upset over the mule. After all, what is a mule? He wouldn't be happy in the plane and anyway we could not get him into the fuselage." He was talking to me like a child—like a doctor talking to a mental patient—and all my hate of the man flared up.

"How would you like to run from the lava trailing a broken cart and then at last be overrun by it and die, smelling your flesh burning?"

"You have too much imagination. That was always your trouble, my friend. You forget it is an animal, not a human being."

I had a sudden wild idea of leaving the damnable little doctor harnessed to the shafts of the cart. The mere thought of it brought a bubble of laughter to my lips. I heard him say, "Pull yourself together, Farrell." He was speaking to me as though I were mad. I saw his eyes dilating in sudden fear of me, saw the way his nose had been twisted by Roberto's fist, and then I saw nothing as I drove my own fist with all the force I possessed into his face, lusting in the feel of pulping blood and tissue, the satisfying thud and crunch of impact and the beautiful pain of my knuckles. Then I was looking down at him, sprawled on the sheet-metal floor of the fuselage, his face broken and bloody. I was trembling. The details of the plane began to swim round in my eyeballs, nausea crept up my throat and into my brain. Very far away I heard my voice say, "Get the mule into the plane." Hacket and Reece were staring at me. Then without a word they climbed out.

Seeing them go like that without question gave me a sense of command, and with it confidence. I jumped down and found some planks to form a ramp. Hacket came into the barn leading the mule, its cut traces trailing behind it. I went up to the animal and rubbed its velvet muzzle, talking to it, calming it with the sound of my voice. It baulked at the ramp, but pushing and pulling we got it up and into the plane. I backed it so that its rump was against the toilet at the rear and we roped it. I stood talking to him for a bit and then I turned to go fo'ard to the cockpit and found myself face to face with Sansevino. He was holding a bloodstained rag of a handkerchief to his broken face and his eyes looked from me to the mule with a malevolence that halted me. "You touch that animal," I said, "and I'll kill you."

He smiled and said nothing. I turned to Reece. "Keep him away from that mule," I said.

"The mule will be all right," Hacket assured me.

I hesitated, staring at Sansevino. You can't kill a human being in cold blood whatever sort of a devil he is, but by God I wanted to. Then Hilda was at my side, leading me back to the aircrew's cabin. I heard the door of the fuselage clang to and then I was in the pilot's seat, my hands resting on the controls. "Anything I can do?" It was Reece.

"Nothing," I said. "Go and keep an eye on that damned doctor." I didn't want Reece near me. I didn't want him to see that I was trembling and sweating. He went and I said, "Tell them to fix their safety belts and then shut the door, Hilda."

I heard her passing on the order and then the door to the crew's cabin slid to and she was back in the seat beside me. I pressed the starter button. The port engine sprang into life. Then the starboard motor was turning too. A cloud of dust swirled through the barn. The noise was shattering. I taxied out then, bumping through the ash towards the vineyard. Automatically I ran through the final routine check-up—flaps, rudder, oil, petrol, brakes, everything. All the time I kept the tail swinging back and forth as I tested out the strength of my dummy leg on the rudder.

At length I swung into position at the road end of the vineyard, facing the villa. I put the brakes on then, revving the engines, watching the dials, trimming the airscrews. From behind in the fuselage I thought I heard the frightened whinny of the mule and the clash of hooves on metal. Then I throttled back till the screws were just ticking over and wiped the sweat from the palms of my hands. There was nothing now between me and take-off except the trembling ache at the back of my knees.

Hilda's hand touched mine. I looked across at her. She smiled. It was a slow smile of friendliness and confidence. Then she raised her thumbs and nodded.

I turned to face the runway. It stretched ahead of me, a grey plain of ash marked out with bush vines drawn up in straight, orderly lines, each a drab, pitiful object under its mantle of ash. And at the end was the lava outcrop and the villa. I thought perhaps I ought to take off from the villa end. But then suddenly my hand was on the throttle, revving the motors. If I taxied the length of the vineyard, feeling each bump, I knew my nerve would be gone. It was now or never.

I took the brakes off, felt the plane begin to move, checked the trim of the motors and braced my feet on the rudder bar, my left hand gripping the control column. The thing that worried me more than anything was the ash. How would the plane react when it gathered speed? What bumps did that damned carpet of ash hide? But there was no going back now. I opened out to full throttle. The ash was streaming past us now. Little grey bushes fled beneath us faster and faster, the villa on its lava outcrop raced to meet us. I braced myself, waiting for the tail to lift, my hands on the control column. We began to swing. I checked the swing with my left foot, checked too much and felt the tail swinging across in the opposite direction. For a second all my mind was concentrated on adjusting the rudder. And then at last I had it and at the same moment I felt the tail rise. The villa grew large till it seemed to fill the whole windshield and then I was pulling back on the stick, sensing the sudden lift of the wings, hearing the motor noise soften to a drone, and the red-tiled roof of the villa slid away beneath us.

I relaxed with a sense of relief. Hilda's hand pressed mine. I looked out through the perspex and beyond the port wing tip I saw there was nothing left of Santo Francisco now, just a black welt of lava.

And then some Jinx got hold of the wings of the plane, shook them, slammed us down and then rocketed us up towards the black pall of the sky. I knew what it was even as we were flung upwards. We were caught in the uprush of hot air from the lava stream that had outflanked Santo Francisco. I fought to keep myself from panicking, to keep control of the plane. As the uprush lessened we began to bump about, tossed here and there like a shuttlecock in the turbulence of the air-streams and all the time I was fighting with stick and rudder to hold us on our course. The lacerated stump of my leg was agony each time I had to put on left rudder.

And then quite suddenly I was at home there in the pilot's seat—at home and at ease. I knew we'd get through all right. I knew I could still fly. And as though in conquering myself the elements recognised defeat, the turbulence suddenly ceased and we were flying straight and steady without a bump as though we were floating in space.

It was then that Hacket burst into the cockpit. "Farrell. There's been an accident. That damned mule. Can you land as soon as possible?"

"What's happened?" I asked. I was banking now, turning away to the sea, clear of the lava.

"It's that doctor fellow. He's badly hurt. The mule kicked him."

"Kicked Sansevino?" I suddenly wanted to laugh. "That mule's got sense."

"Don't be a fool, man. He's pretty bad."

I straightened the plane up, flying along the coast, headed towards Naples. "What happened?" I asked. "The mule couldn't have kicked him unless he was behind it."

"It was when you hit that updraught of air. Sansevino had got to his feet to see that Maxwell was all right. Then he lost his balance, the plane tilted and he went slithering down between the mule's legs to the back of the fuselage. The mule was lashing about and whinnying. If he'd lain still he'd probably have been okay. But he tried to get to his feet. The mule caught him as he got up. He's lying there now close against the rubber dinghies. He's unconscious and it looks as though his head's badly battered. We can't get to him because of the mule."

"Well, for God's sake don't try and shift the mule," I said. "Wait till we've landed."

"Okay. But hurry. He looks bad."

I was swinging in towards the Vomero now and all Naples lay below me, grey with ash, the roads out of the city blocked with traffic. "Go and sit down," I said. "And see that everybody's got their safety belts fixed. We'll be landing at Pomigliano in a few minutes now."

He left then and I heard the connecting door to the fuselage slide to. I sat there, my hands on the controls, staring out ahead, searching for the airfield, and there was a feeling of complete calm within me. I think I knew Sansevino was dead. I felt as though a chapter of my life was closed now, as though the hand of God had been stretched out and had closed it for me. The past was dead. A new life stretched ahead. I had only to land the plane safely....

I saw Pomigliano then, a grey, flat circle like a huge arena. I thrust forward the undercarriage lever. Through my side window I saw the port wheel come down into position. "Check that your wheel is down," I called to Hilda. She glanced back through her window and nodded. I circled the airport, losing height. I felt no sense of nervousness. The calmness that had come over me with

187

the news of what had happened to Sansevino was still with me. But through that calmness I was conscious of an aching tenseness in all my muscles.

There was no aircraft on the runway or lined up for take-off. I swung away towards Vesuvius, banking for a westward run-in. Then I had the flaps down and we were coming in to land. There was little wind and the plane was quite steady. I misjudged slightly and had to come in rather steep. The grey edge of the landing ground came rushing towards me. For a moment I felt a sense of panic. Then I pulled back on the control column. The wheels slammed on the concrete. The plane lifted. Then the wheels were firm on the deck and I was braking. We stopped well short of the runway end and I taxied in towards the airport buildings. A truck came out to meet us. I stopped the engines and sat there for a moment in a sort of daze, a cold nausea sweeping over me. I think I was sick. I know I fainted for when I came to I was lying stretched out on the canvas seats in the fuselage and Hilda's voice, very far away, was saying in Italian, "Nervous exhaustion, that's all."

After that I had only moments of half-consciousness in which I was being bumped about in a smell of disinfectant. I could feel that somebody had hold of my hand. The fingers were cool and safe and I kept trying to tell them not to hurt the mule. After that I remember nothing till I woke up in a room full of soft furnishings and the cool of blinds drawn against the daylight.

Somebody moved in the shadows and then I saw Zina bending over me. "Where am I?" I asked her.

"At the Villa Carlotta. It is all right, Dick. Everything is all right."

"Hilda?" I asked.

"I tell her to get some sleep. Now you must also go to sleep." Her hands were stroking my forehead. My eyes closed. From far away I thought I heard someone say, "Good-bye, Dick." Then I slept again.

I woke to sunshine and the friendly bulk of Hacket sitting beside me. I rubbed my eyes and sat up. I felt damnably weak, but my head was clear. "How long have I been out?" I asked him.

He said, "Well, between drugs and sleep you've had about fifty hours."

"Good God!" I said. And then I remembered Sansevino.

But when I asked about him, Hacket shook his head. "You can forget him now," he said. "He's dead. They buried him as Walter Shirer. Maxwell's orders. He thought it was easier that way."

"And the others?" I asked.

"Maxwell's doing fine. He's in the next room. He insisted on staying here. The Countess has gone to Rome to join her husband. Some nuns are looking after the little Italian kid and all the others are fine."

"What about George?" I asked. "They didn't—do anything to the mule, did they?"

He had risen to his feet. "You don't have to worry about George," he said with a grin. "I guess George saved everyone a lot of trouble. Right now he's stabled in the summerhouse here. You're at the Countess's villa, by the way. And the eruption is over." He turned towards the door. "Now I must get the nurse."

I heard the door close and I lay there for a moment blinking at the sunlight that showed through the slits of the Venetian blinds. Then I pulled back the bedclothes and put my foot to the floor. The tiles were wonderfully smooth and cold to the touch. There was no grit in the room. It was clean and clear of ash. The left leg of my pyjamas had been cut off short and I saw that the stump of my leg had been bandaged. I got hold of the back of a chair and manœuvred myself to the window. I hung there for a moment, panting with the effort and feeling very weak. Then I pulled up the blind and sunshine flooded into the room.

For a moment I was blinded. Then as I got accustomed to the glare I saw the sea glittering below me and away to the left the ash-heap of Vesuvius. It was no longer a pyramid. It seemed to have been distorted into the shape of a camel with two enormous rounded humps of ash. It looked remote and unreal without even a wisp of gas coming from the crater. It was hard to believe that those twin hills had been spouting fire and ash only a few hours ago. The scene was placid, tranquil. The whole thing was like a nightmare dimly remembered.

And then in the garden below I saw the mule. His neck was stretched out and he was eating the wistaria that still cascaded over the summerhouse as it had done that day I met Zina to go out to Casamicciola. So little time had passed and so much had happened.

The door opened behind me and I turned to see Hilda and her father. "What are you doing out of bed, Dick?"

I started to move towards the bed, not wishing her to see me standing there with only one leg. And then I stopped for I saw she had on a white overall and carried an enamel tray with bottles on it. "Have you been nursing me?" My voice sounded angry.

"You and Max—yes."

My hand touched the stump of my leg. It was she who had put the bandages there. A sort of thankfulness swept over me. I didn't even have to worry about that any more. I reached for the bed and sank into it, feeling as though I wanted to cry. Jan Tuček came forward and his hand gripped mine. He didn't say anything and I was glad. I couldn't have borne it if he'd said anything. He was very pale and the bones of his skull seemed to stare through the fleshless skin. But his eyes were quite different. They were no longer haunted, but full of confidence. And Hilda, who had put down her tray and was holding on to his arm, was different, too. The harassed look was gone. Instead, it was the smiling face of the photograph on her father's desk that looked down at me. "You were right," I said to Tuček. "She's got freckles."

Hilda made a face at me, and then she and Tuček were laughing. I don't think I've ever been so happy as I was then, seeing those two laughing together.

She came round the bed and handed me my jacket. "I think, Dick, you have something for my father." It was still torn and dirty, just as it had been—and the pockets bulged. I put my hand into one of the pockets and the first thing I touched was Zina's automatic. I put it down softly on the table beside me and then I got out the two packages that had been hidden so long in the shaft of my leg. I handed them to Tuček.

He took them and stood staring at them for a long time. Then he put the oilskin package in his pocket and tossed the chamois leather bag on to the bed. "That one I think we will split fifty-fifty, Dick."

I stared at him and saw he meant it. "No," I said. "I can't——" And then I stopped and glanced at Hilda. "All right," I said. "I'll accept your offer—provided you let me trade back my half in exchange for your daughter."

"For that," Hilda said, two spots of colour showing on her cheeks, "you get another injection, my boy." And for the second time within a few minutes I saw Jan Tuček laugh. "I think it is a bad bargain you make," he said. "But all right."

Hilda took hold of my arm and jabbed the needle into it. And then she bent and kissed me. "I'll see he gives me some of it for a dowry," she whispered. "I still want that thatched cottage near to the sea."

THE END